The Destined SEAL

Also by Rachel Robinson

All The Way Under

The Real SEAL Series
The Forgotten SEAL
The Playboy SEAL

The Destined SEAL

THE REAL SEAL
BOOK 3

RACHEL ROBINSON

For those who persevere regardless of circumstance.
Never give up.

The Destined SEAL

Prologue

HARPER

SHE FLOATS DOWN THE AISLE. It would be a cruel stereotype if I said she looked like an angel, but she does. In every sense of the word. The ivory empire waist gown hugs every curve just so. Her smile is all white teeth and exhilarating excitement. Mostly, above everything else, you can see happiness and love washing every tiny molecule that forms her as a human being. She is radiant. It's her wedding day, so the breathtaking glow makes every bit of sense even if I don't like it.

It takes a full five seconds for me to swallow the lump down my throat before I let my gaze find what it so desperately seeks. I'm convinced that best friends have another sense. A weird electric connection that brings you to each other regardless of the gravitational pull. I meet his eyes, and he senses my small movement from the other side of the aisle—the pastor stands in between us. He's the groom, and while I would have had no qualms about standing on that side, next to him, when she asked me to be her maid of honor, I had to say yes.

So, here I stand, wearing a rose-colored midi-length dress that's actually cute, carrying a swath of flowers, watching Ben, my best friend since age three, marry her.

He smiles at me, and I see everything behind it. I know him like the back of my hand, like a conjoined twin, like the only man I've ever loved. I force a small smile, a show of confidence, and thank God she arrives at the altar to block his view because it's in that second my eyes glass over. Ben's smile wasn't the same as hers. No, it conveyed an entirely different story. One that only I'll be able to tell.

I fix the train on her dress, and she turns her megawatt happiness on me, and says in a bubbly tone, "Thank you, Harper."

I nod and smile and embrace the razor blade pain slicing through my chest as I accept her bouquet.

I take my place behind the bride and inhale a deep breath. I can live with the agony. Him bearing witness to it is a complication neither of us needs. Tilting my head down, I pretend to be grossly interested in the florist's work as the pastor begins the ceremony. It's small and intimate, which I'm thankful for. I don't dare look at my parents, or his, for fear of losing my mind completely. The spiral on this particular blush rose is perfect. I trace it with my eyes to distract myself from the ugly truth.

I should be in that dress, oozing love and affection, attached to Ben forever. Our timing has always been off, and our near hits equal our near misses. The score was tied, ready to be broken. It needed to be settled. Then she got pregnant. I chance a glance up and find Ben gazing at her stomach. She was able to hide it easily, as she's tall and glamorous, and no one is looking at her stomach when her face looks like that, anyway. She worried about it for no good reason, now that I think about it.

I can't even be upset with her. She's that nice, and as much as I hate to admit it, they're good together. The night before she broke the baby news, Ben and I were at a bowling alley, drinking cheap beer and throwing gutter balls during Glo-Light hour. He told me he loved me.

2

We've told each other those three little words a million times over. Maybe even a billion. That's what happens when you have a person in your life for so long. But that cheap bowling alley "I love you" was different. It was the first forever one. The kind you say when you know you want to take someone and keep a piece of them forever.

Ben looks away from his bride and meets my eyes. It's a brief, time-freezing movement, I'm sure no one else noticed, but in that still frame, I saw and understood all he meant to convey.

The pastor pronounces them husband and wife, and I let my eyes flutter closed as Ben leans over to seal their marriage with a kiss. In that look, Ben told me he's sorry, that he wished it were me, that everything will be okay, and that he loves me—the forever kind. My stomach knots as a sheen of sweat breaks out across my forehead.

That's the thing with love. Life doesn't care what you love. It takes it away anyway.

A tear slips down my cheek and lands right on that perfect rose. I see a flash of a past that held promise of a future. Bubble gum. A cloud. A promise. A kiss. A pact.

I'll forever hold my peace, but that doesn't mean my heart didn't ice over when he said "I do."

CHAPTER ONE

Harper

THE PAST

WE RECEIVE our acceptance letters on the same day. Sitting cross-legged on the floor of his living room, we make a ceremony of opening the envelopes together. Benny's eyes are focused like lasers on the seemingly harmless paper object in between his fingers. I toss mine in the air and catch it by a corner. I repeat the trick a few times, watching the stamp in the corner as I go.

"One...two...three," Benny says, glancing up to find my gaze. We never thought to consider one of us wouldn't get in. There was never any question, really. We're those types of people. We go together. We conquer Harvard like freaking elitist bastards and then move on to world domination. Plus, both of our envelopes are fat.

"Go!" I shout as I carefully slide my forefinger under the side of the flap and tear across. Benny does the same, pushing his glasses up his nose using one finger. Our parents, all four of them, are seated on the long sectional couch, breathing heavily, eyes wide in anticipation. I think it's just for show. They know there's no question as well. We're not secretly driven. Everyone and everything that surrounds us knows it as a fact.

When Benny and I were eight, we performed a knock-down, drag-out, awesome play of *The Lion King*. I was Simba, and he was Zazu because he had a better pretend accent. Our parents sipped the iced tea we made and clapped along the entire time. I made the costumes, and Benny wrote our lines. It was a team effort. All of our lives it's been a team effort.

"I got in!" Benny yells, holding the thick piece of paper up in the air.

I can't help it. I can't. I stop unfolding my letter and watch him bask in this moment. His smile is wide, and his face is at the pinnacle of happiness.

"Open it, Harpee. Read yours!" he says when he sees my pause. Our parents are congratulating him, my father shaking his hand and both mothers crying like the sappy people they are. They became best friends by proxy of Benny's and my friendship. We always understood they would have become best friends without us. They are so alike it's scary.

I follow Benny's order, smiling when my eyes find the part that says, Congratulations! Standing, I meet my parents' gaze, and as levelly as I can manage, I say, "Your daughter is going to be a Harvardian."

The room breaks out into a roar. Someone knocks over a drink. My father picks me up and spins me around like I'm five instead of eighteen. Whoops of gleeful cheers bounce off the walls, and laughter steals any foul thoughts from the atmosphere.

"Dad, you realize this means I'll be in debt until I'm thirty. Even with my scholarships. You shouldn't be so happy," I deadpan. My stomach is bubbling with joy and satisfaction, with validation. All those years of never fitting in and working hard have finally paid off. If I can downplay the emotions coiling in my system, I won't embarrass myself. I'm not a person who shows my true feelings. Even the good ones.

"Oh, hush your mouth, Harper, we're so proud of you, honey," Mom says. She looks at Benny. "We're so proud of both of you. You're going to do great things." She shakes her head. "I can't believe you're leaving us already." Tears well in the corner of her eyes, and it's time to close my own eyes. Mother tears are dangerous and contagious.

My father releases me, takes the letter from my hands to see it for himself, and my mom absorbs me into her arms. "I love you, Harper Jean."

I respond to her sentiment, but Benny catches my eye.

He's hugging his mother but peeking at me over her shoulder. I stick my tongue out at him, and he crosses his eyes. His glasses slide down his nose. I peel up my top lip to expose my front teeth. He mimics my gesture, except he flares his nostrils, too. "Harvard," I mouth when our dumb face match has ended.

His mom releases him at the same time my mom lets me out of her proud clutches.

"Tequila!" Benny's dad roars, and we both shake our heads. Our parents are celebrating our accomplishment. It makes little sense to me. The four of them find their way to the bar area, a place we frequent when they aren't home, and Benny and I are left vibrating with excitement.

"Harpee, this is the best thing ever," he says.

Sliding his hands into his pockets, he starts bobbing up and down. I notice the muscles in his arms bunch at the movement. Girls look at him more than they ever did before. It made me jealous for a spell because I didn't understand why boys weren't noticing me. I'm not flat-chested anymore, and I let my practical haircut grow longer. My aunt showed me how to wear tasteful makeup. Benny laughed off my concerns and said it was probably because I had a boy for a best friend. He said it was like a dog peeing on a hydrant. The territory is marked. I argued that dogs pee on the hydrant over and over trying to cover up the other dogs' scents and accused him of comparing me to a hydrant. He said he was the dog in the analogy, so I shouldn't get my girly emotions in a twist. I agreed with him.

I put my hands on his shoulders. He's bigger now— taller and broader than he used to be. "Benny," I say, biting my lip. "This is going to be the greatest adventure of our lives!"

He picks me up under my arms and spins me around, the smile on his face comforting and familiar. He sets me back down, and we do a stupid dance all the kids at school are doing. Our parents are lost in their drinks, watching us over the rims of their glasses as we act like geeky, Harvard-bound fools.

"I think this calls for the understated elegance of song," Benny says, taking my hands in his. They're warm, and for a second I get lost in his touch. It happens more and more, and I'm not sure what it means. He denies any sort of realization of things changing between us, so I try not to bring it up.

I cross my arms, and he crosses his and grabs mine. At the same time, we suck in a huge giant breath. "Harbenny, Harbenny, getcha, bitchen some, we rule the world, who is number one?" We raise and lower our hands in our secret song handshake as the words spill from our lips. We repeat it one more time, louder this time, and at the end we're laughing so hard we fall back against the couch, one of his hands still lying atop mine.

"Life is finally starting," he whispers so no one else hears. The happiness in this moment is fleeting, because it reminds me of how shitty of a time we've had up until this point. The bullying and the not-so-veiled insults slung our way mean very little in the big scheme of things. We were lucky enough to realize that from a young age. We clung tight to each other and the promise of more. The promise of this feeling, in this moment, right here. It was all worth it.

I don't say anything in reply because he already knows my sentiments reflect his. I squeeze his hand instead, comfortable merely breathing together with thoughts of a thrilling future.

Smirking, I turn to look at him. "We're going to rule the world, Benny. Just you wait and see."

Benny wrinkles his nose. "I smell popcorn," he remarks. I point a finger at our parents as they shovel popcorn in their mouths alternately between their adult beverages. They look at us every so often. "What are they going to do when we leave them to their own devices?"

"Finally live?" I offer, shrugging my shoulders.

They've been great parents. All four of them. When the neighbors in our middle-class neighborhood were busy having scandalous affairs, they pretended nothing nefarious ever happened. They sheltered us. They understood that as long as Benny and I had each other, somehow we'd be okay. When I got my period for the first time, Benny's mom sent him to have a sleepover at my house. It might seem weird to most people, but I was relieved. It saved me from having to discuss these things with my mom, and by that time he was eager to glean knowledge about the opposite sex even if it meant hearing about blood that comes out of the vagina like the great flood.

We don't censor our friendship or build barriers where the typical boy and girl friendships would have them. He tells me with little heartache when he splooges all over his bedsheets, and when Jenny Megley wears a short skirt to school, he bombards me with the gory details. In turn, he drives me to the makeup store and tells me what lipstick complements my complexion.

"They're gonna be drunk in thirty minutes. What do you want to do tonight to celebrate?"

Drumming my fingers on the leather next to me, I contemplate the various ways in which we could mark this momentous occasion. "We could drive down to the water tower and throw rocks? Get Slurpees and Ho-Ho bars and binge until we feel sick and throw up from such great heights?"

"You're such a geek."

I fix him with a glare fitting for an idiot. "You asked. What do you suggest we do?"

He's teasing because my response was dripping in sarcasm. It's a defense mechanism that rises even when there's no threat. It's what happens after being the ugly duckling most of my life.

"You could paint my toenails," I say, grabbing his knee.

"We aren't eight anymore. I can think of one thing we both need to do before we go to college." Benny smirks and slides his glasses up his nose again. Sighing, I tell him he needs to go get them tightened before he makes me crazy. He snarls in response.

"Basketball!" he proclaims loudly.

Our parents watch us as we head out through the garage door. Benny swipes the orange ball from the floor, and I follow him onto the driveway.

"Now that we're out of earshot," he says, trailing off.

"Oh, god, Benny, what now? I don't want to hear about Jenny Megley's pubic hair again!" I steal the ball out of his hand and start dribbling. "You saw it once when the skank didn't wear panties. Surely you don't still think about it?"

It's a shame he was so puny most of his life, because Benny is phenomenal at basketball. His physical confidence kept him from trying out for the high school team. I couldn't push him even though I knew he'd make it because I wouldn't play a sport either. Those kinds of people scare me.

Benny laughs. He's tall and confident now. Or at least that's how I see him. "Virginity clause, Harpee," he says, his voice deadly serious, but his mouth smirking.

When I stop, shocked, my jaw open, he steals the ball and nets a three-pointer. Swallowing, I try to right my attitude and veer into a conversation I knew was coming.

"You're serious?" I cross one foot over the other, as if to subconsciously guard the V he's talking about.

He dribbles the ball around me in a circle, his dirty, white Converse sneakers making me dizzy. "You weren't serious when we made a blood pact at age thirteen? We made a promise."

My stomach falls to my feet.

Leaning over, I make an attempt to snatch the ball from him and miss. "I didn't think about it after that, honestly." Lie. I was just hoping he wouldn't bring it up, because God knows I wouldn't. "I signed it so you wouldn't feel badly about Sophia turning you down."

Benny spins on me. "You're telling me you'd rather go to Harvard a virgin than have coitus with me?" He waves his arm from the top of his head down, like he's presenting a showcase prize in *The* Price is Right.

Leveling him with my gaze, I don't let my true emotions show. I think I hide them, anyway.

Benny narrows his eyes. "You can't lie to me. I know you better than you know yourself. It's no big deal. It's just an act. Like dribbling a ball or taking a test. Or getting into the best school in the world!"

"I'm glad you hold my virginity in such high regard," I remark.

Sweat slides down the sides of his face. He takes his glasses off to dry them off, and I catch my breath. "I'd be lying if I didn't say I think about it more now that you look like that," he says. "I hold your virginity in the highest regard. I'm paying for it with mine. That's sort of a big deal."

"Looking like what?" I ask, scrunching up my nose. I'll ignore the rest if he's going to compliment me.

Benny sighs, turns around, and shoots another basket. "Never mind. I'll keep working on Jenny. She'll give in eventually. It's only a matter of time now. She's skilled, too. That's a better option for a stud like me."

Blood boils at 212 degrees Fahrenheit. Mine is boiling right now. "No. You won't give that wench your virginity!" I shout. "Looking like what, Benny?" I raise my voice even louder. "Don't be shy now."

Benny laughs and points at the front window, where our parents are gawking at us, drunk smiles lighting their faces. "Keep it down unless you want them to know about the virginity clause. I had a feeling you'd say that. So, you're game then?"

Folding my arms, I eye him suspiciously. He works me so easily. "It will be like making love to my brother, but fine. Like you said, it's just an act. Why aren't you answering my question?"

He's a genius at avoiding topics he decides to shun. Unfortunately for him, I know when he's using avoidance.

He celebrates my acceptance by palming the ball and jumping up to dunk it in the hoop with a loud whoop. His dirty Celtics tee rides up to expose his lean waist and abdominal muscles and the spry patch of hair that cropped up a few years ago. Closing my eyes, I swallow down a ball of nerves and remind myself it's Benny. "You know you grew into your body over the last year or so? You look...pretty. Hot, even," he goes on to explain. "That's all I meant. Don't go overanalyzing it."

Blushing, I turn away. Ignoring his compliment, I say, "It won't change anything, right? Just an act?"

Dribbling the ball over to stand in front of me, he fixes me with an excited stare, his eyebrows raised in reassurance. "Always. Just you and me, Harpee. Come on. You should know that nothing can tear us apart." He tucks a piece of wayward hair behind my ear and gives me a warm smile. "Not even fumbling first time sex and definitely not Harvard."

Breathing out a sigh of relief, I nod. "Best friends for life," I affirm.

"We've known each other our entire lives. Every single first in my life has involved you in some way, shape, or form. Why would this be any different?"

While he's distracted by thoughts of sex, I take the ball from him, holding it at chest level. It smells like dirty, burned rubber. I like the smell. It reminds me of Benny because this smell clings to his clothes. "I have to go to my aunt's fancy birthday party the weekend after next. She sent an invite to me specifically. Like I'm an adult or something. You'll be my plus one?"

Benny rolls his eyes, steals the ball back, and dribbles it by his side. "This is your counteroffer. I like your style."

Groaning, I slap his arm. "You should like it. I learned from you. You're invoking the virginity clause, so I feel like I should get something I want out of it as well."

He palms his chest with his free hand. "You're getting me!" he exclaims, his sarcastic smile touching his eyes.

It's my turn to roll my eyes.

"Is it a girl party?" he asks, wrinkling his nose.

I shake my head. "It's an everyone thing. She's

turning thirty-five and wants the world to see how young she still looks."

Benny shoots a three-pointer but doesn't make a move to get the ball. He stalks back toward me, picking up his baggy, dirty jeans as he goes. He places a hand on my shoulder and grins.

"Well?" I ask, widening my eyes in irritation.

"I'll be your plus one."

CHAPTER TWO

Ben

THREE YEARS LATER

"I'VE BEEN DRINKING HEAVILY since I became a SEAL. I don't need to go out tonight," I say, holding my stomach at the reminder of alcohol. "Last night I tied one on so hard my intestines are still violently angry at me."

Harper moans her dissent about the situation. "It's your twenty-first birthday. Did you take a beer shit yet?" Harper asks. "You have to eat cake. We'd eat cake if I were there." She swings from topic to topic so quickly it makes my head spin.

"You sound like such a kid when you ask me questions like that. Was beer shit something you overheard in class, Harper?" I smile. She hates when I single her out as different from her peers. Funny, it's the reason we've stayed friends all this time. I shift the phone from one ear to the other. She called to sing me happy birthday, like she does every year. "I'm sorry." Apologize before she rebukes. I've learned that about her. Harper can't get mad after I say I'm sorry.

She sighs. "I've been to plenty of college parties. Maybe not the kind of parties you go to. I'm not into

15

hookers and blow," she remarks, a hint of ice in her voice. "We're more refined than that."

Low blow. She goes straight for the jugular by bringing up the life I could have had if I hadn't joined the Navy instead of going to Harvard with her.

The terror attacks that rocked the world did so in an all-encompassing, freedom-stealing manner. I watched the widespread destruction sitting on Harper's bedroom floor. We spent weeks, right there, in that same spot, watching the President of the United States give speeches and news reporters with terrified faces offer updates on the death toll. Harper's aunt was killed in a parking garage at the mall here in San Diego.

Our friend Peter's mother and father were killed when their cruise ship was hijacked by terrorists. His grandma stepped in as both parental figures after. The attacks were widespread, encompassing every country and almost every city in the world. Every form of destruction was used, from a simple automatic weapon to car bombs and IEDs strategically placed to cause the greatest amount of death.

My hackles didn't go down as the world changed, and as I watched tears pour down Harper's face as we buried her aunt, mere days after that fancy dinner birthday party, I'd silently made up my mind. I didn't tell anyone of my decision because they'd try to sway my mind. Mostly I didn't want to disappoint them, because I knew without a shadow of a doubt I wasn't going to Harvard. I was going to join the Navy and be a goddamn Navy SEAL.

Destiny was forced by the terrorists' hands. It wasn't easy to get in the physical shape required for BUD/S and Hell Week. In fact, the process was the hardest thing I'll ever do in my entire lifetime. The number of Americans wishing to enlist were pouring in after the terrorism washed across the world. Patriotic men and women, just like myself, switch plans to make their lives better used. Harper didn't talk to me for a full week after I told her about my plans. My parents went into a somber period where I'm sure they mourned the life they thought I'd have. Explaining I would have a more fulfilling experience serving my country did little to quell their fears. With good reason.

Our world fell apart that day. Nothing will ever be the same. It's an impossibility. Martial law lasted so long that we stopped counting months when it seemed commonplace. Curfews and roadblocks were the new normal. Grocery stores were wiped out, and you found fresh produce when you were lucky. Some of the power plants around the US were affected, and some citizens went months without power. It reminded me of the apocalypse —or some TV show where zombies lurk around corners waiting to chew off your face.

Harvard seemed so far away. Who goes to school to learn when national security is threatened? It was surprising how quickly life returned to something familiar. Harper left on time, and something resembling our old life resumed.

"Your birthday is coming up. Want to fly to come see me? I'll buy your plane ticket," I offer when the conversation falls into a lull. We live two completely different lives. Harper has her nose stuck in a book while I have my gun shoved down some asshole's throat. I grew up fast, and sweet Harper is still catching up in all of the ways she's always lacked. "We can celebrate both of our twenty-first birthdays then." It's a peace offering.

"I guess," she says.

I tell her I have a long weekend next month, and we talk logistics in case I'm not able to pick her up at the airport. My job in the military is steady. My schedule isn't something I can ever count on, though.

"Do you have your own place again or are you sharing with…those guys?"

Laughing, I try to picture her crinkled nose and upturned lip. "You know rent is crazy expensive out here. I'm rarely home. Rest assured I do have my own place again." I lived with a few SEALs right after I graduated BUD/S. Harper came down with her parents to visit me, and she was horrified. Mostly because it was her first glimpse of my life after her, and it was nothing like it was supposed to be.

She grumbles under her breath. "They looked at me like I was lunch. Right in front of my dad!" Harper exclaims.

"I told them you were single. They asked."

"I don't need your help with men, Ben. Please."

She doesn't date. I know it for a fact. "Mark your calendar then. I'll get your ticket squared away and email you the confirmation. We'll have cake and whatever else you deem birthday-worthy."

"I can live with that. What's your new place like?"

I make my way to my bathroom and glance around. "Uh, I'll have to clean up before you come."

She scoffs. "Still not a housekeeper, huh?" It's been a whole year since I've seen Harper. We have one of those friendships that never changes. She'll arrive, and it will be like no time has passed at all. "Am I sleeping on the couch?"

I should have known that's what she was fishing for. "No. Sleepover in my bed, of course. Flashlights and Captain America comic books." I bite my lip to stifle a laugh.

"Ha. Ha. We're not kids. We can't sleep in the same

bed anymore. That's just weird. Boy,-girl platonic relationships don't function that way."

I'm not sure how else they'd function. We've made it
work our entire lives.

I tsk her. "It's only weird because you said the word.
It's completely normal. When do you finish your exams?"

Harper starts in with her college talk, telling me of her
exams and her linguistics professor and the boy she
studies with, who has bad breath. I've named him Stinky
Stuart, even though his name is Marcus. It irritates her
when I don't use his real name. It irritates me that even I
can tell Marcus wants her for more than studying, and
she doesn't realize it. I don't tell her that either. I don't
have rights to Harper in that regard anymore.

She's the pipe dream I gave up when I became a
SEAL. My cell chimes with a text message. It's from a
number not saved in my phone.

I had fun last night. Call me later?

Swallowing hard, the memories from my drunken
escapade last night come rushing back. My hands in
blond hair. Her mouth on my dick. I swipe to delete the
message quickly.

"Benny, I have to go. My Jazzercise class starts in
fifteen, and I'm about to blow a gasket with these
upcoming tests. I might even stay for two classes."

Shaking my head, I reply, "Still with the Jazzercise? I
may not clean well, but at least I don't participate in the
geekiest thing alive to combat stress." I can't make fun of
her too much because I used to go with her when we
were growing up. Her mom would drop us off out front
with our sweat bands strapped to our foreheads. We'd
wave her away, with gritted teeth and red faces. Wouldn't

want ol' Mom to embarrass us at Jazzercise class, now would we?

I ask if Harper remembers it, and of course she does. We end our phone call the way we always do, with laughter and good memories. I feel so much better after we talk. The fuzzy, familiar feelings only she can give vanish bit by bit until I'm empty and alone again. Soon, she'll be here, and I'll be able to fill the reserves again.

The random number texts me again, but I delete the message before reading it in favor of looking up house cleaning services.

Sweat drips down the sides of my face as I hold my breath and steady my gun. The wet wood and drywall surrounding us makes for a horrendous smell, and I can't help but wonder how many mold spores I'm inhaling in this abandoned, nasty building. As a kid, I was obsessed with geeky things like Stachybotrus chartarum, better known as black mold. It can cause cancer and infections that take over an entire human body. Puffing out my cheeks, I try to hold my breath a little longer than I should.

My buddy Tahoe is in front of me. He squeezes my thigh with his free hand, signaling we're moving into the next room. I reach behind me and return the gesture to the SEAL behind me. We're stacked against the door, silently pursuing the people hiding behind it. We're not in a third-world country stalking evil predators. We're in a fucking abandoned office building in Florida. This is our new normal. Fighting on American soil, in seedy places, taking out those who threaten our fucked-up freedom. When people talk about the price you pay for freedom? Yep, that's me. Paying that shit a million times over.

Someone from inside the room fires a gun, and the bullet whizzes by my shoulder and lodges into the wall across the hallway. I can't let the near hit affect my mind-set, though. I take a deep breath and confirm I'm okay with a brisk head nod. Tahoe grabs my arm and looks me up and down. It's a frantic gesture as he scans for blood or anything amiss. I hiss out a long breath as the front man gives the order to move in by signaling a hand gesture. It's only been a few seconds since the bullet flew through the wall, and we're obviously compromised. The scent of gunpowder fills my awareness, and in response I tighten my grip on the weapon.

With precision and speed, the first SEAL enters the room, and gunfire lights the atmosphere like the Fourth of July. I keep my gaze focused at the door opening as my three brothers enter before me, folding around the door, each heading in separate directions to clear the room effectively. Voices cascade around me as I enter the dimly lit room for my turn. They took out the bad guy the millisecond they entered, so by the time I entered, the threat was gone. This time, at least.

I'm still breathing hard when someone yells, "Clear!" And we set out for the other rooms in this hallway. The Intel crew sweeps in behind us to case the room and the body to find anything of use. It's become an exhausting effort to root out the people responsible for the terror attacks that rocked our world. It's not just the terrorists, it's also those who helped fund it and those who helped organize the attacks.

All in a day's work. I tell myself this on repeat as I try to forget about the stray, deathly bullet. The rest of the rooms prove less hazardous, and we're on our airplane heading somewhere else just as dusk sets.

My friends talk about the mission and pat me on the shoulder as they pass by my seat on the plane. I'm solemn, a little more silent than I usually am. I'm an extroverted introvert on a good day. Keeping to myself comes naturally, but when close calls rear, like they've done before, I shut down almost completely. Tahoe flashes his phone in front of my face. It's a pair of big, fake titties. He spits into a clear soda bottle and then takes a seat in front of me, our friendly exchange all but over.

My cell phone is in a dirty backpack sitting in the seat next to me. I pull it out and open up the notes to write a message that will never see the light of day. Sometimes I need to write things down to remind myself that I'm still breathing, that my reality is firmly planted in the same place it has always been.

When the light fades and the mute darkness washes over me, I don't think of anything except every memory that has you in it.

CHAPTER THREE

Harper

"MARCUS, I know what I'm talking about. Trust me, I'll be fine." I sigh, folding my arms across my chest. He doesn't think a visit to see my best friend is a good idea. I mean, we're dating, so I get his hesitation. He's putting his girlfriend on a plane to see her lifelong best friend, who happens to be a Navy SEAL with a friend's stable filled with vagina-hungry, muscled monsters. Marcus doesn't have muscles. He's kind and he's thoughtful—more intelligent than I am, if we're being completely honest.

"I don't want you going. I don't know why you even want to go!" he says, his voice loud and tenor demanding.

I wince. "Don't yell at me. If you don't understand why I'd want to see my best friend for his birthday, then you don't know me at all." This is officially our first real fight. "It's a trip back home for me." Mostly to see Ben, but it's still within driving distance to my parents.

Marcus has dark, chocolate-colored skin and the most beautiful smile I've ever seen. He's wearing a plaid button-up shirt and a pair of pressed khakis. He's the poster child for Harvard in every way, shape, and form.

His father attended, as did his older brother, and Marcus is...safe. He lives a secure life, free of any encumbrances that could affect our relationship negatively.

His brown eyes turn down in the corner. "You're right. I'm sorry, Harper. You mean so much to me. It just worries me. That's all." If the tables were turned, I know I'd feel some hesitation in letting Marcus go. "Don't forget about me, okay?" He cups the side of my face and leans in to peck my lips with a warm kiss. I stiffen a little because his mood swings give me pause. I'm not well versed in relationships, but I have certain expectations regardless of my experience. No yelling is certainly on that list.

I kiss him back, wrapping my hands around his neck. "You're going to be soaking in texts the entire time anyway. You won't even know I'm gone," I reply. "Ben needs me, Marcus. He always has." Admitting it out loud forces a lump in my throat. I smile through it because Marcus is studying me with a critical twinkle in his eye. He asked me straight up, before we made our union official, if I had feelings for Ben. I told him I didn't, but that was a surface answer, because of course I have feelings for Ben. I've tried, and I'm not sure how to not have feelings for him.

Standing on the edge of forever, I can only save one person from spiraling into the abyss. It will be him.

Always him.

Even though that answer may never change, I'm able to live with it now in a way that makes it bearable. Ben chose his life, and I chose mine, and those decisions weren't conducive to anything more than a long-distance friendship. It would be a bold-faced lie to say I'm not nervous about seeing Ben after a year of separation.

Marcus leans away from our embrace and sets his hands on top of my shoulders. With a wide grin, he leans forward and presses his lips against my forehead. "We can order takeout. We can rent that rom-com you wanted to see. How does that sound?" he asks, eyes hopeful.

My stomach flips, the excitement of seeing Ben tomorrow encompassing everything else. "That sounds great, Marcus. Chinese from the place next to campus?" I ask.

He nods. "Surprise me," he replies, pulling his wallet from his back pocket. He pulls out a few crisp bills, all neatly organized by denomination, and slides them into my hand. "Something with chicken, maybe?" His last test is tomorrow, and I finished mine today. It makes sense he'd send me for food. Marcus returns to his contemporary desk by the floor-to-ceiling window of his condo and bends his head down to examine his textbook and notecards.

I grab my oversized bag and sling it over my shoulder and lock his door with the key I keep on my key ring. We're close to campus, so I rarely use my car. It stays in Marcus's parking garage. His apartment is beautiful compared to the block cell dormitory I share with a nympho named Nancy Cartgrove. She squeals like a pig and peeps like a baby chick during intercourse, and the noise-canceling headphones Marcus gifted me for my birthday aren't strong enough to block out her sex life. Mostly I stay at Marcus's apartment now. When his parents come to visit, I have to hide my toiletries and empty my drawer.

Marcus says they're liberal-minded, accepting folks, but I'd never want them to think I was that kind of girl. I haven't even told Ben about the relationship yet. At first it was mostly because I wasn't sure if it was going to last, and now it's because so much time has passed, the awkwardness has reached a fever pitch.

My phone chimes from inside my cavernous bag. I

dig my cell out as I walk toward the restaurant, pausing every city block to wait for the crossing signals.

> I'll be able to pick you up tomorrow!

The text from Ben reads. Butterflies invade my stomach again, and I actually skip a little. He wasn't sure he'd be able to get out of work early enough. The exclamation point tells me he's just as excited. He never uses them.

Cars honk, and the cross light is still red. I tap back a quick message.

> I'm so excited!

A card shop with a bright pink sign outside flashes at me as if to signal divine intervention. Stopping, I peer in to check out the display of pop-up birthday cards. One immediately catches my eye, and I run inside to buy it. I already sent him one on his actual birthday, but I don't want to show up empty-handed.

I pick up the Chinese food, a few various dishes I know Marcus will like, and head back. He studies for another twenty minutes after I return, and we end up having to reheat our dinner in the microwave. The movie isn't as funny as it was slated to be. It's one of those movies that shows all the funny parts in the previews, and memories distract me from the screen in front of me.

It's a good thing the movie is a comedy, because in no time at all I'm smiling like a lunatic as I remember birthdays from my past. When I turned fourteen and the girls at school made fun of my flat chest and pretty much everything else about me, Ben raided the girls' locker room to put frosting inside their shoes. It was during the wedge clog phase. Ben was never very stealthy, and I remember being worried he'd be caught and would get in trouble.

That was a birthday he single-handedly turned around, by himself. My cell phone vibrates with a text in front of Marcus on the sleek coffee table.

Leaning over, I scoop it up quicker than I should have. The message reads,

> Don't be shocked. I even washed the sheets on my bed.

It's from Ben, and my smile fades into a blush. My pale skin proves an awful, telling quality. There's never any question if I am embarrassed.

"It's Heidi," I say, biting my tongue. The lie came too easily.

Marcus is laughing at the movie and shrugs. I'm unsure why I even told him who it was to begin with. Reporting to a man isn't something I ever want to do.

"I have to use the restroom," I say, because I obviously tell him way too much anyway.

Marcus nods but doesn't take his eyes off the TV, the blue light casting his face in shadows.

Shutting the door behind me, I sigh. That's totally inappropriate. I send back,

> I'll pack extra sheets for the sofa

My thumbs hover over the buttons to type more, but I hold back.

> If you don't think you can keep your hands off me, then do what you must

Ben replies.

Shaking my head, I laugh. The knock on the door makes me jump.

"What are you laughing at, Harper?" Marcus asks, voice aimed at the doorjamb.

My heart leaps into my throat. "Nothing. I'll be out in a second." Slipping the phone into my back pocket, I turn on the sink and wash my hands. Marcus is waiting when I sling the door open, a small smile plastered on my face.

He unzips his jeans and lifts the toilet seat.

"I can Uber it tomorrow morning," I say, trying to change the subject.

"I'll bring you," he replies, looking at me over his shoulder.

Smiling, I nod. "Is the movie over? I nemessaed to finish packing."

"It's paused. Go pack. We can finish watching it later," he says.

I go into the bedroom and slide my phone out of my pocket, hitting the vibrate button before setting it on the dresser. I open the leather weekender and toss in a bottle of perfume.

Marcus saunters in a few seconds later, and his eyes land on my cell phone. I swallow hard and a chill hits me. "Say goodbye to me properly?" I offer. "What do you say?" With a soft hand, I graze the side of my body and unbutton and unzip my jeans. His eyes follow my red fingernails.

He crosses to me, wraps his arms around my waist, and pulls me to his chest. When his lips hit my neck, the rush of fear is disguised by the pretense of lust. I can't describe what he's making me feel, but the way my nerves are frayed, I'd call it a near miss. Ben is joking, but his texts would seem like something more sinister to Marcus. It's because I lied about my feelings for Ben, and no one knows it but me. A dirty secret that will torture me for the rest of my life. It affects me even when I take away its power and call it friendship instead.

It's the only logical explanation.

Marcus makes love to me slowly, languidly, and completely. I forget why I was uneasy in the first place. Still, after Marcus falls asleep, I go to the gym and chassé step and jazz square until I can't breathe.

I shift uncomfortably in my seat as the pilot tells us we'll be landing soon. Marcus's words as he bid me farewell still linger in my mind. He told me not to do anything he wouldn't do. I'm not even sure what that means, so I called my friend Heidi to ask. Heidi is a serial dater, she's Harvard pre-med, and she knows men. Some people are born with the gift, and others struggle to cobble together the man formula. Unfortunately, I fall into the latter category. We spoke until I had to board my flight, and she told me Marcus has a typical, nothing-to-worry-about case of jealousy.

I'm also seeing my parents while I'm back west, and she thinks that factors into why he's upset about me going without him. He hasn't met them. I'm not sure I want him to. That would make our relationship something I'm not sure I'm mentally ready for. One thing is for sure: boyfriends should respect the best friend status. Heck, they should respect their girlfriend enough to trust their decisions at the very least.

It's almost a shame classes are out and I have more time to worry about stupid, trivial things like this. The fact that women have these worries on a daily basis shocks me. Maybe it's because boys were never on my radar growing up. Maybe it's because my best friend is the opposite sex, but I've never given relationship issues the ability to worry me.

Now that it's here, I wonder if it's because Marcus means more to me than past flings. The realization sends my heart into a mass exodus of beats and pounds. That's the other thing about me. I'm not in the habit of letting people get close to me. That guard definitely came from being bullied while growing up. It's not a flaw, though. Quite the opposite. It's made my skin so thick nothing can penetrate into the fortress of my heart. Once there, you'll never leave.

Shaking my head as I toss my pretzel bag into the flight attendant's trash bag, I vow to push Marcus and relationship issues from my mind in favor of enjoying myself with my time away from school. My classes are paused, and I'm finally free from tedious obligations. I help head the Naturalists Club, and I'm a part of the yearbook staff at Harvard. When you pair classes and my part-time job at the cafeteria, my time is rarely my own. This is the first real break since Christmas vacation. I enjoy being busy, filling my days with things and people I enjoy, but there's nothing like going home.

Home for me is both people and a place. You wouldn't believe how hard it is to have my schedule jive with Ben's. It's why it's been a year since I last saw him, and as difficult as that's been, I know as soon as I see him it will be like no time has passed at all. That's when you know you have something that will last forever. It's as if that little piece inside you that's reserved for that person, and that person only, recognizes the little piece inside them, and they acknowledge each other. You become whole.

I pick my cuticles and wonder how much he's changed this time. I've seen photos of him and via video chat, but Ben changed almost completely when he became a SEAL. His physical appearance morphed into what you'd expect and something he'd never in his wildest dreams thought possible. He had LASIK done almost immediately, so his face isn't hidden by a pair of dirty glasses sliding down his nose. That was the easiest change to swallow. His long, lean muscles grew and grew until I accused him of using steroids one day while we were chatting via video. He laughed and flexed a bicep and then told me steroid use is illegal for SEALs.

I guess blaming medical enhancers was easier for me than acknowledging he'd become an entirely different person. Ben looks the part, he isn't an impostor any longer, and that, on some subconscious level, distanced him from our friendship...and me more than the 3,040 miles of space.

The plane's wheels touch down, and the pilot begins taxiing to the gate. My nerves strum along because I'm finally here—in the non-stop sunshine of Southern California. I switch my cell off airplane mode and stare at it, waiting for my missed texts and emails to bubble up.

I tap out a quick message to Ben. Landed, and send it quickly. My thumb hovers over Marcus's name, but I don't tap it. I'll call him later when I'm settled. After six and a half hours, I'm still not sure what I'm feeling about Marcus or why I'm feeling anything other than normal. Time away from the situation is exactly what I need.

The aircraft comes to a stop at our gate, and then I hear the resounding clicks of seat belts unfastening even though the fasten seat belt light is still illuminated. Mine stays snugly wrapped around my waist. I send a text message to my mother to let her know I arrived safely and I'll see her soon, and then reply to an email from a potential club member.

Ben's text slides down from the top of my cell phone.

> What are you wearing?

Shaking my head, I reply,

> Tanning oil and a bathing suit.
> SUNSHINE!

I'd never admit I prefer the seasons of the East Coast. Not out loud, at least, but the tumultuous weather suits my personality. The snowstorms are fun, and when the leaves change color in the fall, I can't stop staring. After living in Southern California all of my life, with one season, the sun season, I was surprised to find how much I missed out on. I text again quickly.

> A black tank top and jeans.

> What color is your sweater? I know you aren't sitting bare armed on an airplane seat.

Standing from my seat, I grab my bag and make my way, like cattle herding, to exit the plane. I laugh to myself as I think about Ben's message. I tuck my phone into the oversized beige sweater and readjust my leather weekender on my shoulder. Ben would find me first even if I dyed my hair pink and gave a false description of my outfit, so there's no need to respond.

A lightness takes over as I head toward baggage claim, where I'm meeting Ben. I pass people wheeling heavy suitcases and families toting tired children, and by the time I step foot on the down escalator, I'm vibrating with excitement.

"Harper," Ben calls. I don't have to look far. He's standing at the bottom of the escalator holding up traffic, holding a huge pink balloon that says "Happy Birthday," and he's written my name at the bottom. Well, it says Harpee, a name he hasn't called me in a long time. The fear and anticipation turn to dust the second I throw myself into his strong, familiar arms.

I bury my face in his chest and breathe in the scent of Eight & Bob. He's worn the same fragrance since the day he discovered it was JFK's signature aftershave, and I'd be lying if I said it wasn't the most comforting smell I've ever encountered. Ben pulls me to the side to let people pass, but I still cling to him.

"Let me get a look at ya," Ben says, leaning away, handing me the balloon.

I press my lips together in a firm grin as I take the stupid balloon from his hands. "Ben," I say, swallowing over three hundred sixty-five days down and letting right now soak into awareness. "Pink is my favorite color," I drawl, yanking on the ribbon.

Ben shakes his head. "I hate to admit this, but Boston agrees with you." His eyes flick to every part of my body but hold on my face. "You look beautiful, Harpee. I like your style, too." This isn't Ben flirting, like it would seem to a stranger. This is Ben, the kind man who understands how to treat a woman. Even a woman best friend. He always has a compliment for me.

"You don't look so shabby yourself. Switch up your steroids? Your arms look big." I quip, grabbing his biceps with my hands. "My fingers can't even touch anymore!" I exclaim with mock outrage.

He rolls his eyes. "Your fingers could never touch." Leaning in closer, he whispers, "If you think my biceps are thick, you should see my—"

I clamp my hand over his mouth before he can finish.

Shaking my head, I ignore his joke. "My fingers could touch. Don't lie. You're not some high and mighty hero in my eyes. I know the person suffocating in all of that muscle tissue." I let go of his arms and take a step away from him, suddenly worried what people might think.

He laughs, tilting his head back and flashing his bright, white smile. His jaw is perfectly square, and he has dimples by his eyes when he smiles wide. I learned early on he hates those little dents, but seeing them now, on the person he's become, makes me realize those smile marks might be the only cute thing left about him. He's handsome. Ben is tan and tall, and every woman who passes looks at him more than once.

"Let's get out of here," Ben says when I stay silent. "I'm illegally parked."

"You did not!" I chirp as we start walking. I'm the one who lives and dies by the rules, and he's the one who makes his own. Question everything, Ben once told me. *Don't take everything at face value. Just because someone says something doesn't mean there aren't other ways to do it better.*

Sure enough, a cop is circling his pickup truck when we step through the automatic doors.

"It's my girl's birthday, and she's been flying all day," Ben says, jogging up to the officer and motioning to my balloon. I manage a weak smile but feel like I might combust from anger. This is a typical Ben move. "Please don't give us a ticket on her twenty-first birthday, sir."

The cop looks at me over the bed of the truck. I flash a weak smile. I know exactly how to get my barb in during this situation.

"He's a Navy SEAL, sir. He's used to doing things a little differently than the rest of us. He would have never parked here if he didn't think he'd be late for me. His muscles might have gotten in the way of the *No Parking* sign, you know?" I let my smile filter wider. The cop grins at me. "Please. It truly is my birthday, and I assure you he won't ever double-park again." Not in this spot, at least.

Ben's face is red and his lips are pursed, his gaze lighting me on fire. I dropped the SEAL word in conversation with a stranger. I lick my finger and hold it next to my head while the officer turns to head to his cruiser parked behind Ben's large, black truck. He snarls at me but can't hide his smile. Ben drags his thumb across the front of his neck and points at me with his forefinger at the same time.

The officer returns with a warning, wishes me a happy birthday, and leaves to attack another car double-parked several feet up.

"You're welcome," I say when we're situated in the cab, my balloon bouncing off the ceiling behind our heads. "I should have let you flail, Ben. You know how I am about the law."

"You don't have to always be so perfect, you know? It wouldn't kill you to let loose every once in a while." It's easy for him to say now that he's this beautiful, glorified man.

"I'm still the geeky girl I've always been. It's not so easy for people like me to let loose."

Ben pulls into traffic and looks at ease behind the wheel of the big vehicle, one bulky arm propped on the top of the steering wheel. It smells like him in here, and I take in a deep breath and relax a touch. "But I'm only here for a weekend, so hopefully we can let loose as long as it doesn't involve anything illegal."

He chuckles. "I'm employed by the government, Harper. I don't break any serious laws. I double-parked because I wanted to see you sooner. I'd also like to point out that you don't look like a geek anymore, so you should probably stop referring to yourself in that way. It looks desperate."

He glances over, a grin in place. His brown eyes flutter a couple times before he turns his attention back to the road, waiting for my retort. "It doesn't matter what you look like, Ben. It's what's inside."

"I beg to differ. I'm a prime example," he replies, palming his wide chest with a free hand. "You know I'm the same person even if I don't look anything like what I used to. People treat me one way because they don't know who I really am. You've never known how beautiful you are. It's so bad that people probably think the low self-esteem thing is for attention."

I scoff. "That's not even close to the truth. I'm confident."

He nods. "I know that, but do others?" I fold my arms across my chest, and he continues on. "I got us concert tickets for tonight. We'll go see our parents now to get that out of the way."

I laugh. "I do actually miss my parents," I say. "What concert?" I ask, my voice a little too loud.

Ben laughs. "A wee bit excited, huh? Just your favorite indie rock band of all time," he says, sighing in a big, exaggerated way.

"No way," I say. "Cold War Kids?"

"Yes way. We need to be pre-gaming by five, so I hope you don't want to spend too much time hanging out with the parental units."

I squeal so loudly, I have to cover my own ears.

"You better wear something illegal," he replies, wincing at my excitement.

CHAPTER FOUR

Ben

I TRIED to take the third glass of whiskey from her hand at my place, but she insisted on swallowing it down. Her cheeks were already red, so I should have known to force the issue. She promised to tell me if she got the spins. That was my last concession before we dumped ourselves into the back seat of an Uber and made our way to the concert venue. We're right next to the stage. My buddy Tahoe has Harper on his shoulders so she doesn't get squashed, and because I didn't trust her on the floor by herself while I went to the restroom.

Seeing her after all this time does weird things to me. It's a nostalgic feeling of being home, just by being in her proximity, but there's also more—a longing so violent, I'm unsure how long I can stave off the desire. The band starts playing the song "First," and I can hear Harper scream from my place several feet to her right. Her lithe arms are in the air and her cropped shirt rides up, showing off even more of her tight stomach. I glare at Tahoe when he catches my eye. He shrugs and makes a crude tongue gesture. I roll my eyes and shake my head. He'd never touch her. He knows Harper is everything to me.

I want her on my shoulders and I'm about to tell Tahoe to hand her over, when Harper's voice cuts through the air, "Ben!"

I smile and tilt up my chin to let her know I heard.

"Take a photo! It's my favorite song. Take a photo!" she yells, making a goofy hand motion like she's snapping a photo.

Nodding, I slide my phone out of my pocket, hold it up, and snap several photos. Swallowing hard, I scroll through them and give her a thumbs-up. She's already staring at the band, the excited light in her eyes, her lips mouthing the words to the song. Harper is beautiful—a step beyond stunning and bordering on scary attractive. I post one of the photos on my Instagram account with a simple caption: #twenty #plusone. She's smiling wide, her arms lifted high above her head, and half of her face is masked by a cascade of wild hair.

Harper doesn't do Instagram, her social media prowess is limited to Facebook. She logs in there just because her college groups are active participants and it's mandatory to keep up. She's had the same profile photo for over a year. It's a black-and-white candid photo taken of her profile. I never asked who took that photo, but I love it. I'd probably be a little sad if she does change it just because it's something I associate with her. I, on the other hand, love social media of all sorts. As long as I keep my filters and privacy settings strong, I can post what I want, where I want.

I return to studying Harper in person. Her long chestnut hair hangs halfway down her back in waves, and every curve on her goddamn body was sculpted to my exact preference. Tahoe sees me staring and motions for me to grab her. He lifts her tiny frame off his body and places her in front of me. I can't take my eyes off her moving lips as the words from the song feel like they were meant just for us—right now. Harper moves toward me, her hands falling on the front of my sweaty shirt. Tahoe rejoins our group of brothers and the women they came with to leave us alone.

I grab her hands and lock them with mine. We stare at each other and don't say anything at all. The music says everything we can't...or won't. The buzz of life and energy around us is electric, and the second she leans up toward me, I think it's finally going to be it. This will be the moment we'll call ours. Then the song ends, and hesitation lights her eyes as she pulls away from me. Harper swipes a hand across her forehead.

"Feeling okay?" I ask, leaning into her ear so she can hear over the roar of applause. "We can get some air."

"I need another drink," she replies, trying to distance herself from my body.

I catch her hand in mine. "Hey," I say, pulling her back. "It's me."

"I know," Harper says, her eyes brimming with tears. A far-off look washes her features, and it's not the blatant drunk eyes. She licks her lips and says, "It's you." She nearly chokes on those final words, and I'm left wondering what she means.

She swallows hard and turns to flee. I follow her out into the lobby, where they're selling T-shirts and stickers and beer. "I need a shirt," she says, unfolding a wad of cash she pulls out of her tight jeans.

"Okay," I reply, my ears fuzzy now that we're away from the amps. My hearing won't ever be the same after the blasts and explosions I've been around. She buys an oversized black shirt with a simple logo and pulls it over her head, effectively cutting off my view of her tight stomach and the outline of her tits. "Everything okay?"

"I will be. Let's get another drink?" she asks, flitting over to the alcohol line before I can respond. This is

Harper trying to do avoidance. "This is so great. Thank you, Ben. For tonight. It's really...awesome."

I'll let her get away with it for now, so she feels like she has some control of her emotions, but when we're alone tonight, in my bed, I'm going to call her the fuck out. "Happy Birthday, Harper. It needed to be something to remember. It is your twenty-first. Memorable?"

"Did you hear them? They're so amazing in person. This is more than memorable. Maybe even the best birthday ever." I can think of several awesome birthdays and there's only one way this one will take the proverbial cake, and I need to make it happen. Fate is in my hands.

Harper orders a couple drinks, throws too much cash on the bar, and then pushes a drink into my hands.

"I'm not sure more alcohol is the answer," I tell her, sipping the top so it doesn't spill any more than she already has. I grab the bill the bartender is trying to hand back to Harper and slide it into my pocket, shaking my head.

She takes a few long swallows. "The answer to what?" she asks, quirking a brow. A slight sheen of sweat glistens on her face, and it reminds me of when she's working out. That thought moves to other more inappropriate thoughts, and by the time she asks me her question again, I've already mentally undressed her.

"Uh, do you want to get out of here now? I think they're finished after this song." I check my watch and glance up to meet her eyes. A little line appears between her eyes as she thinks, and she stumbles back. I grab the solo cup from her hands and dump the remnants into my cup. She's done.

"Yeah, if I'm going to get sick, I'd rather be at home." My chest puffs out. She called my place home. Then I realize she mentioned getting sick. Her cell phone chimes, and she fumbles to get it out of the top of her shirt. The iPhone falls to the cement floor. Face down. We all know how that ends.

I stoop down and pick it up. "Shit, it's cracked," I say, a second before I see the dozens of texts from some dude named Marcus. The stream of texts goes a little like this:

Where are you?

Text me back.

Where are you?

What are you doing?

You better text me back right now.

Call me.

FUCKING CALL ME.

"Who the fuck is Marcus?" I ask, and the second I say his name, I know who it is. The guy she studies with. I gulp in a huge breath as the significance of this hits me full force. "Harper," I say her name like a question. "Why is he texting you like this?" I flash the cracked screen at her face so she can see his obviously angry messages.

She looks away, to the right. "Do you think we can get it fixed tonight? I bet some place is open." Taking the phone from my hand, she licks her lips and examines it closer.

Grinding my teeth, I take her hand in mine. "Let's go." I text a group message to let my friends know we're taking off because Harper is drunk. A few inappropriate emoji messages flash up immediately. Even in a venue such as this loud, raucous theater, my brothers are tuned into their surroundings and their phones in case of emergency.

Clutching my arm in a death grip, Harper lets me

guide her out into the street. I pull up my app and call for an Uber while seething in her direction. "What are you keeping from me?" I interrupt. Harper is talking to me about a club at school and how her mom gave her a bag of goodies we should eat when we get back. "Avoiding the subject isn't going to fare well for you."

Her head whips in my direction, hurt shining in her eyes. I open my mouth to apologize, but the white sedan squeals around the corner. Twenty-five security guards who pace the exterior of the theater are automatically on alert at the quick, asshole maneuver. Their guns are drawn, and gazes slide to our proximity. Even halfway in the bag, I'm aware of everything around me. I hold up my hand to show the guards everything is okay. "Ubers. Time is money, right?" I call out. Security doesn't look amused with my lowbrow jab and continue to monitor our every step.

"Are you okay, ma'am?" a guard asks Harper as he approaches us.

"Me?" Harper looks alarmed at the attention. Her eyes flit to the gun in his hand. As do mine. For a different reason. "I'm fine. I drank too much, but it's my birthday and the band was amazing. Are we in trouble? It's all his fault if we are," she says, hiking a thumb over her shoulder awkwardly. "Everything is always his fault. He never does anything he's supposed to."

I groan and lean over to talk to the Uber driver, who rolled down the window. To the guard I say, "I'm trying to get my friend home, sir."

He nods and holsters his gun and then warns the driver to slow down. The guy looks scared, and if I was already concerned about putting Harper's life in the hands of a strange driver, now I'm even more so. "Harper," I say, guiding her into the back seat. My hand accidentally brushes her bare stomach, and she freezes at the touch.

She straightens and slides into the seat with a clumsy slump. I wish the officer good night and sit next to Harper in the back seat.

"You really could use some driving lessons. Didn't you think about where you were picking us up? Guards crawl all over crowds. Use your head a little. You have one job."

He looks abashed. I'm not sure if it's because of my size, the fact I'm leaning into the front seat, or the threat behind my words, but it works. He drives the speed limit all the way to my place. Harper is asleep, draped across my lap when he puts the car in park. I pull her out of the car as gently as I can. She rouses and swallows, wiping the corner of her mouth with her forearm. "That was a quick trip," she mutters, fidgeting with the phone she has tucked in her top.

The car pulls away slowly, and I lead her up the cobblestones of my front walkway. It's a cottage, a small house with one bedroom and few furnishings. Harper was impressed when we stopped here earlier to drop off her things. She said it reminded her of a hobbit house and skipped across the hardwood floor like a Disney princess. I pull my key out of my pocket and try to keep one arm on her as she leans against the doorframe.

With her head against the dark gray stone, she lets it fall to the side. "You're cute when you're furious," she says, slurring every other word.

I close my eyes, take in a calming breath, and push the door open. I hold out my arm like a good gentleman should and tamp down on the boiling rage I feel thinking about the text messages and her meek attempts to avoid the subject. "After you," I say, prompting her when she doesn't make a move.

Her eyes scan my face, and her gaze falls to my lips. My heart hammers, and that uneasy, questionable feeling enters my bloodstream for the second time tonight. "I should stay at my parents' house. Think that driver can come take me there?" Harper asks. After her question is out, she begins humming a song from Cold War Kids.

I shake my head. "It's late. I want to talk to you. Go in, Harper."

Sighing, she flicks her gaze over my chest and midsection and then walks through the door, ambling to the brown grocery sack on the counter in the kitchen. She pulls herself up on the barstool and dumps the bag with the grace of Ben-Hur. "Come eat some of this with me, Benny."

My anger subsides a touch when she uses my old nickname, but I wonder if she's doing it purposefully. I know her well enough to know how well she knows me. "Marcus," I say. One word. "Start talking."

She spins on the stool, a string of licorice in her hand, wielding it like a weapon. "He's my boyfriend, Ben. What do you want to know?"

I'm drawn to her, and even though I don't remember moving, I'm standing in front of her in seconds, her eyes looking up at me and my frame in between her legs. "Let's pretend for a second that he is really your boyfriend, which I have a hard time believing because you haven't mentioned that. Why is he texting you like a ragey asshole? That's not okay. Even less okay than you having a boyfriend to begin with."

She scowls. "You're not my father. You can't tell me I can't have a boyfriend. Heck, even my father can't tell me I can't have a boyfriend. I'm an adult the last time I checked."

Shaking my head, I say, "I never said you couldn't have one. I said I don't like it."

Harper catches her breath and holds it. After a beat of two, she brings the red candy to her lips and bites off a piece. Chewing with her mouth closed, she watches my face. After she swallows, she says, "I've been with him for a while now. I told you we studied together, and that wasn't a lie. We have classes together. Same major. As for why he acted like a complete moron in those texts, well, I can't say for sure. Though I'm not sure why, but I think jealousy might have something to do with it."

"Can I call him?" My heart is hammering. No one talks to Harper like that. No one touches Harper. No one loves Harper. No one but me.

Her eyes widen, then she relaxes a touch. "What do you want to talk to him about?"

I walk into the kitchen and pour a glass of water and slide it in front of her, then open the cabinet and take out a bottle of whiskey and pour two fingers into a glass and gulp it down.

"I get water and you get alcohol? That's not fair. It's my birthday."

"You can't handle your liquor like I can." I shrug at her expression. "It's the truth. Deny it."

She doesn't. Instead, she pulls her phone out of her little, tight top and slides the cracked device across the counter. "Call him then. Maybe he'll chill out."

Or maybe I'll kill him via telekinesis. I pick it up, find his number, and hit the green button. Harper shoves a whole licorice stick in her mouth and grins. I walk into my bedroom, shut the door, and sit on my bed.

"Where the fuck have you been?" Marcus says.

"Who the fuck are you to talk to Harper like that?" I seethe, trying and failing to keep my voice low.

"Who's this?" Marcus asks.

"This is Ben."

"Oh," is his response. Oh. Like I'm some fucking

afterthought. I've been her only thought for as long as she's been alive, and this motherfucker is going to settle into the place I give him. "Where is she?"

"We were at the concert tonight. For her birthday. She didn't have her phone on, nor would I assume she could hear it in that madness. We just got home. Now, answer my question. Why the fuck are you talking to my girl like that?"

He laughs. "Your girl?"

I swallow down the bitter pang of reality. She's not my girl, but somehow along the way I've forgotten that fact. "Yeah. My girl."

"She's my girlfriend, Ben. She sleeps in my bed. Harper and I have more in common now. You're her childhood best friend. You're her past, bro. I'm her future. Move your muscles out of the way for a second or two and you'll clearly see she's changed. I didn't want her to go. So, yeah, I'm pissed off she's ignoring me."

My breath stalls, and it's because there's truth in his words. "She's not ignoring you," I say, swallowing down all of the insults I was planning on saying. Marcus is merely jealous. Harper was right. He obviously cares for her. I can't say I'd be acting any differently if the woman I loved was spending the weekend with a man like me. I sigh. "I'll always be in her life. Always. Better learn how to like me."

He laughs. "Where is she? Put her on."

My fist is balled so tight I have to work to loosen my grip before I punch a hole through the wall. "She's indisposed at the moment," I whisper, hoping he assumes the worst.

"We're talking about the same girl, right? She'd never do anything with you. It doesn't serve her moral compass."

Now, I laugh. "I am her compass. She'll always come back to me. Remember that."

I click off the phone before I let him say another word that will pick at the threads of my relationship with Harper. Sure, things have changed, because we grew up, but our friendship will always remain. Even if she's dating a dickhead. It's a dickhead who obviously knows her.

She peeks her head into the door. "Did you verbally assault him? Is he scared straight?" She laughs. I smirk and hang my head, and she sits next to me on the bed. "I had some of your whiskey."

Groaning, I look at her. "Don't puke everywhere, okay? That's way worse than beer shits."

Harper laughs, her pretty face lighting up. "We have a lot in common," she explains after a long, silent pause. "Marcus and I work out because we have many of the same goals, the same friends, the same interests."

And he's there. With you, I think.

She sets her hand on my leg. Glancing her way, she's looking at me, eyes full of every damn thing I try to forget. I angle my body to face her. Harper blows a huge, pink, sweet-smelling bubble directly in my face. Her mom really did fill that bag with treats.

Her eyes slant in a smile around the round balloon. She pops the bubble and slides the gum back in her mouth with a few big smacks. "He'll never be you," she says, her voice low. Leaning into my embrace, Harper lays her forehead against my chest.

All I can smell is the gum. All I can feel is her lips.

Spin the Bottle

BEN

THE EMPTY, green box of Ecto Cooler is sitting by her knee, the orange straw brushing her bare leg. "I practiced on my hand. I feel like this should be easy," she says, her eyes wide and fixed on mine. Licking her lips, she tilts her head to study my lips, like I'm some science experiment.

I nod. "You can't be that bad at it. You didn't have to practice on my account."

"If we're ever going to one of Jenny's parties, we need to know how to kiss. They play seven minutes in heaven and spin the bottle, Benny. We need all the practice we can get. My hand is always around. You're not."

Imagining my first real kiss always involved Harper, but in my dreams it wasn't as unromantic as this. We're sixteen, and instead of making out in the back of a movie theater like most kids our age, we're in the old wooden treehouse my dad built us when we were seven. "If you want to make out with me for practice, I'll be around more," I say, waggling my eyebrows, grinning.

"Gross. Don't make this any weirder than it has to be. I want to be skilled. Maybe then the boys in our class will want me." A pang of envy slices through my chest, and the smile fades from my face. "I mean, that's what they want, right? Good kissers?" She's misreading my facial cues. Thank God.

She has full lips and perfect skin. That's not what they want, though. Harper has an ass and body on her that should be illegal. I know that's how I've tagged her because she's my best friend. All of the guys want her. Every single one. I'm weak, ol' Benny, so it's just a matter of time before some jock comes and takes her out of my treehouse and life. I won't be able to do anything to stop it, but I can make sure I have her first kiss. "Right. That's what they want." And sex.

She gets up on her knees and takes the empty juice box in her hand and places it between us. "Spin it. We'll practice like it's going to be the real thing." Her cheeks are red now. When I comment on her flustered appearance, she swats me on the shoulder and tells me to grow up. "Spin Slimer, Benny. This needs to be somewhat legitimate so it's not two desperate teens practicing kissing for a cool kid's party."

Swallowing, I scoot closer to the box. "What if it's not just practice for me? I'm desperate," I reply, looking at her.

Harper raises one brow.

"I'm desperate to kiss you," I say, my voice cracking.

She chews her bubble gum a few times, and her eyebrows pull together. Harper isn't confused, she's trying to figure out the meaning behind my words. She's self-conscious, so I know where she's going to jump first. I hold out my hand, the first move. "Because I want to kiss you. Not because I want practice for any other girl."

Her jaw stops working. "Benny. I'll kiss you no matter what. You don't have to pretend." She puts her hand in mine, and it's electric—a jolt of testosterone and pride and every other thing she makes me feel. Alive.

I walk toward her on my knees, and I think my heart might explode out of my chest. I never see her this close up, and it's a crying shame. The way her soft eyelashes flutter when she looks away seems like a movement from a dream dimension. I grab her chin when she's close enough and tilt her chin to look up at me. Shaking my head, I say, "This isn't me pretending."

My black glasses slip down my nose. Harper grins. Familiar territory. With soft hands, she reaches up and takes my glasses off, folds them, and sets them on the windowsill. "You're not like…you right now," she says. That's exactly what I want her to feel. I want to be the man she wants, not the boy she's known. "It's hot."

"Do you want to kiss me?" I ask. It's mostly out of curiosity, because I can't get a read on her. Is she playing?

Licking her lips, she sticks her tongue through her bubble gum and blows a bubble, her eyes slanted in thought as she studies my face. The bubble gets so huge I know I could pop it and it would cover her face. I don't, though. I wait for her to bite the bubble and recapture the gum in her mouth. Harper takes the gum out and sets it on the side of the juice box and takes the final step on her knee to put us chest to chest.

Her breaths come faster now, and I want to say something to calm her. To let her know I'm just as nervous and how much this means to me, but words don't come. Blood does, rushing to my dick faster than when I look at my dad's tittie mags he keeps in the bottom of his bathroom drawer. Harper puts her hands around my neck, and my hands automatically lock around the bottom of her back, one hand creeping down to her ass.

"I want to kiss you," she says. Her voice isn't confident. It almost comes out as a question. "I've always wanted to kiss you," she finishes.

Her hands slide up the back of my head, and a bolt of

pleasure washes over my whole body. It tingles and my hard-on pounds and she's in my arms and I can feel the heat of her skin through the thin white shirt. Her eyes are locked on mine, and it feels surreal, like we're adults, like we're finally doing something because we want to, not because it's what we should do or what's expected of us. She breathes out, and I smell Bubble Yum, and my mouth waters.

Because I'm trying to be the man and not the boy, I run my hands up her sides, and the simple movement elicits a sigh from her, and my head swims a little. Can you black out from anticipation? From all the blood traveling to my cock instead of my brain? Is that possible? I should know something like this.

"Benny," she moans out, her eyes closed and her forehead pressed against mine.

"It's me," I reply, returning my hands to her lower back.

I tilt my head to the side the tiniest of degrees and press my lips against hers. She responds right away, opening slightly. I follow her lead and move my lips in sync with hers. She clutches my neck tighter, and I pull her against me closer. My mind clears. It's amazing. At any given moment, my brain is filled with a thousand video clips of worries, concerns, or just noise. My concerns about ruining our friendship by mixing kisses disappear. Softly, I bring my hands up to cradle her face and use my thumb to pry her mouth open a little wider.

I want everything. All of her. I slide my tongue out tentatively, and she jumps a little, but after a second she meets me with her tongue, and it's so soft and so wet, and it tastes like Harper and bubble gum, and I forget to breathe. I forget everything except what's underneath my hands.

The kiss turns a little more frantic as we both gain

confidence. Her hands leave my neck and travel down to the bottom of my tee. Harper runs her fingertips under my shirt, against my skin, while keeping her lips against mine. In a quick blast of panic, I pull away, my eyes still closed and my chest heaving.

"My god," I say, swallowing, holding Harper by her shoulders. When I let my eyes open, I notice her eyes are heavy, her pink mouth open and swollen. She's staring at me with a hungry look in her eye. Everything about this moment is perfect. We're not kids anymore. The switch flipped. All generators are running on high. Words aren't needed. We can read each other without even trying.

She leans in and kisses me again. This time we know what we're doing a little more than last time, and when she breaks away to catch her breath, I feel more than everything. I pull her against my body and my raging hard-on.

"I love you, Benny," she whispers, hugging my neck like a spider monkey.

"I love you, Harper Jean."

She pulls away, grinning like a maniac. We're such rebels. "I also love those Bubble Yum lips," I say through a wide smile. "Give me some more of those?"

She does.

CHAPTER FIVE
Harper

I STRETCH my arms over my head, and my hands run into the headboard. Not the familiar wicker headboard from my apartment or the cool steel of Marcus's. My eyes pop open and I roll over and slap Ben in the face. "Sorry. Sorry!" I whisper-shout into the dark bedroom. "Ben! What are you doing in here?"

"It's my bed. What are you doing in here? That's the question," Ben says, voice hoarse and drowsy—utterly mouthwatering. Let's be honest, here. Everything about him does things to my body that I work hard to deny. It's harder when he's next to me. In bed. When I'm wearing...wait. What am I wearing? A crop top and a pair of lacy white underwear. Perfect. I'm barely awake, and I already feel like the whore of Babylon.

One of his arms juts out, and he pulls me against his body. "I left all my clothes on. I know your prude sensibilities, but the sofa wasn't long enough to hold me."

There's no use struggling against his snuggle, so I go willingly, letting his cozy body heat envelop mine. He smells like Ben. A hint of his signature scent mixed with the indiscernible smell that is him—home.

"This is so inappropriate. I'm going to hell," I groan,

trying to think of the last time I called Marcus. I can't be sure, but I'm almost positive I win the award for world's worst girlfriend. Guilt lies heavily on my chest as the whole scenario of my time here is realized.

Ben cuddles me closer, his lips at my ear. "Do you think I'd do anything untoward while you were blitz-faced drunk? Come on. You know I like my ladies willing participants."

I cringe. "You're such a dog, Ben. I have a boyfriend." His body stiffens. Not his penis. No, that's been hard since the moment he woke up. "One who would cast me to the dogs if he saw me right now. Best friend or not, a hard dick this close to my ass has to be a deal breaker for most people."

He laughs. "Fine. Fine." He slides away, and I roll to face him. "I can't believe you didn't tell me, Harper. I thought we were closer than that."

Sighing, I contemplate every single word I'm about to say and the many ways in which they can be misinterpreted.

"It got weird. Too much time had passed; I fibbed once, and it kind of snowballed." My purse is sitting on the nightstand, and my eyes widen as I make a grab for it and pull out my birth control pills. I swallow the one meant for last night without water and realize how dry my mouth is. It's a desert, California in the middle of drought, death. "I need water," I croak.

Ben watches the whole thing, and pain flickers across his face. I have to physically remove myself from him before I comfort him. That would be inappropriate. "You're sleeping with him?" His eyes crinkle as he asks. It's almost humorous, because how in the world could I not be sleeping with my boyfriend? Ben will always see me as ten years younger than I actually am.

Sighing, I run a hand across my forehead. This isn't a

conversation I'd have with anyone, let alone Ben. Though, maybe he can help me figure out if Marcus is jealous. Best friends do that a lot, right? "I live with him. Sex is sort of a given. I'm twenty-one, not fifteen. Sometimes I think you forget that I grew up the same time you did, with you."

Ben folds his arms behind his head, and he looks so damn hot I have to stand and turn away from the bed. The first time I slept with Marcus, I was completely uncomfortable. I didn't really want to do it, but he was persuasive, and I knew it was time to let my old dreams die hard. "I picture you at school, at class, and going to your clubs and study groups. I never thought you'd live with a dude. Fuck another dude."

"Was I supposed to wait for you?" I ask, swallowing down broken dreams. "You know what? Never mind. Want breakfast?" I ask, desperate to change the subject. Jealous Ben isn't fun. He never has been.

Turning, I hit him with my biggest smile. I've never quite been sure where his jealousy stems from. He doesn't want me romantically, I don't think. It's more of a claim thing. He claimed me as his, and because he's male and they bang on their chests, jealousy is akin to breathing.

We're both aware he doesn't answer my question, but unlike him, I'm not going to force him to say anything. That answer isn't good for either of us.

"Yeah. Let's go eat. I need to erase the images flashing through my brain." Ben runs both hands through his hair, back and forth several times.

I know how to stop the flood of images, but I can't fix it for him. Not right now, not at this stage in our lives.

His cell phone rings, he mumbles something under his breath, and he walks into the bathroom.

Digging through my suitcase, I find a pair of sleep

shorts and pull them on. It takes longer than it should because I'm lost in my thoughts of Ben and me in bed, in my underwear, and what all it implies. All I wish it meant. A flash of a future so muddied by life lights my senses and then promptly turns to dust.

He clears his throat. "We didn't do anything, Harper," Ben hisses from the bathroom doorway, body propped against the frame, startling me from my daydream.

Glancing over my shoulder, I catch sight of him. He's shirtless now, because that's his natural state. I have to remind myself he's always walked around shirtless after he transformed into a perfect male specimen. He truly did wear a shirt to bed because of my prude sensibilities. I wish I wasn't that kind of girl. The meek, do-what-you're-told, type. Old habits die hard, and I should praise Ben for realizing that as much as things change about me, that one facet never will.

"You wouldn't tell me if we did. Don't lie, you perv." I knock him off balance on my way out of the room and into the kitchen. I duck out of his grasp as he tries to catch me around the waist. My cracked cell phone sits on the counter, a glaring reminder of the person inside of it.

"If you get everything out for me, I'll make breakfast. I need to make a quick phone call." It's so late in the morning that it's already an acceptable time to call the East Coast. Marcus will be up, sipping his morning tea and watching the news, a textbook sitting next to him.

"Make it fast. We have big plans today," Ben growls, laughing. Our uncomfortable exchange is already buried. In record time, no less. We're able to hide almost anything inside the confines of our friendship. It wasn't until recently that I realized that's not always a good thing. He's still thinking about me and Marcus together, and I'm still thinking about how I wish it were him.

Savagery.

I hit speed dial number two, and Marcus answers on the second ring. "There you are. Are you okay? You had me worried last night." His words are mashed together in one long wind. To his credit, he does sound worried. His text messages were so rude and unlike him that I was afraid to call him at first.

I close my eyes. All this guilt. I didn't do anything to feel guilty about, and yet I feel it all the same. My heart is a traitor. "I'm so sorry, Marcus. We did have so much fun, though. My screen is cracked. I'll take it in to get fixed today, so I may be unreachable for a while." I listen to him breathing for a moment or two, then continue, "What are you up to today?"

"That's all?" he asks after a few more silent seconds. For me, those seconds are loud and unbearable. What will he ask next? Can he see his imprint on my soul? Does he have that unquantifiable sense I don't? I'm always a step behind, socially.

"Yeah. The concert was awesome. Then we came home and went to sleep."

"Hmm," Marcus replies. He doesn't believe me, and I want to scream out all of the truths.

Ben is watching me over the rim of his drink. When I catch him looking, he looks away and pretends to be busy.

I yank on the hem of my short shorts self-consciously.

"I miss you, Harper. I know how much you like that band. I'm glad you got to see them while you were there. I, uh, wish I were the one who took you." Jealousy. It seeps in enough that even a dull wit like me can recognize it through a phone call.

"Maybe we can go together when they're on the East Coast," I offer. "I'd see them a million times. You spoke with Ben last night?" I edge, while he seems to be engulfed with missing me. Ben is

57

banging a frying pan around on the stove. I cover the ear not holding a cell phone and glare in his direction.

"I did. He seems like a...nice guy."

I breathe out a sigh of relief. I didn't hear what was said last night, mostly because I was drunk and in a candy haze, but Ben was upset after the conversation, so I couldn't be sure.

"I won't pretend to know your relationship with him because it seems complicated. I didn't know that a male-female relationship could ever function platonically into adulthood, but I'm going to trust you, Harper. I'm an intelligent man. I know he's in your life to stay. I hope I am, too."

I smile. This is the charismatic man I fell in love with. "Of course you are. How was your last exam?" I ask. Flopping down onto the couch, I listen to his story about the exam and how he had to guess on the last question. I reassure him by giving a statistic on what his chances are of selecting the right answer. He laughs a little, and as I lie back on the arm of the couch, I find myself smiling at the ceiling.

I tell him about seeing my parents, and although I wait for it, he doesn't ask about my sleeping arrangement at Ben's. I end the call with a good feeling about Marcus—all hesitation erased. I walk into the kitchen warily. "Over medium with toast?" I ask.

He clears his throat and nods. "Marcus makes you happy," Ben says.

If he'd asked me this question ten minutes ago, I'd have had a different answer, but I have to tell him the truth. Ben is a hero. He lives and breathes in a world that's equal parts destroyed and perfect. I live in the perfect version, and he's not my superhero. Ben can't be. "I'm happy, Ben. I need to be a good girlfriend for him.

Give him a chance, yeah?" I nudge him with my shoulder.

He shoulders me back, his bare arm sliding against mine. "You leave me no option. Now cook, Suzy Homemaker. Man is hungry."

"Oh, piss off, Benny," I squawk, laughing at his stupid joke he knows will offend me. "I'll poison your food."

"Tahoe is on his way over to pick up my bag."

I crack a couple eggs on the side of the pan and listen to the fizzle and pops. "He reminds me of Arnold Schwarzenegger in that movie where half of his face is a robot. He's scary."

Ben laughs, tells me to flip the eggs because he's micromanaging, and says, "Tahoe is solid. A lot of these guys have been doing this job for such a long time. They teach me a lot. They were SEALs before the attack. Can you imagine? Just normal SEALs."

I laugh. "As opposed to what? Hybrid SEALs?"

He sighs. "Nah. Just less…risk."

At the tenor of his voice, I turn to face him, and I raise one brow. "How much risk are you in on a normal workday, exactly?"

He cranes his neck to look at the eggs in the pan. "Less risk than those poor eggs are currently enduring."

Rolling my eyes, I scoop the eggs out and onto a waiting plate, but I can't shake the uneasy feeling. "Seriously. Be honest with me."

"Ah. Ah. Ah. We're not completely honest with each other anymore. Remember?"

"Touché. Fair point, but I need to know how much danger you're in. For my own sanity."

The doorbell rings and Ben escapes my glare. Tahoe ambles in, his large frame hiding the sunlight. "What's for breakfast?" he quips, flicking his gaze my way.

"Eggs?" I ask, holding up Ben's plate.

"No, that's mine!" Ben says, reaching over the counter to take the plate from my hands. "I'll cook you something if you want, man," Ben says, nodding at Tahoe.

"Nah. I'm going to meet a girl at Hash House," he replies, a predatory smile stretching across his face. "What are you two kids getting up to today?"

I drink a sip of Ben's orange juice and skirt around the corner, self-conscious about my shorts. It was fine to sleep in my underwear with Ben, but a strange man can't see me in my pajamas. I realize the twisted hypocrisy. "He won't tell me. Evidently they're pretty terrific, though." I laugh a little. "You don't strike me as a man who brunches," I add on.

"I'm getting my greens in. Their Bloody Mary counts as vegetables, and they serve beer in brown bags. So, yes, I do brunch."

"And I'm sure her tits are dessert," Ben adds, butting in.

Cringing, I shoot him a dirty look. "Don't be crass, Ben. It doesn't suit you. It reeks of desperation."

Tahoe laughs as he looks between us. "Ben didn't lie then," Tahoe remarks. Then to Ben he says, "Where's your bag, dude? I'll get it packed up when I drop my stuff off later. You got that new Kevlar in there? Don't want you getting any holes in your pretty, perfect body."

Ben looks at me, eyes wide. "He's joking. Of course he's joking," he says, glaring at Tahoe for a second before turning his gaze back to me and my gaping mouth. "I'll throw it in your truck, dude."

Tahoe looks taken aback, and he realizes what he's said.

"Sorry. I'm not used to filtering. You understand?" he says, eyes softening. "Ben's body repels bullets. He can't get shot even when he tries."

"Oh my god, Tahoe. Shut the fuck up, dude!"

"Did you almost get shot?" I nearly yell. It's one thing to suspect things given his job description, but it's quite another to hear them spoken about as truth. My heart hammers.

"Which time?" Tahoe laughs.

Ben punches Tahoe's arm. It's lighthearted because they're laughing, but I feel like someone signed my death sentence. Ben's death sentence. I'm still breathing heavily when Ben returns from bringing his huge bag outside as Tahoe's loud truck pulls away.

I'm standing in the same spot. Tahoe said his good-byes, and I must have mumbled through them, but I don't recall just what I said. Visions of Ben bleeding out, bullet holes peppered throughout his body, overtake all sane, rational thoughts. My perfect life has never been more glaring than right now, when I realize that while I'm worrying about exams and jealous boyfriends, Ben is dodging bullets and praying he escapes with his life. The attacks changed everything in our world, but in my universe, they damaged the one thing I hold dearest.

Ben and I aren't the same anymore.

The door slams behind him, pulling me from my nightmare. He's breathing heavy from toting his huge bag, and his abs flex and cave as he breathes. "Get dressed. First up is the comic book store. Then the beach and ice cream," he says, waggling his brows.

Swallowing down the lump in my throat, I throw myself into his arms. "Maybe we can do some Jazzercise first?" I whisper through ragged breaths.

He chuckles under his breath. "Sure thing, geek. I'll dig out my sweatband."

CHAPTER SIX

Harper

"THAT ONE IS DEFINITELY Jim Carrey from *Dumb and Dumber*," I say, pointing at a cloud. We've played this game since we were small. Animals are too easy, so the clouds have to resemble characters from movies or shows. "Ten points for me."

"Yeah, I see that. Ten points awarded," he mumbles, irritated I'm ahead. "The clouds are always best at the beach."

He has a huge blanket spread on the soft sand. It's a beach on his base, so it's empty but for us. It's strange, to be honest. I grew up here, and we never had military access, so we were always packed into the popular beaches like animals.

I think about how fluffy and beautiful the clouds are on the East Coast, but I don't say it. It would make this moment less somehow. "Yes. Especially when we don't have to worry about people stepping on us."

"It's nice, huh?" he asks. He's actually curious. I haven't been exposed to his military world, and I can tell he's doing it incrementally.

Rolling toward him, I prop one arm up on my head so I can look down at him. "When I can't hear gunfire, sure, it's nice. Are you happy? Does this kind of life make you happy? Happier than you'd be with..." I say, almost saying me. "Than college and studying stuff that interests you? Don't get me wrong, Ben. I'm proud of you. So proud. But as your best friend, I need to hear you tell me you're happy with this life." My gaze skirts to the dark buildings on the horizon—the place the bullets are firing.

He turns to look at me, squinting in the sun. He refuses to wear sunglasses. He says after years and years of wearing corrective lenses, he'll never wear glasses of any sort again. While it's idiotic, it also makes sense. I shade his eyes with my palm so the sun is deflected, and he smiles.

"They're practicing right now. I'd be at the range if I wasn't here with you. I'm not sure how to answer, Harper. I'm happy knowing I'm making a difference. Before you ask, yes, I am making a difference. Will I go down in history books? Who knows?"

He licks his lips, and I keep my hand in place. "You know I had a hard time understanding your reasoning, but I give you credit. You've been steadfast with your decision for a few years now. Will you stay in the Navy forever, then? Is this it for you?"

"Deep questions when I have a belly full of salted caramel, Harpee," Ben replies, sitting up. Now he's looking down at me, so I sit up as well. "I'm happy." I want more, and he knows it. Biting the corner of his lip, he adds, "I don't think school would make me happy knowing how messed up the rest of the world is. I'm not faulting you for your choice, but knowing what I know now…it changes everything. There's so much bad in the world. Stuff civilians have no clue about. Stuff that would change everything."

I pick up the Spider-Man comic book sitting on the blanket between us and page through it. "Yeah, that's true." I whisper the words. "I want the best for you." For so long I thought I knew what that was. Seeing him here in this element proves me wrong and tells me he's where he needs to be regardless of how I feel. "Are you safe?"

My thumb lands on the page where Spider-Man defeats a bad guy, and I sigh. I meet his gaze. I've ignored Tahoe's comments from earlier all day. Right now seems the best time to bring them up. While I'm listening to guns firing.

He grabs my face with his thumb and forefinger. "Don't worry about me."

I'm indignant. "Someone has to! Telling me not to worry has never worked," I sling back, chewing on my thumbnail.

Ben gives me a crooked grin and grabs my wrist to halt my bad habit. I remember when that same grin went from a geeky smirk to a panty-scorching smile, and I blink away the memory from long ago. "I have, ah, girl-friends. I'm not lonely. Is that what you're asking? If people worry about me?"

"Ugh. No. I don't want to know about your girl-friends. More than one?" I ask. "Wait, I don't think I want to know the answer. I'd hate you for it."

"Oh, come on!" he pleads.

I hold up a palm in his face and close the comic with my free hand. "Don't." I laugh. "Not only do you look like one, you act like one, too," I remark, smiling.

"Act like what? A badass with an awesome person-ality that the ladies love?" Ben kisses his bicep awkwardly, then waggles one brow at me. "Give me some credit."

Sighing, I lean back on the blanket but startle when a cacophony of gunfire ricochets in the air. Ben puts his hand on my stomach. It's flat and warm. He's calming me, not doing anything untoward, but I can't help but realize what this would look like to any outsider. Now that I'm not sloppy drunk. "Act like a womanizing perv," I say, tossing his hand away.

"Harper, Harper. Are you jealous?"

I shrug. "You've never had luck with girls. It makes sense you'd sow your wild oats now that you've"—I pause, unsure how to phrase it—"grown up."

He coughs. "It was weird," he says, lying down again next to me. "Women wanting me for what I look like and what I do. I thought it was a joke, you know? They told me about these Frog Hogs, these women who want to date and have sex with SEALs. Totally real, Harps. I was so stymied when I met my first one I probably stared at her for an entire minute before I responded to her question."

"Which was?" I ask.

"Oh, her question?" he asks, obviously lost in thought. "She asked if I was going to buy her a drink."

My eyes are closed so he can't see me roll them. "Classy," I remark. "Then what? You took her home and had dirty, wild, frog sex?"

"Pass me the comic," he says.

I reach next to me and hand it to him. He opens it in front of him. It blocks the sunlight beaming into his face.

"Are you really going with no comment on this one?"

He laughs. "Yeah, I took her home." Ben pages through to a random page, and I wonder which one it is.

Gross. His answer shocks me a little, and it picks at a thread of our unraveling friendship. Old Ben would have never had a one-night stand. I'm not brave enough to ask if it's a regular occurrence. "There's so much wrong with that, but we don't have time to dissect it right now," I remark, sighing. Since Ben, I've only been with Marcus.

"I'd prefer we never dissect it," Ben replies.

So would I, come to think of it.

We talk a little bit about his father's promotion and my parents' new deck that wraps almost all the way around the house. Something my mother has asked for since we moved into that house. We're supposed to make it there for dinner shortly, but I'm so comfortable here I know for a fact we'll be late. I don't get this sense of self and freedom frequently, so I have to drink it up while I can—while being late doesn't matter.

Ben pretends to read the comic bubbles through squinted eyes.

"My graduation is rapidly approaching. You're going, right? Maybe if you start planning for it now, it will work out."

He's a slave to the Teams and their schedules. I'm never one hundred percent sure where Ben is at on most days. He travels around the US tracking down people and then…exterminating them. Shivering, I lean down to see which part he's at. I point at a joke and laugh. He grins, but it falls quickly.

Ben shakes his head. "You know it doesn't work like that. I've put in a request to be on the East Coast for the week before the graduation and the week after. That means I could be anywhere from Maine to Florida. Atlanta has been a fucking hot spot lately. I'll give it a good college try," Ben quips, turning to look at me. "I wouldn't want to miss it for the world. You know that, right?"

I think it's a double entendre. How he wishes he wouldn't have missed his own, not even happening, college graduation, but he's going to settle for mine.

I nod. "I know. It happened fast. I've been so busy with classes and meetings and everything else, being finished with this degree snuck up on me." Enter the real world. A place I don't function very well. Inside Harvard walls, I am

Harper, a student. Outside, I have no idea who I am. I'll be a linguistics graduate with a ton more schooling to finish before I arrive at my ultimate goal. "I got into the program at USD. Not sure if I mentioned that yet." It's a fib. I was planning on broaching the moving subject during this visit.

He turns his head. "You're coming back to the West Coast?" Ben's eyes light up. "For your master's?"

I nod and try not to show him how pleased I am with his response. "Yeah. They have a linguistics assistant professor job available. I can do that while I take classes and finish school. I need that PhD after my name." I grin. He knows I'm not being a snot. He felt the same way in the past. "Marcus got in, too."

"Oh. Gotcha. It's a lovers' move. Not a move for you to come back home." What he failed to say, and I know was there, is that I failed to come back home to him.

I push his shoulder, and I'm again reminded about his muscles. "You're constantly away anyway. I figured it was time to be closer to my parents, and I've been away for a while already, you know? Nothing is holding me anywhere. It was a good opportunity one of my professors set me up with, and that's it."

"Nothing to do with me then, huh?"

Of course.

"No, Ben. The world doesn't revolve around you. Didn't you learn that lesson when you were three? I'm allowed to make decisions that benefit me, just like you make decisions that benefit you."

"My decisions benefit the rest of the free world, but who's counting?" he jabs.

"I do miss you, and one of the first things I thought of when the opportunity was presented was you," I hiss. "But if you're going to be such a jerk about it, I'll cancel the thought and replace it with disdain."

"With your boyfriend, though. Not sure how I like that."

"You don't have to like it, Ben. You have to live with it," I explain.

He shakes his head. "No more boyfriend talk. I'm sorry. Rewind. Congrats on your new endeavor. The best coast is happy to have you back. So am I."

Smiling, I lie back down next to him. Our hands touch in a lazy, comfortable way. With one finger stretched out, I point at the passing cloud cluster. "Who do you see?" I readjust my thick black sunglasses.

"Buttercup," he says matter-of-factly.

The Princess Bride. I was obsessed with that movie and the unconventional way Westley expressed his love. Ben watched it with me more times than I'm comfortable admitting. My heart hammers out the familiar rhythm called my repressed feelings for Ben. "It's not her. No points," I whisper.

"You're awfully sure it's not her."

Clearing my throat, I say, "It can't be her. It looks like the Tasmanian Devil."

He tilts his head to look at the cloud from a different angle. "As you wish," he says.

Narrowing my eyes, I glare at him. He smiles, acknowledging his heinous crime.

"If that's what you want it to be, but no one is getting points for it," Ben replies. His cell phone is pumping music out from the bottom of the blanket, and the song changes to one of my favorites. I sing along in a low tone while I contemplate a million different things.

"One last cloud, and then we need to get on the road. Hell hath no fury like your mom when she's made her famous consommé and we're late to the party," Ben says, bouncing his foot up and down to the beat.

"Oh, god. She made consommé? How did I not know

that?" I roll up to a sitting position and start gathering our stuff. The gunshots have receded from a rapid fire to a few piercing shots every few seconds. "They must have killed whatever they were killing."

Ben laughs. "If they're killing anything over there, we're in trouble, Harps," he says, handing me the comic book to put into the big tote bag. We came here after a Jazzercise class. Just as he promised, he participated and didn't laugh once. I think Ben likes Jazzercise as much as being a SEAL. I'll never call him out on it, though.

"Do you wish you were with them?" I ask, standing to brush off sand. Taking a deep breath, I inhale the fresh, saltwater air. It's one of the purest scents on Earth. To me, it smells safe and constant. Who the hell knows what the world will look like next week or year? The ocean will smell the same, though. "Don't you like to practice killing things?"

"I took some time off while you're here. I never take time off." He raises his brows and blows out a breath. "I needed this." Looking up at me, I see the cost of his breakneck-paced lifestyle. "It's constant, you know? The second we rat out one guy, we're focusing on the next."

I nod, lean over to grab the corner of the blanket, and pull as hard as I can. He rolls off into the sand. "Don't feel sorry for yourself. Consommé, remember?"

He plays at mock outrage and rolls around the sand, making a big deal out of my ceremonious dumping.

"You're going to get your truck full of sand. You know that, right?"

He waggles his brows, folds his arms behind his head, and says, "Not if I take my clothes off before I get in."

Folding the blanket, I stuff it under my arm. "Better get on with it then," I quip.

"You're so full of it," Ben says, standing in one fluid motion. "You'd lose your mind if I took my clothes off."

With one hand, he reaches to the back of his neck and pulls his T-shirt over his head.

Looking away at the safe, constant ocean, I say, "Whatever. I'm not full of anything except brains."

He laughs, but I hear his zipper, and then his pants hit the ground. "You've seen it all before anyway." It's both fact and fiction. I haven't seen this version of Ben naked. "Look at me." He shakes off his clothes, the fabric flapping in the wind.

I do, trying my best to seem uninterested in his sculpted body, as my gaze wanders. He has things I've never really thought much about. Intelligence and goals are sexy. Things that further you in life. Surveying Ben's qualities, I realize maybe there's something about the physicality of a man I might find attractive. Chiseled abs. Broad shoulders that curve into lean forearms and thick wrists. His boxer briefs ride low on his waist and wrap around thick thighs. "What's the big deal?" I ask.

"You tell me," Ben says, tucking his thumbs into the band of his underwear, teasing.

"Let's go. You're high on testosterone right now. It's the only excuse I'm willing to accept. You're not going to take those off," I deadpan, meeting his cocky gaze.

"Oh, no?" he replies.

I start walking to the parking lot and hear him follow. No one is here, so I know he doesn't care about being in his underwear. When we're at his truck, I spin on him. "Do it then. You say you have no problem riding bare-assed in your truck, then do it."

"Uhh," Ben says, looking at me like I'm from another planet. "You want me to?"

It's my turn to laugh. "I know you won't put your bare asshole on your truck seat, Ben. Tell me I'm wrong."

He thinks about it, I can tell. In the end, I'm right. Ben

jumps into the driver's side scowling, wearing his boxer briefs.

I lean my head against the window and soak in the air conditioner blasting through the vents. "I'm always right. Don't forget that," I say.

Ben grumbles. And then says something magical. "You're right."

CHAPTER SEVEN

Ben

"YOU DIDN'T TELL Harper about your plans?" Mom chirps from around her wineglass.

Harper glares at me from the other side of the table. We're talking about Harper's newest West Coast plans. Our parents are proud and excited to have her back in their lives on a more regular basis. From that, my own plans, which I was hoping to keep secret, went on blast.

I take a bite of bread. Empty carbs. I never allow myself something so silly. My diet is stringent ninety-nine percent of the time. This weekend with Harper I've broken every single nutrition rule I typically abide by. Stuffing another bite in my mouth, I smile around the food. "No," I say with my mouth full. "I haven't gotten the chance, and you know how things work. Nothing is for sure yet."

Harper leans back in her chair and folds her pretty little arms across her chest, her tongue smoothing over her front teeth. "Tell us, Ben. What 'maybe' plans?"

I catch her intonation when she says "maybe." She keeps things from me. Huge things, like serious boyfriends that she intends to move across the country with. Asshole boyfriends who swear at their girlfriends out of jealousy.

"Go on," Harper prompts, sipping her wine.

It's nice outside. The sun is setting, and her parents have a beautiful table out on the new deck. I shrug. "I was trying to switch coasts to…ahhh…be based over there."

"To be closer to you, Harper," Dad says, like he's being fucking helpful.

I glare at him. He turns his eyes down to his plate. It's like we're all seven again when we're together. I have to remind everyone we're both competent adults.

"And for different job opportunities," he adds.

Harper's face changes. "Seriously? Why would you want to be over there?"

You. For you. For only you. I need you. To be close to you. For my sanity.

"Like Dad said, there's other stuff I could do if I'm stationed on that coast. Who knows, I haven't had to go overseas yet, so I might do that instead."

"No," everyone basically screams at once.

"I mean, don't do that. I'm coming back here," Harper says, leaning toward me, cutting everyone else off.

The news plays reels of our efforts in other countries. That's where men like me go to die. America has been restored to some semblance of rule. Our democracy keeps things moving efficiently. The rest of the world didn't fare as well after the attacks. Terrorist strongholds are harder to eradicate overseas. Our forces and troops are busy dealing with our issues. We haven't had men or resources to help out other nations as much.

We're just now trickling into European borders, and I can't even count on my fingers and toes the funerals I've been to since the infiltration began. Harper is still going on and on, listing all the reasons why I need to stay in the

States. Most are selfish reasons, but she doesn't realize it, and I wouldn't expect her to, so I can't fault her.

I hold out both hands. "I don't have much say in it. Now that you're coming back here with your boyfriend, you wouldn't have to worry about me stealing any of your time." I sound like a jealous boy, but I don't really care. I don't have to care about these people. They're mine. They will always understand me and us.

"You're being dramatic. Harper will always have time for you," Harper's mom says, laying a hand on mine. I glance her way and smile. Harpee resembles her mother more and more as the years pass. Most of the sweet and lovable qualities came from this woman. "Don't say stuff like that. If you can help it, stay in the States, Benny. We don't want you coming home in a body bag."

I shudder. It's not visible to anyone except Harper, who's watching me like an evil woman eagle.

"You two kids need to get together already and put us all out of this misery," Dad says, laughing as he looks between us.

My mom hits him in the shoulder. "Harper is attached. Don't say that," she scolds.

"Yeah, Harper is attached. I should attach myself too. What do you guys think about that?" I meet them all face-on, one by one. "Should I just fix all of this and find a girlfriend?" I ask, staring Harper in the eye.

Our parents busy themselves complimenting the meal and the wine and the deck, but Harper is silent.

"Yes," she says simply. She looks away, focusing on the conversations happening around us.

I nod. It's been years of this. Since that first kiss. Since my pulse started hammering jaggedly anytime she came into view, since my whole heart was taken by a woman I'd never fully have.

We finish dinner and move into the house for drinks.

Harper pulls me aside in the kitchen. "Maybe I should stay here tonight?"

She should, my god, she should, but I'm greedy. If this is all I'm getting of her, then I'm taking every single second. "No. We have cake plans. No drama. Promise."

Harper looks hesitant but agrees. I have to listen to our parents praise her accomplishments and all her future holds. When they speak of me, their voices change. It is worry and uncertainty. They fear for my life and for my sanity given the circumstances our world is in. It doesn't matter how much I assure them, I'll always be the reckless child with a penchant for adventure instead of stability. Everyone respects my decision to become a SEAL and will regale my military accomplishments to anyone who will listen, but it's understated bragging.

Harper doesn't smile for the rest of the visit with our parents. That fact makes me happy.

We read comic books and eat vanilla cake straight from the bakery box. It's both of our favorite, and I couldn't help the falling, dying feeling settling in my stomach as we finished up. I promised no drama, but all the words I should be saying are eating at me. We're analyzing a scene from one of our favorite comedy movies when she finally breaks our mundane conversation streak.

"Our timing will never work out, you know? This newest blunder is evidence. Me moving back, you moving to where I just was. I think we need to let go of the pipe dream of forever after, Benny." Her eyes glass over.

"Yeah?" I ask.

She turns away, and her long ponytail swings,

brushing an exposed shoulder. When her hair is up and she turns her head just so, a muscle moves in her neck. It's long and elegant, and it reminds me of a swan. I've come to realize it's because she wore her hair up for an entire year while she waited for it to grow out. Ugly duckling. Swan. Yeah, really deep. It's not the same as the haphazard blowjob ponytails and tight neck muscles I see in the women I'm with these days. They don't have swan necks that make me stare. They have nothing. In their defense, Harper already has everything.

"You're right," I say, pulling her against me on the sofa.

She leans her head against my shoulder, and I wonder what her neck looks like right now.

"I need to get to bed. Your flight is early."

She sniffles, and I feel her nod against me. "I'll miss you."

If I hadn't just promised to keep things simple, I'd tell her how I feel dead when I'm not with her. How inconsequential life seems without her to share it with. No one understands me, knows that weird, quirky person buried deep inside. Instead, I kiss her head. "I'll miss you too, Harps. I'll see you soon, though. Graduation or bust, you nerdy, awesome person."

A quiet laugh rolls through her. "You know I don't want it to be like this, right? I'd fix everything and make life simpler, the way it used to be, if I could."

"Who is saying we can't fix it now? It's never too late. Kiss me. Kiss me and tell me you feel nothing." My heart is hammering. I'm asking something of Harper that I know is a hard limit, but sometimes you have to push limits to know you're wrong. "If you feel nothing, then that's it. I'll let you go this time, and I won't look at you this way again." As if it were an option. I won't let her know, though. The innuendos and the thinly veiled propositions will be gone for good. I will be only her friend.

She scoots to face me, her knees folded underneath her small body. My heart might explode—the percussion hammering against every pulse point in my body, the whooshing of every beat in my ears. The look on her face tells me she's willing to break moral code, and I hope I can stop myself—can hold off from taking everything I want from her, because as much as I'd like it, I know she won't recover from something like that. Harper is fragile. I'm asking too much already.

Before I can say another word or tell her she doesn't have to because my idea is idiotic, she wraps her arms around my neck and leans in to kiss me, her lips opening immediately. She straddles my lap, and I forget what to do. Like I'm sixteen again and I have some untouchable *Playboy* model splayed on my lap. What do I do?

Grinning against her teeth, I remember. I remember everything. Her kiss is like coming home after a really long trip in a cold, cold climate when I've had zero human contact and haven't spoken a word. Now, my lips finally get to say everything by not uttering a word. The kiss feels like fire, warming me in record time. I touch the sides of her face with my fingertips, and she slides her hands in my hair. Little gestures that happen on their own but feel grand in the scheme of things. What would sex with her feel like now that we're not clumsy teenagers? *Some out-of-body experience I could never erase.* My subconscious answers the question for me.

Slanting my mouth over hers, I take control. I remind myself to keep my hands above her waist. She's wearing a pair of jean shorts that leave little to the imagination. Her tan thighs are on either side of my legs, and from my peripheral vision she looks naked, and my cock hardens further. Harper leans into my body until there's no space between us, her chest rising and falling against mine.

Try as I might, I can't keep my eyes open another second. My eyes flutter closed, and I'm lost to a landslide of emotions. The overwhelming sense that I need to keep this. Keep her. Hold onto this feeling and never let it go. Some proverbial tapping on my shoulder, as if to remind me that this electric current streaming from her body to mine can't be duplicated. All things that are deeply hidden are forced to light by a mere kiss from her lips.

Harper's hands become more frantic as she tugs at my shirt, and my breathing speeds even as the warning bells start ringing in my head. Even as I envision us going too far, her small, creamy pale body underneath mine as I enter her in a swift, soul-searing thrust, I know I won't do it.

"Hey," I say, breaking the kiss. She's inhaling and exhaling at warp speed, and her eyelashes are lowered. I push a tangle of long hair out of her face. "Hey," I repeat.

She swallows, and wetness shines in her eyes. She'll blink in a couple seconds, and the first tears will fall down her round, perfect cheeks. Three. Two. One. "I'm not even sorry! I kissed you like that, and I can't even be sorry about it!" Harper wails.

I wince, because her voice is loud and screeching as her crying becomes more jagged.

I hear the guilt in her voice. I could tell her that it was just a kiss and that kisses only mean things to teenagers and actors on sitcoms, but we both know I'd be lying. That kiss left a black mark on my soul. With one arm, I pull her against my chest and cradle her head with the other. "It was just an act. It doesn't have to mean anything."

She calms under my touch as she mentally sifts for the rightness in my words. "Regardless of what you want it to be, I think we have an answer to our age-old question."

She sniffles into the crook of my neck, and my cock jerks. Harper shifts, moving her knees so we aren't lined up anymore. "What question?"

"You didn't feel anything abnormal in that kiss, did you?"

She shakes her head. "Of course. I felt everything! It still doesn't matter."

"You'll do the right thing even if it means giving this up forever?" My voice cracks, but I cover it with a deep swallow.

She's the girl who turned Paulie R. in to the teacher when she saw him cheating in fourth grade, the woman who pays for her fountain drinks in her school cafeteria even though she works there. She's the woman you want till death do you part. The saint. The angel. She's my devil incarnate. My darkest, dirty secret. It will always be her.

"You're with some dude right now. It's not the end of the world. You break up with him, and we continue down our merry path." Holding my hands out to the sides, I bring them together.

She leans away, her eyes wide. Slowly, as if realizing her mortal mistake in increments, she slides off my lap and backs away from me like I'm holding a live grenade. "I know who I am, and I'm not this type of woman, Ben," she says, voice quavering. "This whole trip was a bad idea. We aren't just friends anymore. Were we ever just friends? Have we been lying to ourselves all this time?"

Yes and no. It took extensive physical contact for her to see what I've known for quite some time. "Harper, please. You're my best friend. You'll always be my best friend."

"When kisses feel like that, how can you look at me

and call me your best friend? Your dick was literally begging like a dog to come out and play. My mouth waters when I think about your lips. This is a case of built-up sexual frustration."

Her words are sharp—and true. "There are two options," I say, smirking. She called my dick a dog. The smile is a necessity. First, it will keep the mood light, and second, she has an option to take my offer seriously or dismiss it as garbage. I explain, "You teach the old dog new tricks, and we get this out of our system." Harper balks, as I knew she would. I continue, "Or we cool it. Take a break for a while. You throw yourself into school and whatever that stank-breath boy is called, and I'll find someone. But this is your decision. Not mine. Not what I want. You need to understand this."

If we were both thirty and in different places in our lives, maybe I would have laid out the proposition differently, thought about it longer, and been more thoughtful with my word choice. Harper has always been there. She'll continue to be there. "I'm going to bed. You're right. My flight is pretty early. Want me to sleep on the couch?" She leans away, on one foot, like she's heading to my bedroom.

She took a fucking page out of my playbook and ignored my questions altogether.

"Of course not. Let's go to bed."

Harper crosses her arms under her chest, forcing her shirt to rise and expose a sliver of tight stomach. "Don't make me sound like some immature child."

"You said that, I didn't."

Rising from the sofa, I shift my semi-hard dick. Her gaze flits down and then quickly away. Harper licks her lips. She shifts from one foot to the other, deciding just how badly she'd rather sleep in a bed than out here on the couch. How virtuous can she be?

With a hand of fingers splayed in her face, she whispers, "Please don't touch me. I can't. I need to be me, and you are—"

"Studly? Irresistible? Chess champion in three different divisions? I know. I know. Ladies can't keep their hands off me."

Sighing, she brings her hand to her chest. It's still rising and falling quicker than it should. I've affected her more than I thought a mere kiss could. Marcus must be a loser, selfish asshole in the sack if I can get her this riled up. Or, it's just us. My money is on us, and I'm not a gambling man.

"I'm serious, Benny. Just let me have some space tonight. I hate feeling so conflicted."

I hold out my hands. "After you," I say. "Everything is settled. I won't ever touch you again. Not like that."

Harper's back straightens, and it reminds me of what happens when she's scared. Not the type of scared that happens when you watch a scary movie. The kind that happens after you've taken an hour-long P.E. class full of verbal abuse and you can't take much more without falling to pieces. I never wanted to see her like that, and if I had been a different man back in high school, I would have done more to protect her from cruel teenage ways. Now? I have the ability to protect her in every way, shape, and form, and she's rejected it in favor of doing the right thing. I think.

She spins and faces me, one hand extended between us. "Friends," she says.

I take her small hand in mine right away and look her straight in the eye. "As you wish."

CHAPTER EIGHT

Harper

NYMPHO NANCY IS HAUNTING our dorm room more than she usually does. It's only an inconvenience because I'm actually staying here instead of at Marcus's. Also, my parents are in town. I'd rather they not have too much contact with my sex-fueled roomie lest she spill the beans that I'm never here. I tap the stylus on the edge of my iPad as I stare at her Johnny Depp poster. It's an old-school version of the man who now dresses like a pirate on hallucinogenic drugs. The scent of weed filters down the hallway and seeps under the doors. It's graduation week, and rules don't exist anymore. It's sort of unfortunate, because I love rules.

Marcus texts me, the message flashing on my iPad app.

> I miss you. Can't you come over after your parents drop you off at your dorm after dinner? I'll meet you if you don't want to walk it alone.

I smile as I read his message.

When I returned from San Diego, Marcus took on a new approach to dealing with my weird friendship with

Ben. He didn't care. Better, he didn't bring it up or even acknowledge it existed. I don't know what Ben and Marcus's phone conversation consisted of, but I'd be lying if I said I wasn't curious. I didn't have the heart to tell him that Ben and I are taking a mild friend break in light of a kiss that changed the world. A kiss that I envision anytime Marcus kisses me for any length of time. It upset me for a while, then I got used to it. Sort of like a hallucinogenic freak in emotional denial. Sighing, I glance back at the poster.

Ben and his kisses will never fade, but his presence in my life will. When we don't talk constantly or video chat, he kind of fades into the background. Seeing in person how much he changed made me realize I might not be good enough for Benjamin Brahams anymore. Not in the way he was asking for. Ben's looks and sexual presence dominate everything in the space surrounding him.

In my moment of guilt after the kiss, I also felt self-conscious. I'm still the geek, and Ben has somehow morphed into the man I always knew was inside him. We ran into one of his many admirers at the concert. She was beautiful, and I could tell by the way she looked at him that she's tasted him in the same way I want to. As much as I try to forget the way that quick, painful moment made me feel, it validates my decision to stick to the safest path. The known quantity. Ben loves me, but I don't think he'll ever be in love with me. Not like Marcus is.

Marcus is perfect for me. That one solid fact stands out among everything else. This is a relationship that deserves my time and energy. He's a man who'll move across the country to make me happy and help my dreams come true, a man I have so much in common with that silly memories and inside jokes are insignificant. Ben and our lifetime of memories is my past. Marcus is my future. All of it.

I tap back a quick message to Marcus using lots of sickening emojis and bounce off my bed to swing the door open. Pinching my nose, I peer outside my dorm. "Would you go outside? It stinks!" I call out, my words sounding more like a grandma sucking on helium than an annoyed woman. The hallway is empty and gray—absent of everything except the bright light that filters in from the large window at the end of the corridor. Someone laughs. The volume of the music lifts in response, and I slam our door.

"If you can't beat 'em, join 'em," Nancy says, spinning in her computer chair to face me. "You should be more excited. We're graduating. Let loose a little, Harping Harper."

I despise that nickname, but literally seconds before, I was harping.

Crossing my arms across my chest, I glare at her. "I'm only staying here until my parents leave. I'm not joining in any of this debauchery. Why would I risk it?" In a way it feels like high school graduation. I'm not even close to being finished. This is the beginning of my college career. This degree is the foundation for everything that follows. "I'm surprised you're not celebrating," I say, lifting my chin toward her bed.

"That comes later tonight," she says, smiling. "After you go to sleep." Yes. Exactly like high school. "Unless you want to watch? Join in?"

I stoop down to pull my full suitcase from under my bed and rustle around until I find a long black maxi dress that's suitable for dinner reservations with my parents. My iPad pings with a message as I'm loading my bathroom caddy, and I grin, thinking it's Marcus returning my last lewd message.

I see Ben's name instead. Not sure I'll be able to make it tomorrow. Sorry, Harp. My stomach sinks lower, and a bit of nausea hits me in a rush. We haven't spoken in a while, but never for one moment did I think he wouldn't make it. Anger replaces disappointment. He can do a million different dangerous things all across the world, but he can't make a ceremony that lasts a few hours? I swallow the lump in my throat as my eyes water.

That's fine, I reply back. Ben doesn't have his read receipts on, so I have no idea if he's still by his phone or if he's already busy. Graduating Harvard is NBD anyway. See you in a few weeks? Marcus and I are moving right away.

Nancy is cackling as she watches stupid videos on her laptop. I have no idea how she's graduating—how she got accepted here. She's one of those smart people who don't have to try. The kind who exist in their intelligence without even giving it a second thought. Ben is like that. It's why he's so good at whatever he devotes his life to. It's full-minded focus. I'm not a part of that focus these days. Ben doesn't text me back, so I take a shower and take my time doing my hair and makeup.

My mom calls when she's outside waiting for me. I check my phone as I trot down the stairs to the exit of my red brick building. Ben texted back, and all it says is, I'm so sorry. If I could see him right now, I'd know exactly how sorry he was. The rest of the night is a blur of disappointment and agitated nerves.

Marcus picks me up outside of the quad after I've finished dinner. He knows right away that something is off-kilter. It's a quality you hope for in a mate, someone who can read you without effort.

"I'm fine," I say, locking my hand with his. We wave at a group of our friends as they pass by.

Gently, he squeezes my hand. "Dinner was that bad, huh?"

The false smile I plastered on my face for my friends fades.

"Nah. I'm kind of nervous for tomorrow. Nothing abnormal."

"Nothing to do with Ben not being able to be here for you?"

I stop walking.

I'm glad it's dark so he won't be able to see the multitude of emotions that are surely trickling across my face. I look at him and narrow my eyes.

He smiles. "He called me to let me know, too."

He didn't call me. "Oh," I say. "He didn't tell me why he couldn't make it." Do I sound desperate? Old Harper would call and demand answers. I know it wouldn't be healthy for me to talk to him while I'm in any kind of emotional state, and guarding my heart is of the utmost importance. I can't mess up what I have with Marcus. "Do you two talk frequently? You never mention him."

He's still smiling, and I take that as a good sign. "He's on the right coast. So making commencement is a possibility, but I don't think he can be certain he'll be able to get out in time." He sighs. "He didn't tell me what he was doing either. I'm not sure that's something he can tell anyone." Marcus's voice holds a tinge of admiration.

Ben would tell me. If I called.

"He said you guys hadn't spoken in a while," Marcus hedges, squeezing my hand again. "Today was the first time he called me. We don't talk regularly."

"Yeah, we've both been pretty busy. Me with exams. Him with killing people and saving the world. You know that's not why I'm upset. It's the move and everything. It's a lot to plan for and think about." Marcus will buy this lie. I know it. These are legitimate concerns.

He releases my hand and puts his arm around my shoulder instead. "We have this. The hard part is over now. You just have to show up tomorrow. Focus on that. Let me worry about moving. I'm the man. Let that be my job, okay?"

I nod against his chest, and I'm wrapped up in his sheets and arms and kisses in no time at all.

I've never been so nervous in my life. My black gown is oversized and smells like starch. The trees are beautiful in the Harvard Yard. The day is perfect, and everyone is happy—smiles as far as the eye can see. I'm fidgeting in my seat as I listen to the commencement speech. My mind wanders, though. It wants to think of everything else instead of what's happening right now. In a moment I should be proud of, a moment I've waited my whole life for, I'm thinking about what could have been, what should have been.

It's all so anticlimactic in nature. Maybe it's supposed to be this way. An indication that you've finally grown up and realize how insignificant you are in the grand scheme of things. When I was a sophomore in high school, I researched Harvard's commencement procedures and glamorized it in the way most girls dream about their wedding day. "I'm here," I whisper to myself, trying to force the awareness I crave. The graduate sitting next to me glances over and quickly away. I need to stop talking to myself.

I cover my mumbling by readjusting the dark maroon swath of fabric around my neck just as my cell phone buzzes in my hand. Taking a deep breath, I peek at the phone and see the text from Ben. It's not words. Just a photo of two horribly drawn stick figures wearing graduation caps. Hot tears prick my eyes at the stupid drawing meant to calm me. It does, though. I feel calmer.

The speech finishes, and after another ravishing, uplifting speech from the valedictorian, we return to our houses to get our individual diplomas and have lunch with our guests. I'm distracted, wallowing in a place of pride in my accomplishment but sorrow that this moment didn't live up to what I dreamed of all these years.

"We're so proud of you, honey," Mom says, folding me in a hug. They're always proud. I never give them a reason to be anything but proud. Maybe even to a detriment. Do they appreciate this straight and narrow life I live less because it's what they've come to expect? Do I?

"Thanks, Mom," I whisper.

She senses the melancholy like a bloodhound.

Squeezing me a touch tighter, she says, "You are the favorite part of my life."

I kiss her cheek and pull away. The crowd of black and maroon cascades around us in a sea of humans. Everyone is warier now than they would have been before the attacks. Large groups like this aren't something anyone likes. Even happy gatherings carry risk, and you have to balance the reward to compute if it's worth it. I know at least twenty students who were having small parties at their homes with their parents and were forgoing commencement altogether. The thought is a reminder of my aunt, and my sadness deepens.

"Auntie would have loved to be here," I say, my eyes turned down to the ground.

We find a bench that overlooks the yard in front of the house and sit. My father is happily engaging with any other parent who looks his way.

"She would have worn something tight and then

bragged when the college boys looked her way," Mom says, a small smile playing on her lips, and then laughs. "She wouldn't have given them the time of day, though."

My hands folded in my lap, I try to stifle all of the memories that contain my aunt. She was the first one to show me how to do my makeup, the first one to come to my aid when I chopped off my hair and needed it to look…girly. My aunt was my feminine hero—the woman I secretly always wanted to be more like. She was confident in her looks and carried herself in a way that let everyone know she knew exactly who she was and what she wanted. "I bet she's here, though. I just wish…" My words trail off as I see him. Through a throng of gowns and smiles.

Ben.

He's buttoning the top button of his light blue dress shirt, while his eyes scan the crowd for what seems like forever, but I know it can only be seconds. His gaze, narrowed in a harried rush but so familiar and calming, lands on mine.

I cry. Because that's what I do when I'm angry and relieved at the same time. Ben's mouth quirks up to one side, and the crowd parts for him. He walks toward me, I stand, and his pace quickens. I take one step forward, and he stops in front of me. I'm aware people are staring at us, mostly because he's so huge and out of place here, but I don't care. Relief folds over me like a sedative.

I see him sweating and breathing heavily and wonder what he had to do to make it here.

"You got my text?" he asks, breathing out.

Wiping under my eyes, I grin. "I got it."

He takes me in his arms, pulling me against his body, and finally. Finally, I celebrate.

Save the Only Dance

HARPER

I'M ALL ALONE. Standing against the glass wall like one of those geeky girls in the teen movies. The girl I told myself I wouldn't be tonight. On the night of my senior prom. All of the disastrous dominoes fell in rapid succession. My date, a first-chair violinist in our high school's competition orchestra, got the flu. When he called me to tell me this morning, he barely got the words out before vomiting in exaggerated stereo. He felt awful, both figuratively and literally, so I'm not that mad at him.

My dad dropped me off in front of the aquarium. For some unknown reason, I wanted to come here regardless of being the solitary hermit. He opened the car door for me, kissed me on the cheek, and told me I was the most beautiful girl in the world. I didn't miss the sadness in his eyes. His only child. His baby girl. Forever the loner. Not the most beautiful girl in the world by a long shot.

My mom brought me to the custom dress shop all the popular girls go to for their pageant dresses. I chose a two-piece emerald number. The skirt is long and flared out like a mermaid tail, and the top is cropped, showing a sliver of stomach with long, tight, lace sleeves. It was too beautiful to let anything stop me from wearing it. Puking dates aside.

The student president of our senior class was seated at a table when I walked in. She was taking tickets, looking just as stunning as she always does. I'm self-conscious as a general rule, but being here by myself dressed like someone I don't feel like turns my nerves on their head. She takes my ticket while eyeing me up and down. I smile and tell her to have a nice night, even though at the moment I wish I were the one home with the flu.

Heads turn when I walk into the large room glowing with the blue light from the floor-to-ceiling aquariums surrounding us on all sides. Of course Harper Rosehall entering her senior prom by herself is something worth watching. My face heats under their stares, and I do my best to keep my head high as I head toward the edge of the room and pretend to be overly interested in the sharks swimming by.

A few guys wave, and a girl from my calculus class grins in a polite hello. Reaching into my skirt pocket, I pull out my cell phone. The DJ plays a song with a fast beat, so I text, instead of call, Benny in a rush I'm sure I'll regret as soon as I hit send. This is awful. Will you come, please?

Ben refuses to do anything school related. Prom is equivalent to the second ring of hell for him. He didn't understand why I wanted to go in the first place. I think he was even a little upset when I told him Jeff Golden asked me out. He seemed surprised. I yelled at him for being so rude and he apologized and told me I was reading it all wrong. He never explained further, though. I'm waiting for him to reply with an I told you so, but no text message comes.

Ben does.

Walking through the same entrance I came through

only minutes before. His hair is gelled in a way that makes him look suave, and he's standing tall and proud —a feast for any girl's eyes, but he's not looking at any of them. He's here for me. I watch as he takes his cell phone out of the pocket of his tuxedo pants and smirks as he reads my message.

He looks up from the phone and tilts his head to peer around the room. Everyone is staring at him. My guess is no one recognizes him. Ben fumbles with the button on the top of his shirt underneath the green bow tie—the bow tie that matches my dress perfectly.

I step away from the aquarium, using the cool glass to push off of.

I walk slowly, taking in only him—trying not to let anything else filter into my awareness. The crowd of sparkling teenagers parts, and I'm standing in the center of this stunning room. I've never been the center of anything, but right now I feel as if this is my moment. My hands in fists by my sides, I flex them open and smooth out the sides of my skirt. Ben kissed me, and it changed everything. I kissed him, and I fell so hard I can't dig myself out of this rut of confusion and desire.

Standing before me is both the boy I've liked all my life and the man I love more than I can comprehend. Ben's gaze scans as he still messes with his tie, and when his eyes fix on mine, his mouth drops open and his eyes widen as he sees what I'm wearing. I smile as tears fill my eyes. I won't let them ruin my makeup, though. Not tonight, after my aunt spent an insane amount of time contouring me like a Kardashian sister.

When he doesn't make a move, I approach him and stop when we're inches apart. "People are staring." I lick my lips and flick my gaze to each side.

"Because you look like a goddamn angel."

I blush. "Thanks. You got my text?" I smirk.

He nods. "Your mom called my mom this morning when Jeff left you high and dry." Ben reaches out and gently lays his hand on my shoulder. "Sorry I couldn't get here sooner."

I shrug. "Everyone stared at me like I'm some freak with three heads. Nothing new."

He reaches into his pocket and pulls out a pen. "Harper, people are looking at you because you're the most beautiful girl in this room—probably even the world." He means every single word.

My heart rate speeds up. It's this buzzing feeling because I can smell his cologne and see the honesty in his eyes, and that's all I want. All a person really needs in another person. Truth. There's an honesty in his kiss that I know I won't find anywhere else, regardless of how many boys I kiss.

He slides his hand down to my wrist, then up the lace sleeve. "Thanks for coming, Benny," I say again, louder this time so he can hear me over the music.

"I'd never leave my girl to the wolves," he says, swallowing hard. His gaze flicks down to my empty wrist. "I have something for you. It's not what I had in mind when my mom demanded I save you, but it's all I have time for." He smirks and raises one brow. I nod.

Leading me by the hand, he moves us closer to the shark aquarium. Sliding the light lace around my wrist up my forearm, he bends over, pen in hand, and starts drawing on my skin. "You're tickling me," I exclaim as I watch him work.

Ben moves my arm as he draws. He bites his tongue and bottom lip as he concentrates—his gaze intent like a furious artist.

"Done. It's totally worth the tickle factor. What do you think?" he asks, bending my arm so I can see my wrist. He clicks the pen closed and slides it back into his pocket.

He leaves his hand in mine as he watches me appraise his handiwork.

I swallow down the lump in my throat. "It's the most beautiful corsage I've ever seen." It is a horrible drawing that wraps my entire wrist. "Daisies?" I ask as I narrow my eyes. "Or a rose hybrid?" I sniff my wrist. "The flowers smell so lovely. You shouldn't have. Thank you so much." Doodles. The man can cheer me up with doodles. Always has and always will.

"If you don't sweat your ass off like it's an underground rave, you might be able to keep the flowers all night," Benny replies. "Dance with me?" He extends one hand and raises a brow. I say a silent prayer, thanking God Jeff got the flu.

A slow song trickles through the speakers, and I can't get into his arms fast enough. We sway to the music, the side of my face pressed firmly against his chest. "How did you rent a tux so fast?" I ask. This is the first time I've seen him in a tux, and it just might be the most handsome thing I've ever seen.

I can feel him raise and lower his shoulders. "Maybe I always wanted to come to prom with you, Harpee."

All he had to do is ask and he didn't. That means the kiss changed things for him, too. My whole body glows with anticipation. "Thanks for breaking your rule about no school functions. The sharks aren't good dancers." I tilt my head to the side of the room where the huge, lithe creatures swim above our heads.

"Neither are the wolves," he growls, eyes darting around the room. "You should have known Jeff would end up puking on prom night. He's that type of guy."

Laughing, I pull myself against him tighter. He presses against me, and my mouth waters. The need to kiss him wars with my sensibilities. "Careful, little lady.

Unless you want a true prom night." Ben pulls back to peer in my eyes. When he sees my panic, he winks.

I can see the doodle on my wrist all night long, my hands twining around his neck. It's the best night of my life. For the first time ever, I belong somewhere. Our peers whisper and stare and it's not because we're different, or weird.

It's because we have something none of them ever will.

CHAPTER NINE

Harper

IT FEELS SO good to be back in San Diego. Marcus and I have settled into a comfortable lifestyle in a small two-bedroom craftsman house near the college. We're so busy we rarely have time to do anything other than mandatory obligations. I have Sunday dinner at my parents' house every weekend, but I rarely have time for my friends in a non-school setting. My mom called last week and mentioned Ben was dating a girl, and they're pretty serious. It's the first time I've gleaned facts about his life through another source. It was odd.

I ignored the familiar sting, but it made all the pieces fall into place. The no contact. Not even so much as a text in weeks. I've made other truly good friends, and it's nice to have an adult circle of like-minded individuals to brighten the monotony. A Harvard degree didn't make me an adult. Life did. And I'm so busy living it, sometimes I forget to enjoy it.

I'm in our office at home when Marcus drops into his chair across from me. We've fit two desks and three bookshelves in here. We're the epitome of master's students. We live and breathe school. "We should do something fun this weekend, Harp. It's been so long since we've done something for us. With friends."

I nod, spinning in my swivel chair to face his side of the room. "The workload is incredible. I moved here hoping to spend more time with family, and I might have to cancel Sunday dinner again this weekend. I have to grade those exams, and this paper is acting like a bogus clown. I can't get it to behave."

"I saw the paper earlier today. You left it up on the laptop. It's not bogus at all. It's solid. Don't worry so much. You've got this." He clears his throat. "When's the last time we've hung out with friends?"

I lay a palm on my forehead. "It's been forever."

"Let's make dinner plans for this weekend. Call Ben and see if he wants to come along. Let's let off some steam. What do you say?" My first thought is that he's crazy. The second is that I want nothing more than to relax for a few hours without thinking about anything taxing. "Drinks and tacos. You can't say no." He's making a rolling gesture with his arms, and I laugh at how goofy he looks.

"The fact that you're the one proposing this says a lot about the dire need of a night off." I'm usually the one begging off to do something fun. Marcus is all work and no play.

"Proposing, huh?" Marcus says, smiling that wide, beautiful smile. It's malicious this time. Calculating. I'm not giving him something he wants, and I'm unsure how long I can hold out without causing an enormous rift.

I throw a wadded-up ball of paper at his head. "Stop. I don't want to get into that conversation right now. Nor do I have the time."

He holds up both hands. "Fine. Fine. Just thought I'd bring your Freudian slip to your attention."

Marcus wants to get married. While I'm not opposed, because I honestly don't know who the hell else would marry a person like me—a person enraptured with success and my career—I just can't agree to it. We've been together for years, and I know he's getting pressure from his parents. There's something, and I'm not sure what, holding me back from pressing the gas pedal. Most would tell me I'm being childish, but I'm stubborn enough to trust my gut. I need more time. After my master's I can slow down and marry Marcus. I've told him that a half dozen times, but he shakes his head and tells me there will never be a perfect time. Sort of like a robot, but with more feeling.

Shouldn't there be, though? A perfect time? Shouldn't something like a wedding day be perfect? Free of all encumbrances of a harried, busy life? Free of all notions of what's supposed to happen and when it should happen? Love doesn't happen organically twice. It's an impossibility.

Marcus changes the subject to his brother's impending visit.

In lieu of stressing about a family visit, I reply, "I'll call Ben." I turn in my chair so I can hide my face and every emotion I don't want him to see. "If he's away on a work trip, it can be a date. Just you and me." I hear him open a textbook, and I take his silence for what it truly is. A promise to bring up the marriage thing again as soon as the time arises. Maybe it doesn't have to be perfect, maybe it just has to work.

Before I lose my nerve, I dial Ben. He picks up on the first ring.

"Harper. Fancy hearing your ring in my ears."

His voice, after some time has passed, makes my heart race. Graduation was a much-needed visit. We laughed and talked about the old days, and then it ended and he left to go do God knows what. His face was stoic as he said goodbye, and my stomach filled with dread when I saw it. We don't talk about those things anymore. They make our parents worried, and they make me plain, ol' terrified. Ben knows it. His life is a secret because it has to be, and because he's sparing our feelings. I realize how selfless an act it is. How difficult it must be to keep your entire life shrouded in a rose-colored cloth for the benefit of those you care about.

I laugh. "How are you doing? It's been a while. Can't call a best friend on a more frequent basis?" Even as I give him a hard time, I eye the stack of unfinished work on my desk. I'm just as much to blame for the friend absence. "I win, by the way. I called first." My stomach falls when I realize my tone has changed completely and Marcus is listening to every joy tinged word fleeing my mouth. I swallow and try to compose myself.

Ben's returning chuckle warms my stomach. "I'm good. Lots of trips. You caught me at home, though. You got your radar on me?"

Clearing my throat, and my nerves, I get it all out in a rush. "Want to go out to dinner with Marcus and me? Mom says you have a girlfriend now, so it could be a double date."

"The timing is too good to be true. Sure. Where?"

My stomach sinks. I didn't realize I wanted him to deny the girlfriend until right this second, when he doesn't.

"It's time you met Norah. Give her the official Harper stamp of approval."

She has a place in his life, and she has a name. A pretty one.

We hash out the details, without consulting our significant others, and he ends the call with a cheery goodbye. I knew it would happen. I was surprised it took this long, but it truly wasn't until I told him to move on that he did.

Ben deserves happiness in whatever form he can find it in.

"We all set then?" Marcus growls from the other side of the room. The consternation in his words pricks my whole body with unease. Every once in a while, when he's tired and worked to the bone, I see the side of Marcus I experienced right before I flew out to visit Ben. Luckily, it's not frequent, but when it happens, it does make me uncomfortable enough to smile at his grimace and leave the room and eventually the house with some lame excuse about needing coffee from a shop instead of a pot.

Brooding on his side of the room, I give him the details while focusing on the framed drawing of a park above his desk. He holds his pen up in the air to let me know I'm dismissed, and I leave the room quietly, respecting his need to get stuff finished.

I make my way out the back door and flop down in a chair on the patio, a stack of papers as my only company. Concentrating is hard. For the first time in my life, I feel something other than excitement and happiness at the prospect of seeing Ben.

I feel a swirl of anxious dread. Norah. I wonder what she looks like. I wonder if she's seeing the smile that belongs to me. I wonder if Ben is finally in love.

Ben is gesturing wildly. "He turned around and said, 'Don't touch it unless you can fix it,'" he says, finishing some story he heard from his friends. "Not since before the dawn of time has anyone used an axe as a weapon," Ben adds, shaking his head.

Everyone is rapt. Especially Norah. She watches Ben,

chin resting on one hand, like he hung the moon. I can't look at her longer than a few seconds without feeling something akin to buyer's remorse. Marcus asks Ben lots of questions, and because Ben is so effervescent and malleable in any situation, he makes this whole thing seem as easy as walking down the street on a sunny day.

I sip my drink and smile. Marcus keeps his hand on my knee for a long time. When he finally takes it off when our appetizers arrive, there's a sweaty, warm spot that reminds me of a swamp.

"Tell us about yourself, Norah. You've been so quiet," Marcus says during a lull.

He's irritating the hell out of me, but right now I could kiss him. Aside from a brief introduction in front of the hostess stand, I haven't heard her speak. Ben wraps an arm around her chair, as if Marcus's question reminded him she existed.

Norah grins at the subtle touch from Ben. She loves him. It's so obvious to me. I wonder if it's obvious to a stranger. I look at Marcus, but he's staring at the couple with an air of indifference. "I'm a veterinarian at an animal hospital down the street from Ben's house." She's smart and committed. And beautiful. Expecting anything less wouldn't have given Ben enough credit.

I can't keep the rabid curiosity at bay. "How did you two meet?" I ask.

Ben looks wildly amused as he tilts his head toward my voice. He reads beneath the surface of my question, and I might as well be fully exposed—stripped of the skin that masks my insides.

Ben turns his focus to Norah. "Go ahead. Tell them," he prompts, leaning in close to her face.

She sighs. "Ben found a kitten in a sewage drain by his house. He pounded on the door two hours before my clinic opened. I happened to go in early that day to finish some files from the night before and opened the door when I saw the kitten."

Ben smiles, pleased that he's the hero in this story. "It lived, and now I have a black cat named Pennywise," he explains.

Marcus puts his hand back on my leg, and I can feel his eyes boring into my bones.

I smile because Marcus is watching. "That's a great story," I say, actually meaning it.

Norah continues, her eyes taking on a far-off, love-swept look. "He kept coming back day after day to check on the little guy. God knows I'm attracted to a man who loves animals. Especially one as handsome as Ben. I asked him out the fourth time he came around."

My eyes flare, but I tamp down on the surprise quickly as everyone is watching for my reaction. Marcus, for jealousy, Ben, to see if the story is getting a rise out of me, and Norah, because she's talking to me. I flush.

"He's so charming without meaning to be."

I nod and reaffirm her sentiment. A million stories of how Ben charmed me come to mind, but I realize only one matters. Theirs.

Norah and Ben's story is perfect.

"How did you and Marcus meet?" Norah asks innocently, merely returning the favor to let me wax poetic about my relationship. She doesn't like speaking about herself. I can already tell she's a listener.

I tell them the story about the first day of class at Harvard and how I ran late. Tardiness isn't a trait I'd ever own on a normal basis, so I was flustered, and the professor had already started, and the only seat left was next to a very good-looking man with a bright, wide smile. Marcus whispered where we were at in the text and smirked as he tapped the end of his pen on the correct paragraph.

I wanted to explain to him that I got held up on a phone call, that I wasn't this spaced-out loser destined to flunk out of Harvard before I'd gotten out of the gate. I didn't have a chance, though. I stayed silent and thanked him with a meek smile. "He asked me to study that same day, right after class. The rest is history." I squeeze Marcus's hand on my knee.

"She's a beautiful girl. Can you blame me?" Marcus says, palming his chest with one hand.

Ben looks off to the left. "Nope. Not at all." His usual, jovial smile has vanished, and Norah rubs a hand on his back. Can she tell he's upset because of me?

Does she know how important I am to Ben? The thought makes me feel weak—like a vulnerable calf waiting for slaughter. "That's a great story, Harper. You two have so much in common. You're the best couple ever," Norah coos, clasping her hands together in front of her. Our story reads like a textbook, and theirs reads like a fable.

"Yeah, the stuff fairy tales are made of," Ben adds, giving a pointed wink in Marcus's direction. "It's been a while now, hasn't it?"

Marcus knows down to the minute when our anniversary is, so it's him who answers. I take a sip of my drink and compliment Norah's nail color instead. It's a light mauve, a color my grandma loves. On her, it looks chic and in style. She sidesteps the compliment by gushing about the woman who does her nails and tells me we should go together next week and grab lunch at the pho place next door.

I agree to the outing while Ben watches the interaction with curiosity. I'm sure he thought jealous rage would seep out of my pores and turn to acid. Leave it to him to select a woman so polished and polite that I literally have nothing to hate about her except she has more of Ben's time than I do. We order dinner, and we eat while partaking in overly polite conversation. Marcus kisses my cheek when he excuses himself to the restroom, and Ben seethes at the innocuous touch of his lips.

"Want to help me grab another round at the bar?" I ask, tilting my head toward the crowded corner where people are mingling about, trying to find something they probably won't locate in the wiry, loose atmosphere.

She smiles wide. "Yes. Of course!" she replies, patting the corner of her mouth with a napkin.

The restaurant turns into a club at nine p.m., and the service starts slowing down to a snail's pace. If the food wasn't so good, there's no way we'd deal with it. Norah stands, a willowy, graceful being, and tucks her soft blond hair behind one ear. After Marcus returns, the men give me their drink orders, and we head to the bar. She stays close to my side as we weave toward our destination. It's hard not to compare myself to her for the solitary reason that we are polar opposites.

She sways a little when she walks. Not because she's trying to get attention, but because she has that natural grace some tall women have. She could be a ballerina in another life. The self-conscious part of me recognizes it in her, and I think maybe I finally see what drew Ben in. It's in the way her eyes dart around the room but never land on any one thing for too long.

"Ben talks about you all the time. I can't believe I haven't gotten a chance to meet you yet," Norah says, leaning down to make sure I can hear her.

"Yeah, we're both pretty busy." I'd love to be able to say I know everything about her, but he didn't share this part of his life. My stomach rolls when I realize it's the first thing he's kept from me. "A childhood full of menacing," I joke, turning to the bar to order our drinks when I catch the bartender's eye.

After I finish rattling off the order, I sense Norah's eyes on the side of my face. I turn to her with a smile fixed on my face. "Let's see if he gets it right," I exclaim.

"You're so pretty," Norah says. "And intelligent, and every other wonderful thing that can be used as a descriptive word. I have to admit I didn't believe him when he told me his best friend was a girl," she says, pausing to look over my head. "Or rather, it's possible, but there's always something more." When I don't answer, she goes on. "It truly is just a friendship, though, isn't it?" This is the moment to tell her the gritty truth. That love doesn't exist outside of Ben for me, that the only man who has ever held my heart does so wearing a warm pair of gloves that are fit to size.

The bartender slides two drinks toward me. Swallowing down the fear, I decide on a half-truth. "I love Ben. He's been in my life for as long as I can remember. He'll always be in my life if he wants me there. We're just friends, Norah. I promise."

She smiles as she reaches out to take one of the drinks. "I feel foolish for asking. He told me the same thing. Women's intuition, I guess. It's off!" Norah laughs, and I could shake her. She's not off. She sees what I'm too scared to admit.

The other drinks arrive. "Don't feel bad. We get it a lot. It took Marcus a long time to accept the friendship. It is that, though. Just a friendship." One a lifetime long with more love than most people accumulate in eighty years.

She nods. "Thank you, Harper. I hope you approve of me, because I love that man, and I know he wants your approval. I think it's why he finally let me meet you."

All I can do is grin and tell her there's no way he puts that much weight into my approval. Making our way back to our table takes longer than it should. My feet feel heavy, and I'm not ready for any more of this group date.

Right before we sit down, she whispers something into my ear that makes every hair on my body stand on end. It was supposed to be a sweet sentiment. She laughed when she whispered it—made it seem like a joke. She told me she wanted Ben until death do them part.

CHAPTER TEN

Ben

YOU CAN CHANGE what you want, but you can't change the way you want things. Fuck knows I've tried. Harper calls almost every day now that she knows I'm serious about Norah. While I tell myself I want Norah, I can't squelch the ever-present desire to have Harper. I'm doubtful anything divine or otherwise will change that fact.

Norah is sitting in front of me, cross-legged, her long blond hair piled high on her head. With a mischievous grin, she lays down three kings. "Wasn't Rummy your idea because you thought you could finally beat me on game night?" She's intelligent, beautiful, and has a soft-spoken charm that negates the first two facts. Norah was raised in a middle-class family, the same as my own, and has the same quality that draws me to women. She's searching for something inside of me that will complete her. It's self-destructive, but she doesn't know that. None of them do.

Sighing, I lay down three aces. "It was," I return, leaning over to peck her mouth. I know she has the fourth ace. She will never discard an ace. Which usually always ends up being a detriment when I go out and she has to deduct the points from her hand. "What were you saying again?" I tease lightly. I look forward to this day all week when I'm in town. It's the night where I let myself eat carbs and drink booze and have as much skin-to-skin contact with my girlfriend as I possibly can. I feel human—I'm more than what I do.

Norah's melodic laugh is cut short by the shrill pierce of my doorbell. "I'll get it. Go grab the popcorn from the microwave," she says, laying a soft hand on the side of my face. The doorbell rings again, more frantically—someone slamming it over and over.

Narrowing my eyes, I follow Norah as she rushes to the front door. "Did you order food or something?" I ask, peering out the geometrically printed curtains Norah hung when she deemed my windows too naked last week. I don't see any cars parked out by the street. Nothing to indicate we have a visitor.

"No," she replies, shrugging and throwing the door open with all the care of a bulldozer. A wave of unease filters through the air and saturates the deep breath I inhale.

"Is he home? Is Ben home?" I hear her voice and the tenor and know it's not good. Watching Norah's profile as she takes in Harper confirms my most dismal suspicions.

"What happened? Oh my god, Harper, what the hell happened?" Norah murmurs, pulling her into her arms. "Where's your car?" Norah narrows her gaze out the door and looks both left and right while Harper buries her face in the front of her T-shirt.

"Close the door," Harper whispers. It takes all of these seconds for me to make my brain behave the way it should have—the way it would have if some bad guy with a bomb strapped to his chest came through my front door. Somehow Harper sobbing in my doorway turns my voice box to ice and my feet to lead.

Harper calls my name again, asking for me.

"What happened?" I croak.

She turns out of Norah's embrace and faces me. Her body relaxes almost completely at the mere sound of my voice. The opposite of relaxation washes over me when I see her face.

The second I see her cheek, she turns her gaze to the floor. "I'm fine. Can we talk? I'm fine, really." I know enough about women to know when they say they're fine, the opposite is true.

Harper meets my eyes. Hers are red and ringed with black makeup. Apart from the dark red mark on her cheekbone, there are red splotches on her neck. The very same neck I cherish has been marred by hands. Large ones.

"Come on. Let's talk," I say, gesturing toward the couch.

Harper brushes past me and sinks down into the sofa, pulling one of the new throw pillows onto her lap. She puts her chin on it and keeps her gaze pointed at the floor.

Norah has already vanished into the bedroom. Shaking my head, I sit next to Harper and pull her into my chest. She breathes in deeply once and then falls apart.

"I hope I'm wrong, Harper, but if I'm not, you need to start at the beginning."

"Which beginning?" she asks, sobbing. "There are so many."

"Please tell me you called the cops."

She nods against my chest. "Of course I did. Which makes this so much worse."

I clear my throat. "I need to hear you say it. All of it."

Harper leans away, as if finally realizing our seating position might not be chaste and friendly enough. She pulls her cell phone out of her sweater pocket, hiccups, and scrolls until she finds what she's looking for, and hands me the phone. It's a screenshot of my Insta photo of Harper, at the concert, on her birthday. "He saw it," she whispers. "Marcus saw it. I told him it was nothing, but he's been acting strange since our double date—says I don't look at him the same way I look at you." Harper lowers her voice as her gaze darts to my closed bedroom door.

"I don't have him on my account," I say, with finality in my voice. Like I can erase this by using reason.

She ignores me, still staring off toward my bedroom. "Because I won't marry him."

I close my eyes and blow out a breath. My heart rate accelerates as my mind tries to pick apart every angle she could be aiming for. "We're getting off topic. Tell me what happened." I brush my fingers across her cheek and wince when she does.

Harper puts her face in her hands, mindful of her cheekbone, and speaks low, "You don't have him on your account. You have some bottle blonde named Sexy Jenny, though. He created a fake profile to add you. He thought he'd have a better chance at stalking you if he was a twenty-something chick. And it worked."

My stomach sinks. I know exactly who she's talking about. Even though my profile is private, I'll add people I don't know every once in a while. I remember wondering who the chick was, but I'd had a few beers, and she was blonde and hot.

"He called me a slut. A commitment-phobe who'd rather fuck around with guys like you than marry men like him." She raises her head and looks at me. "He's been under a lot of pressure here," she explains.

I shake my head. "Don't you fucking dare stand up for him." My voice booms, echoing off the walls.

Norah won't come out. She probably won't even listen to our conversation.

Harper takes my hands in hers. "I get it, Ben. He moved here for me, with me, to be with me, and I keep turning him down. I'm not making excuses for him, because we both know there's no excuse for this," she explains, gesturing to her face and then neck. "He saw the photo and got mad." She shrugs. "It happened so fast. We were talking one second, and I was on the ground the next. He didn't hit me. He grabbed me by the throat, told me to stop feeding him bullshit excuses, and then threw me into the desk." She rubs her face. "I caught the corner. Or rather, my face caught the corner."

"This is my fault," I say, nodding. "My photo caused this." I stand, untangling myself from her. I run my hands through my hair and look at the ceiling. With Harper at my back, I listen to her finish the story. She gives me the facts as detailed as she can in between sobs. She begs me not to tell her parents and asks if she can stay with me for a little while. I answer immediately that she can without thinking about any repercussions. Without thinking about the woman in the other room.

"I called Marcus's brother to let him know what happened, and he's going to come out and stay at our place for a while. Try to see if he can help him or...I don't know. Be there for him. Marcus was sorry right away. I'd almost think it was an accident if..." Harper trails off.

"If what?" I spin to face her.

She swallows hard. "If I hadn't been scared of him in the past, too. He's been weird before, and it's worried me. Nothing like this, though. I don't want you to think I'll go back to him. I won't, Ben. I never would have stayed with him this long if he'd shown these tendencies before now. It was always just words and tone."

"And you stayed?" I ask, furrowing my brow. Her statement causes me physical pain. I palm my chest. Lowering my voice, I say, "You got weird vibes and you stayed with him instead of..." I trail off. My insides are coiling in regret. How easily could she have been led away if I had stayed my course in pursuing her in all ways? If I hadn't taken no for an answer. If we'd embraced what we've had our entire lives.

She slams her eyes tight. When she opens them, she's gazing at my bedroom door with a pitiful look in her eye. "I know," is all she says. "The cops came and took our statements, and because of my face, they took him away. Do you know what he said when they were putting him in the back of the cruiser?"

It's rhetorical, because I can see her mind working.

"He told me I could run to you so you can make it all go away—so you could make everything all better."

"I'm going to kill him," I say, my words cracking like kindling hitting fire. "String him up by his toes and bleed him until he's dry."

"He's right, Ben." Her voice shakes. Like the realization is just as bad as what he's stolen from her.

I place my hands on my hips to keep from reaching out for her. "Nothing is right about him. Look what he did to you." The distance is too much. She feels the same because she stands up as I approach, and I fold her into my arms. The Harper well is filling. I breathe in her hair and tuck my face into the crook of her long neck. I kiss her there, where his fingerprints stained her creamy, delicate skin.

"You make it all better," she whispers. It's like we're kids again and I'm helping her with her homework or playing pranks on the mean girls to make her smile. It's not that easy anymore. Life is far more complicated than that.

I hear the bedroom door open as I'm pressing another kiss against Harper's rapid pulse.

"Is everything okay out here? Harper? Are you okay?"

I don't even pull away from the embrace. It's that comforting—that satisfying, even given the horrendous circumstances. Let Norah see it all. She's about to know everything anyway.

"Harper's going to stay here for a bit," I say as an explanation.

Norah comes through the front door pulling the last suitcase. Harper follows a second later with an armful of textbooks. She's parked down the street in an alleyway to hide her car and refuses to move it until she's sure of his brother's arrival. I wish he'd come to my house looking for her, but she's a pacifist, and I know I won't win this argument today.

My anger is tempered by the fact that she's here. More so than she's ever been.

Harper heaves the texts down on a writing desk in the corner of my living room. "You don't mind if I work here?" she asks Norah.

I finally have her where I've always wanted her... where she's always wanted to be, and yet it took far more than it should have.

My girlfriend pats her back. Not in a condescending manner, but in a way that tells me she's as good as I always assumed she was. "Work wherever you want. I don't mind at all. It's Ben's house, after all." They exchange polite smiles, and my fraction of happiness fades as a new realization dawns. Norah might not possess the intuition to understand the severity of what's happening. "Let me know if you need anything. I'm headed into work for a bit, and I can swing by the store and pick up anything you want that Ben doesn't have." Norah glances at me, a small, sweeping smile lighting her face.

I back away, terrified of what this means, knowing exactly what I'll need to do to her. Instead of agreeing with her or replying at all, I grab one of Harper's bags, one I know is her bathroom stuff, and disappear into the hallway.

Norah pokes her head in, her brows raised. Clearing her throat, she says, "Harper didn't need anything. I'll leave you guys alone tonight. I'm sure you have a lot to talk about. She gave me the gist of it on the walk to her car." Norah pauses, waiting to see if I'll offer anything further. When I don't, she whispers, "I can't believe he did that."

Looking at myself in the bathroom mirror, I see a traitor. A coward of a man. A man who protects innocent people for a career but couldn't protect the person he loves the most in the entire world. "I know," I say, voice low.

"Are you okay?" Norah asks, tilting my face to hers, using her soft, cold hand.

"I'm pissed, Norah. That's all. Thank you for being so helpful, but you're right. We have a lot to talk about tonight."

She holds out both palms in my direction. "I won't be in your way. Say no more."

I scowl, eyes narrowed and lips pursed. "A month ago you were badgering me with questions about my feelings for her, and now you're okay with this?" Badgering is the wrong word, she merely asked, but I have a giant case of displaced anger.

She looks away from me but steps forward and closes the door behind her. "You told me she's your best friend, and that's never going to change. Fine. I decided to look at her like your best friend. If she were a man, there would be no issues, so I try to have no issues. Harper told me that you guys were always only going to be friends."

My stomach sinks. "When did she say that?" I already know when, but I don't want to talk, and I need time to compose my thoughts.

She tells me about the double date and what Harper said. I'm irritated that Norah approached her to begin with, but I can also understand it completely. She clears her throat, and I meet her eyes. "I'll ask one more time, Ben. Only because I love you and I want a future with you. Do I need to be worried about your friendship?"

I grab her face with both hands. Her pretty eyes and her thin lips are things I've found comfort in for a while now. A salve. A patch. She arrived in my life at the perfect time. "I love you, Norah," I say, brushing my lips on hers. Her eyes flutter closed and then open again, searching mine in earnest. "But my friendship with Harper is something you should always be worried about."

Pressing her lips together, she leans her forehead on mine. "I already knew that, though. Didn't I? Guess I need some time to figure out if that's something I'm willing to live with."

Maybe it's that I'll never be able to live without Harper. That the empty well inside me only craves one person, and even if I wanted to fill it with someone or something else, it would stay a dark, pitiful cavern of loneliness.

"Any woman I'm ever with will have the same

concern. She was first," I explain, shrugging. "I can't give you what's already gone."

She's too good for me, and I'm left with a fleeting sense of guilt. I wish she were a one-night stand. Maybe then she'd smack me, storm off, and leave a dead fish in the back of my truck. Instead, she leaves the bathroom and my house quietly, asking once more if Harper needs anything before she leaves.

Harper is in the kitchen making herself a sandwich when I finally steel myself away. My cell phone vibrates on the counter in front of her. She doesn't look at it. She maintains pure focus on the ham and swiss on rye. She has her hair pulled over the front of her neck, trying to hide the mark I desperately want to see.

It's work calling. With a pounding heart, I silence the call. Maybe if I had silenced the call all those years ago, this vision in my kitchen would be less of a nightmare. Harper licks her thumb to get errant mayonnaise off and puts the jar back in the refrigerator. "I still have the mustard out. Want one?" she asks, finally looking up. "You still hate mayo, right?"

I nod, eyeing her neck. "No, thank you," I growl.

My cell phone starts buzzing again, and I have to close my eyes and take a deep breath.

Harper puts the knife down on the counter with a loud clank. She pulls her hair back and looks to the side. "What? Just say what's on your mind."

The cell stops vibrating. I can think clearly. "How did we get so messed up? Why did we complicate things? We could have so easily been done. Happily ever after."

"Life doesn't work that way," she whispers.

My cell phone goes off again. This time Harper looks at it. "The truth always hurts more than lies. It's easier to swallow down a bunch of lies than face the one truth that changes everything."

I hold my arms out to the side. "What changes? We'll be perfectly happy for the first time since the last time?"

Clearing her throat, she turns around and leans against the counter with the sandwich in her hand. She takes a careful bite, chews, and swallows it. "Do you remember when I had to take Bobo to the vet to put him to sleep?" Harper turns to look at my face, her eyes turned down in the corner. "You kill people."

"Bad guys," I insert. "What does that have to do with Bobo?" My voice cracks on the last word.

"You kill bad guys for a living, and yet the thought of putting your cat to sleep brought you to your knees. It was easier for me to do it. You could pretend it didn't happen if you didn't see it. You could lie to yourself."

I swallow down the panic the memory causes. My childhood cat lived almost twenty years. Cancer stole his body, but his mind was still there. A nightmare I've had on repeat since I can remember dreaming is that of me in a cold vet's office. I'm standing in a small room, surrounded by white, and I'm holding an animal. It's never the same animal, but my feelings are always the same the moment the doctor walks in holding a syringe needle. Panic. Soul-crushing pain. Fear.

Immobilized by the dream world, I watch through glassy eyes as the breathing creature I love fades away. First the chest stops moving, then the eyes close, and last, the freezing temperature in the room transfers to my fingertips, and the body goes ice cold. Typically, at this point I'd always wake up with a sheen of sweat and terror in my heart.

Harper is the only person who knows of the nightmare and subsequent phobia, which is why she was the person I called when it was Bobo's time. She'd just moved back to the West Coast, and there wasn't a second of hesitation when she came into my house without knocking, hugged me, kissed me on the cheek, picked up the soft-sided cat bag from the living room floor, and left to do the thing I couldn't do. When she returned with his urn of ashes a week later, it was no nonsense for her. A part of life. She never spoke of what happened in that room. I never asked—would never dream of asking. I saw the urn on the fireplace as a weakness. A thing that labeled me damaged. Bobo's ashes remind me I'm human.

Harper clears her throat after she takes the last bite of her sandwich. She's watching me through narrowed, tired eyes. Rinsing her plate, she puts it in the dishwasher.

"The lie is always easier," she repeats.

"What's the lie?" I ask. My phone vibrates once more, and I can't ignore it any longer. It's obviously something important. Holding up one finger to halt her, I answer the call. As I suspected, I have to leave. They've found a terrorist quad in the underground tunnels in Washington State.

Speaking softly, I confirm I'm on my way into work to catch the bird out. Even as I say this, I wish I were lying to Tahoe. Wish I didn't have to tell the truth to everyone else. I hang up and find her in the living room, a photo in her hand. She pulled it out of her open suitcase that's haphazardly spilling across the coffee table.

She hands me the wooden frame. It's scuffed around the edges. It has seen a few moves in its lifetime. "I don't know what the lie is anymore, Ben. Maybe it's time to face the truth." We're graduating high school. Melancholy, forced smiles on our faces, the blue gowns swallowing our bodies. Her head lying on my shoulder.

I study the photo and remember the mix of emotions that day. "I have to go. You'll be okay here? I should be back soon."

She takes the frame from me and tosses it back on top of her jumbled suitcase. "The truth is, happily ever after was shot the second you became a SEAL."

There aren't enough hours in a lifetime to tackle the monumental oceans between me and the person I'm closer to than anyone else in this world. I offer her a weak smile, promise her she'll be safe, and thank her once more for Bobo.

Grabbing my keys off the hook by the door, I turn to face her. She approaches quickly and hugs me. I kiss the spot on her neck one more time, trying in vain to erase the hurt. "I have a work party next week. Will you be back? I don't want to be alone," she rushes out. The vulnerability shows despite what she's just admitted. Perhaps it's in spite of it. We both know the game of cat and mouse has to end eventually. Doesn't it? "Work friends will be there, and I don't want to talk about Marcus. They won't ask if you go with me. That's if Norah doesn't mind."

I reply without hesitation—the way I always will. "I'll be your plus one."

I squeeze her a little tighter and then leave. My mind slowly clicks into another mode, the one in which I hunt down and kill bad men with heaving chests and warm blood.

We kill the quad of men after twelve hours of traipsing through dirty water and stale air. As usual, I feel nothing but pride at our victory. When I'm back to safety, I pull out my cell phone and type out a message. It helps me feel again even if no one else ever sees it.

You are my truth.

CHAPTER ELEVEN
Harper

AGAINST MY BETTER JUDGMENT, I'm blown, polished, waxed, and made up to the nines. Norah and I had a girls' day. Ben got home last night, but he showered and went straight back to work. He said he had a lot of briefs and video conferences to attend. Because people from all over the world sit in on these video calls, sometimes they land in the middle of the night, and quite frankly, international leaders don't care how tired he is.

Norah was more than gracious when I mentioned bringing Ben with me to the party tonight. It was her idea to go shopping and have a day filled with pampering in preparation. She's trying to make me feel better, and it would be a lie if I didn't feel equal parts guilt as I do gratitude.

True friendships have been few and far between for me. Those people I met at Harvard are all busy with their own families and lives. I've been up to my eyeballs in my own studies and career. Studying a multitude of languages takes its toll on one's ability to function in social settings. It's almost as if the part of my brain that's supposed to form real friendships with new people is used for understanding Swahili, Mandarin, and Arabic.

We're sipping cold-brew coffee, browsing dresses in a boutique in the Gaslamp District when her cell rings. I can't help the jealous rage when she smiles and says his name into the receiver of the phone. "Yes, she's going to be ready and beautiful for you by six. You're not going to be late, are you?" Norah's smile fades. "Oh, okay."

I do my best to search the racks, running my hands over the fabrics. The store clerk tells me she has a dress she just got in and hasn't had a chance to put out on the racks yet. It's the perfect excuse to wander from Norah's side and disappear on the other side of the store. By any person's standards, this would be weird. She's shopping for my date with her boyfriend. Somehow, it's not. It is two friends who share a best friend.

I see what Ben likes about Norah and know why he's drawn to her.

The emerald-green dress she presents is gorgeous. "I need to try that on right now," I say, running my fingers along the hem.

"Of course. The color will look beautiful with your hair color." She leads the way to the back, where large billowing curtains are hiding small dressing rooms. I enter with one other dress and the green one I know I'll probably buy.

The mark on my cheek is almost gone and is hidden completely by makeup the heavy-handed artist brushed on my face an hour before. Marcus hasn't tried to contact me since his brother arrived in San Diego from the East Coast. He left the apartment so I could clear out the rest of my things. Most of which reside in a storage unit on Fifth Street.

My parents can never know the true extent of the demise of my relationship. I did have to do a little creative concocting to produce a story believable enough.

It was a lot of time spent curating a relationship to toss away all willy-nilly. Or so my father said.

Leaving Marcus was easy. Living without the security blanket he provided is more difficult than I'd ever imagined. If I were with him, then I wouldn't have to worry about men or dating or my true feelings. Marcus simplified an area of my life that needed an easy fix. I'd feel guilty for the realization if my cheek didn't still throb in the shower. When I told my mother, she smiled to herself, like she was in on some secret, and told me it would get easier in time.

The green dress is stunning. I don't come out of the dressing room to show Norah even though I know she's there, chatting on the phone. I think it's one of the other veterinarians now because she's asking about an animal and giving directions on care. My cell chimes with a text.

> **Ben**
> I'm home. Are you coming home soon?

Home. My stomach rolls in anticipation. The word never sounded so good. I tap back.

> I'm naked right now, but I'll be on my way back soon.

> **Ben**
> Uniform or suit? He ignores my cheeky joke.

Pressing my lips together, I decide on the option that will draw the least amount of attention.

> Suit.

> **Ben**
> Are you still naked?

There it is.

Peeking out from the curtain, I spy Norah wrapped up in her conversation, talking with one hand moving furiously. It's harmless banter. Ben and I have always joked like this. Why does it feel different? Because my security blanket is gone.

> No. But I will be later on tonight.

Ben
I'll be there. When?

> I'll have to shower. Duh. You're such a perv, Benny.

I laugh and toss my phone in my purse. I purchase the dress and a pair of earrings that remind me of pearls, except they're silver and shiny, like alien spaceships about to infiltrate my brain by way of my ear canal.

I wait for Norah to buy a top after she ends her call, and we meet outside.

"Thanks for coming with me today," she says, sighing as she adjusts her huge purse from one shoulder to the other. "I wanted to get to know you better. You seem so familiar to me, but it must be because you and Ben are so close."

"Or we were meant to be friends." I laugh. "Those aren't easy to come by for me. I had a nice time today." A car horn honks somewhere, and our gazes dart in that direction. We'll always be on guard at the slightest disturbance in the world we live in nowadays.

She looks down at the pavement as her smile fades. Like it would be a criminal act if she showed me any side of her personality that wasn't flawless. I wish she would. Give me the ammunition I need to put my silent jealousy to use. "We're taking a break, Harper. Ben and I."

My stomach flips, and I break out into a cold sweat. "Since when?" I blurt out. "It's not my fault," I say, holding out my hands. "Don't tell me it's my fault."

She laughs. "No. Well, yes, it is, but it was my decision. Ben needs to sort his feelings, and I think you might, too." Staring at her, I catch the breath I didn't know I'd lost. At my silence she says, "You need him now, and this is as good a time as any to give him space."

"Excuse me?" What a fine time for jealous rage to rise to the surface. "My feelings have always been sorted when it comes to our friendship. Ben lives inside a tiny corner of his mind where he can't separate fact from fiction—a place that light doesn't touch, a shriveled-up cavern of what might have been. He doesn't live in the present, Norah. His feelings aren't something he can sort, because it's…complicated."

I can tell I've overstepped my boundaries and have hurt her feelings.

"I didn't mean it that way. I meant that now that you're single, you might want to explore other options. He fully admitted he's in love with you. To me. To my face. I love him. More than I ever thought possible. We work well together," she explains. Looking off to the side, she tells me a story about how he brought her to meet his parents. How it felt so seamless and easy up until the second my name was brought up. "The air changed, and you might as well have been standing right there in their living room, Harper."

I wonder which living room they were in and who brought me up. The way Norah's eyes turn down in the corner tells me I've tainted a memory when I wasn't even there. My spirit ruined the damn thing all by itself. "Okay," I state simply. "I wasn't there, and I can't speak for Ben."

We walk toward the parking lot that wraps around the back of the tall brick building. "I still can't believe you want to be my friend," I say.

She shrugs. "You're not the only one bad with friendships. I've been tied up in school and then building my practice most of my adult life. When Ben talked about you like you were some winning lottery ticket, I figured I might get a piece of that, too."

I tell her a lame self-deprecating joke to try to counter the lottery ticket comment, and she laughs. "You look beautiful. Thanks for today. For what it's worth. I've always been honest with you about the friendship with Ben."

She grins, opening her vehicle door. "Oh, I know you have. Ben's going to try to change your mind, though. Mark my words." She gets into her large SUV and pulls away. She has a sticker of a dog paw with a red heart in the middle on the back window.

I drive back to Ben's house, careful of the busy intersections while I'm lost in thought. Norah knows Ben well. Not that it complicates things more than they already are. It merely heaps more guilt on top of a tricky situation.

I decide not to broach his pseudo-breakup separation with Norah in favor of keeping the mood light and carefree. He took his turn in the bedroom getting ready, while I told him all he needed to know about who was going to be there and what I expected of him. According to the online RSVP site, Marcus won't be in attendance.

"And his friends will leave us alone, I'm sure. I made

you wear a suit so you have to act like a gentleman, not a hand for hire."

Ben scoffs audibly. I make sure to keep my tone light. It bothers him when he thinks I view him in any other way than the way I'm supposed to see him. People change, and our times surely have changed, but my perception of Ben is supposed to warp to meet his desires. It's easy most days, because he's always been Ben to me. It's harder now that I'm living here and I see his demeanor change almost completely in the span of a workday.

While he's changing, I pull out the dress and cut off the tags using a kitchen knife. Sliding off my shorts, sandals, and T-shirt, I heft the soft material of the dress over my head, careful not to mess up my hair or makeup. The plunging V-neck dips to mid-stomach, so I remove my bra and toss it over the counter to land on the sofa, my bed.

"You can dress in my bedroom," Ben says, voice low. "You're a woman. You like the kitchen, but some things should stay in the bedroom."

Grabbing the knife I used to cut off the tag, I aim it at him in mock outrage. "Take it back." I smirk. Cursing at him in one of the languages I know he's fluent in, I make my way around the counter. A half grin pulls the side of his mouth up as he replies back, something just as mean.

He raises one brow. "Or else what? You attack me with a steak knife? Sounds like my kind of Friday night." It's now that Ben finally lets his gaze dip to the rest of my body. His neck works to swallow as he takes in the neckline, or lack thereof. "Or maybe we can add something else to the agenda." He licks his lips.

I set the knife down on the edge of the counter. Even I have limits on how far I'll go to prove a point. "You like my dress?"

"It jogs a certain memory."

Picking up the heels—something I almost never wear —off a barstool, I balance on one foot and then the other to slip them on my feet. "I didn't have the rack to wear this back then, but I did buy it for the color."

He's watching my every move—studying every motion and movement my body creates. Sometimes it's like I'm an art model on display for him. If I move just the right way, maybe the spell will be broken, and he'll be unable to remember what he's desperately trying not to forget.

"You look pretty dashing yourself, Mr. Brahams. Thanks for coming with me. It's the culmination of every-thing I've been working toward." I bury the compliment in other mundane facts so I don't have to feel awkward about giving it. He does look stunning, though. Now that he fills out a suit with broad shoulders and thick arms, I know no one is going to miss him regardless of what he's wearing.

"I need you to know something," Ben replies. "Some-thing I want to say that has nothing to do with you, but it probably has everything to do with us."

Sighing, I steel myself for more conversation I'd rather not have. "Can we chat on the way? I don't want to be late. My face will literally melt off at midnight. Like Cinderella, except more real. Like Courtney Love."

He laughs and grabs his keys to lock the door. "Norah wants to take a break from our relationship."

I nod. "We talked today while she was helping me get ready for tonight. Talk about weird. It feels right, though. Being her friend. She understands us, Ben."

"She understands how I feel about you, Harps. Not us. No one else can understand us."

He closes his door to the truck and starts it up. "I need to know where we stand. It's almost as if the stars are aligning right now in the sky we grew up under to make us happen."

Panic sets in. I'm not the type of person who destroys a relationship for the sake of my own feelings. I always put others before myself. "What are you asking?" My words come out in a rush of hysteria.

"It's been a while since we last had this conversation, and I'm dropping it into our space again. For your consideration. You don't have to make any decisions tonight. I can tell you're about to hyperventilate over there, and I don't want one of your tits to pop out in a panic attack. We're not dressed for Jazzercise right now. I'm throwing it out there again. That's all."

He'll throw it out there until the cows come home. Until we're old and gray, and I'm finally brave enough to take what I want. "You aren't officially broken up, though. Are you?" It's a minor detail most people this in love would overlook in light of our situation. I'm wary—in unfamiliar territory.

He furrows his brows as his lips purse. "If you need me to make that more official than the current state, I will. This whole thing with Marcus has made me realize how important you are to me. I stare death down on a regular basis, and I don't bat an eyelash. When your life comes into question, Harper, it's no contest."

I take a deep breath and adjust my dress. I don't want a tit to pop out only because it would prove him right, and right now I want him to be wrong. "I just need to think on it, okay? I haven't been single in years. I need to think. I've had this plan in my mind, how everything was going to be and end up, and in less than a second, he changed everything I thought I knew." The hot sting of betrayal cuts through my chest. I'm not sad about Marcus anymore. The memory of him and what he stole gives me rage. Norah told me I needed to sort through my feelings, and I snapped at her. She's right. "This isn't that simple."

"Let me take you bowling tomorrow. A Ben and Harper simple date."

Crossing my legs, I turn to glance at the side of his face. He's so beautiful it makes my heart hurt. It's a moment of weakness. Of taking what I want for selfish reasons. "Yes. Fine. Bowling." Sighing, I draw his gaze.

Ben bites his bottom lip. "I'll whip your ass like always, and we can binge on dirty water beer and nachos. I bet you won't even get food poisoning this time."

"You make it sound so appealing," I deadpan. The smirk rises to my face anyway. "What's tonight then? A pre-date date?"

"Tonight, I'm just your plus one."

He does so admirably while mingling with my coworkers and superiors. I never thought he wouldn't. Ben is smarter than I am. This was a path he didn't choose but could have easily excelled in. My boss is impressed with his knowledge of a current language study. I sent him the link months ago with a note to give it a read if he had time. Never in my wildest dreams had I imagined he'd give it a second look, let alone read it thoroughly enough to quote passages and dissect nuances. I almost forget this isn't his career, nothing like his chosen profession.

Ben sings my praises, he makes sure my glass of champagne is filled at all times, and he even pretends not to notice when Marcus enters the ballroom from the side door. We see him at the same time, though, so it's obvious he's aware. His posture changes, his stance widens, and his breaths come in a furious succession as he becomes a human shield. One of his arms turns into a mom seat belt as he backs me away from a threat half a football field away.

I never filed a restraining order against Marcus. Not because it wasn't the right thing to do—I should have on principle alone—but I know he's not a threat to me anymore. That moment of hypocritical anger was his moment, the last memory he'll ever have of Harper Rose-hall in his world. Not only that, but his professional life would have been ruined, and my life would have been made more difficult. Facts aside, he wasn't supposed to be here tonight, and that makes my whole body itch with unease.

Looping my arm through Ben's, I guide him to the other side of the room. There's a live jazz band playing softly, several tables with gourmet foods spread throughout the room, all under the beautiful low light of a gregarious chandelier in the center of the room. Ben's whole demeanor changes at the prospect of conflict.

"Time to go then?" he asks.

Coworkers try not to stare between Marcus and me. In the act of trying not to, they do—their heads bouncing back and forth between the two of us. No one but Martina knows all the details about the demise of our relationship, one that was heralded as the most epic love story of all time. The love linguistics department. Not so much. What most are aware of is it went down fast, crashing so hard that we don't even speak anymore or want to be in the same breathing space together.

He nudges me again, his large hand encompassing my whole waist, and repeats, "Time to go?" The taut bulge of his muscles presses against me. An anti-warning because, unlike Marcus, Ben would use his muscles and body to protect me at all costs.

Squeezing Ben's hand, I say, "I really wanted to see

Martina before we left. I bet she shows up shortly. We can eat more cheese," I offer.

When he looks at me, his eyes hold a fear so palpable, it makes my heart rate pick up. "It's fine. Look at this room full of people. Don't be scared of him." It's a joke. Put the men side by side, and you have a laughable match. Ben could squash Marcus with a mean glare.

"I'm afraid of what I'm going to do to him," he replies, teeth gritted.

I tsk. "A gentleman would dance with his plus one. Not get into a"—I look around the room, narrowing my eyes—"well, I can't call it a bar brawl, per se. How about a work function fight?" I eye the band and hold up my arms to the side. "Dance with me?" This is a new territory. Me calming Ben. "Don't even think about him. He's afraid of me. I could have destroyed him." I roll my eyes for good measure.

The temptation to wrap his arms around me wins out, like I hoped it would, and he pulls me into his chest in one big heave. "You should have, Harper. I'll forget it for the moment, but we're coming back to this topic later. You smell so good." Distraction manipulated. One point.

He holds me closer and bends his head into my neck. Ben doesn't spin us, we kind of sway, and I know it's so he can keep his gaze locked on Marcus. I shiver in response to a blast of air conditioning. "He's ruining this for me," Ben growls, his lips barely brushing the side of my ear.

Quickly, I tilt my head away and spy Marcus and his brother, Darren, at the bar, eyes fastened on us on the dance floor. I'm saved when Martina dances up with her husband. She has on her standard black boxy glasses and a dark purple sheath dress. She's tall with quirky black curls that pop out of any updo she tries to contain them with. Tonight it's down and wild.

"You guys win." Martina laughs. "Most beautiful couple. That dress, though, Harper. You're really turning over a new leaf." Little does she know.

"Oh, stop. You look beautiful. I love your hair. May I present you with the Benjamin Brahams," I say, halting our awkward sway.

He reluctantly releases me and saves face with a false, happy front.

Martina gushes and is immediately caught up in conversation about Ben's job. I think she's the first person who knew exactly who he was and what he does. I blush for her. Her husband watches with mild amusement, shaking his head. He raises his brow when he catches me watching him.

"Tough luck with the other one," he says, voice low.

I nod. "Yeah. He wasn't supposed to be here. I'm glad I ran into Martina so we can get going."

He looks confused for a moment or two. "He changed his RSVP when he saw you had a plus one," he whispers.

Martina must tell him all of the gossip. Married people don't have any secrets. I remind myself of this before I get irritated with my friend.

Turning slightly, I find Marcus staring at me. Darren has a different drink in his hand. "That's surprising. He knows who I'd come with."

Martina tunes in to our conversation. "Yeah, a massive hunk of good looks and charm. My word. You've been keeping this one caged for all these years?"

Smirking, I take Ben's arm again, trying to turn us subtly.

"Finally, someone with brains!" Ben exclaims. It seems Martina's own charm has worked to calm Ben's nerves. "I've been trying to get Harper to notice these qualities for the better part of two decades."

I scoff. "Ben didn't have these...attributes for the

better part of two decades. Don't let him fool you. The recent developments are just that. Recent."

"What about my charm?" he asks, palming his chest as if I'd stabbed him in the heart. Martina and her husband laugh. "Haven't I always had that?"

"When you weren't breaking rules. I guess so," I agree. "No breaking rules tonight either." It's a thinly veiled request, and one I know he picks up on. He squeezes my waist.

"Harper. Nice to see you," Marcus rasps from Ben's other side. The reason I was trying to work us to stand in the opposite direction.

Martina's eyes widen. She knows the whole story, which means so does her husband. I'm shoved behind Ben's back before I can get a word out. SEALs give new meaning to the words reflexes like a cat.

"Don't talk to her," Ben hisses. "Get the fuck out of here. Right now."

I can see Marcus swaying, a drunkenness I've only seen one other time—when his grandmother died—visible from my hiding spot. Laying a hand on Ben's back, I try to remind him of where we are. He shakes his head as a response to my silent plea.

"I never want to hear her name come from your lips again. You have nerves of steel. I'll give you that much. Which means you're looking for trouble, or you're a fucking idiot."

Martina grabs my arm. "Let's go to the bathroom."

Ben spins on us. "She doesn't leave my side."

My eyes widen as I take in a side of Ben I don't know. It's scary. It's also undeniably mouthwatering hot. I have to check my psyche another time, because I'm not sure what that says about me. "Go. Get out of here," Ben says, leaning forward to Marcus.

Darren wanders over, feet sluggish and eyes glassy.

His brother's presence is all Marcus requires to leak asinine statements. "I have nerve? I'm the one with the nerve?" Marcus says, voice quavering. "You loved her when she was mine. You had her when she wasn't yours." I can see his neck work as he swallows and shakes his head. "Don't call me a fucking idiot. I know what I want. You're the fucking idiot for not going after what will never belong to anyone else. Maybe I do have nerves of steel, but someone needs to tell you to appreciate what you have."

"You had to hit her to figure out how to appreciate her? That's how it works then?" Ben's breathing heavily, and I can tell the effort it's taking to keep from causing a full-on scene. "You're a pathetic excuse for a man."

Ben ushers me next to him. Marcus's eyes dart to my chest, my body, and finally my face. "Take a look, man. Take a good, hard look. A nerves-of-steel look," Ben quips.

My arms feel like spaghetti, and my stomach has butterflies so wild a bout of nausea takes me over. The room is staring at us. "Hi, Darren," I whisper. He didn't have anything to do with Marcus's reckless behavior, and manners dictate I be a decent person.

Darren nods at me and takes another sip from his clear cup.

Grabbing my shoulders, Ben spins me to face him. "This one is for the fucking record, okay?"

His eyes are pleading, but his features are soft, a complete transformation from mere seconds before.

"Okay," I whisper, unsure what he wants me to say or do. He's unreadable. His hot alpha kill mode has annihilated all of my Ben sensors.

"You hear that, Marcus? This is me setting the record straight for you and for anyone else who doubts what I want. Hell, what we both want."

Ben grabs my face in his hands, his thumbs setting on the top of my bottom lip, one on each side. He smiles. An out-of-place smile that reminds me of the Ben from thirty minutes ago. The butterflies leave, and the sappy, deep emotions I feel for this man soak my awareness. He kisses me, slanting his head to the side. My eyes close, and I feel every single place where his body touches mine. The five o'clock shadow on his chin brushes my soft skin.

I grab his forearms and let him guide the kiss deeper still. I haven't been kissed like this, or felt this much in a single melding of lips, since the last time we kissed. It's like I'm opening a suitcase of emotions and love that's been sitting untouched in a closet, dusty and disused. I've missed out on this all this time. The thought makes me sad, and a tear slips from the corner of my eye.

Ben pulls back, eyes wide, and lips slightly parted. His hands are still on my face, and he brings a finger up to brush away the salty remnants of a memory that is equal parts sad and amazing. I can have this now. Finally. Past relationships be damned. This is what life is about. Grinning at Ben, the rest of the room vanishes. We don't say a word to each other. We don't have to.

I think it's why I wanted to go into linguistics. The silent language I've always had with Ben. We speak without saying a word and understand each other in a perfect harmony no one else could ever decipher. It's ours.

"Record straightened," I whisper, mostly for my own benefit.

"It was better than I remembered," he replies, glancing to the side and breaking eye contact for the first time since we pulled apart.

Sometime in the middle of the kiss, Darren and Marcus disappeared. Those who weren't paying attention before are now. The room is applauding with cheers and whistles mixed in. My blush comes fast and furious, and Ben glows under the attention, waving and shaking both hands side to side like he's accepting an award.

As we leave, I remark that it's like I'm starting over completely. I'm finished with school. The new chapter is starting. A new life, one of my own choosing.

A life I've always dreamed of.

The Virginity Clause

HARPER

"YOU'RE NOT PUTTING those balls inside me, Benny," I say, voice cracking, gaze fixed on the silver orbs sitting on his palm.

Swallowing hard, he replies, "The article I read said it would get you...ready for sex."

I won't give him crap for reading articles. I did the same. I read one about the female orgasm seventeen times. It was in the back of one of my mom's women's magazines. How to cook a great baked chicken, what not to wear to a summer party, and how to have a mind-blowing orgasm. The content of women's magazines is a mystery to me, though I was happy to glean at least a little information aside from the porn GIFs Ben sent me on a biweekly basis.

We're at my house because I have a queen bed and Benny has a twin. The candles are lit on top of my desk, and my parents are away for a business meeting. That's all that's required for this momentous occasion. We're both eighteen—legal, consenting adults who want experience, and while I'm being so candid, we want each other.

Ben puts the balls down on the desk.

"I'm a virgin. That stuff is supposed to be for people with more experience. I doubt balls...well, those balls are required for orgasms and good sex." My voice warbles when I say the word sex, and I realize just how nervous I actually am.

His chest heaves a few times. I grin, relaxing a touch. "You're having a panic attack," I joke. "You're about to pass out, and I'm going to have to resuscitate you instead of having sex with you."

"Shut up!" Ben barks. "I can't believe it's happening, that's all."

"You invoked the virginity clause. If you're not ready, that's okay," I say, meaning it. "I'll wait for you." Standing from my bed, my feet heavy like bricks, I approach him. He's leaning against the wall, hands in his pockets. His gaze follows me as I approach. "Okay?"

Benny closes his eyes. "I'm afraid I'm too ready. Do you know how long I've wanted this? I want it to last forever. Not like...two minutes."

I look to the left in thought. "Probably since you first peeked into the girl's locker room and saw Jenny Megly's vagina?" I let my gaze wander back to his. We haven't kissed since the treehouse, but after that there's been a crackling tension between us neither of us can deny. A few months ago my mom asked if I was dating Ben because of the way we'd been looking at each other.

If she sees it, God knows everyone else must too. I won't go so far as to say that the kiss changed things between us, but it surely made things more. We know what it feels like. The desire. The emotions attached to the act rule our thoughts now.

Ben takes his hands out of his jeans pockets and sets them carefully on my shoulders. His hair is wet from a shower, and it flops over one eye, on top of his glasses. I flick it out of the way. As if as a reminder, he removes his glasses and sets them down. "I feel like you taking off your glasses shouldn't be so sexy," I say, laughing.

"That was sexy?" He smirks. "Wait until I take off your shirt." Ben's smile slips, and a carnal look replaces his mirth. My core clenches, and desire floods my awareness. It's more than want. I need him. Because he completes me in a way no one else can.

I lose my breath for a second, and my heart races along with my thoughts. "I've wanted this with you since we kissed, Harper. If you had given any indication you wanted it, I would have stripped you down, kissed every square inch of your body, and fucked you until you forgot you peed your pants in the treehouse when you were ten."

"Your dirty talk is on point," I remark, nodding firmly once. "Though you could have left out the pee. Pee isn't very sexy." Stepping forward, I'm in reaching distance. His back is still pressed against the wall. He reaches out and pulls me against his body.

Ben leans his forehead against mine. "I'm going to kiss you."

"That's a good place to start."

"Is it a good place to finish, though?" Biting his lip, he swallows hard. He meant it as a joke, but it has the opposite effect right now. It stokes the flames inside me until I feel like I might explode if he isn't inside me as soon as humanly possible.

Slowly he lifts his chin up, and I do the same to match his mouth to mine. It's a gentle peck, his lips barely parted, mine glossed to all hell in preparation for tonight. It's marked on my calendar. I freeze the second his hands slide down to cup my ass. I'm wearing a cotton skirt that skims the back of my thighs. "It's just an act. Remember that," Ben whispers against my mouth.

"Just an act," I repeat. I feel him hard against me,

ready and willing. We've discussed every detail, and we decided against using a condom. I went on birth control three months ago. We're both virgins, so sexually transmitted diseases are off the table. We want our first time to be as perfect as it can possibly be. Skin on skin. Nothing separating us.

The weight of his hands leaves my back, and he slides my shirt up and over my head. He brushes his knuckles against my bare skin as he goes, and a tiny gasp leaves my mouth. I can't catch my breath. "Touch me more," I say. "That feels amazing."

Ben grins and rubs his hands down my sides and slides my skirt off, touching everything as he goes. Stepping out of it, I'm left in my bra—fully exposed to him, willing to do whatever he wants. I'm basically panting, unable to concentrate on anything except the warm feeling flooding between my legs. Backing away, I tug on his hands to guide him to my bed. I'm fumbling and awkward as I remove his shirt and unfasten his pants. Ben likes it—his gaze lighting like fire as he watches my every move, taking it all in. I remind myself that's what matters. Ben. Us. I sit on the edge of my bed as he towers over me, standing in between my knees.

"It's just me," he says when he sees my hands tremble on the edge of the band of his underwear.

"It's just you," I say, nodding. Looking up at him, I'm reaffirmed of everything I've always known about him. "It's just me," I whisper, pulling his underwear down.

"It's only you. Always. Only you," he returns, shaking his head.

I take off my bra after several seconds of Ben trying and failing to get it off, and then he falls against me, lips and passion and this feeling in my stomach no one else gives me. There's no regret or feeling that we may be making a mistake.

Ben is the only decision I've ever been sure of in my entire life. Giving myself to him is the culmination of a lifelong, forever love. Something I'll never be able to give to anyone else.

Lust. Passion. Soul-searing love.

CHAPTER TWELVE

Ben

"TELL ME HOW YOU WANT IT."

Harper is standing in the middle of my bedroom, looking every bit as perfect as she has my entire life, except even more so. Half of the green dress is hanging off her shoulder, exposing her tit, and her hair is as big as a lion's mane from the intense make-out session on the sofa. We barely made it through the door before we went full-on primal.

Her chest rises and falls as her perfect goddamn mouth pants out breaths of seduction. It was her idea to come into my bedroom for more space.

"I don't even want to blink right now," I admit. "You're a vision."

Her tongue darts out to lick her bottom lip. "Yeah?"

"Tell me how you want it," I repeat.

With slow hands, she removes her dress, exposing her flawless skin inch by inch as she goes. "Any which way," she says, meeting my eyes. Gone is any hesitation she's ever had about our friendship and boundaries or even other relationships. No one else is in this room with us, despite the fact that there's a bottle of Norah's hand lotion on one nightstand. When she's naked but for a pair of nude high heels, she draws nearer, eyes like sex-shrouded missiles locked and aimed directly on me. My dick strains against my pants, and I readjust in a squat, grab move.

I still haven't blinked, too afraid the mirage from my wildest fantasy might pop smoke and morph into a normal woman instead of the one I've wanted my entire life. Harper is standing so close in front of me I can smell her desire mixed with her perfume, and the scent makes me delirious with lust.

"No hands," she says when I reach for her tiny waist. "Not yet," she amends when my face falls.

"I never pinned you for a cock tease," I admit, smirking. "How many years has it been?" I ask. "I take it back. You're the cock tease president."

She tells me how long it's been. Down to the day, since the last time I was inside her, my mind and body being indoctrinated with the perfect balance of everything and nothing at the same exact time.

"I've wanted you every second since then," I reply honestly.

Her neck works as she swallows and leans in to kiss the spot beneath my ear. I give in and close my eyes to the sensation of her lips on my skin. My entire body responds—every square inch of skin prickling with heat and desire. More than anything in the world, I hope my damn phone doesn't ring or that someone doesn't ring my doorbell. With steady, deft hands, Harper unbuttons my shirt and unzips my pants. With pure womanly confidence, she slides my boxer briefs down my legs, stooping down on her high heels to help me step out of my clothing.

Standing back to admire her handiwork and my hard

work, she rubs her chin like she's judging a dog show instead of my smoke show.

"Best of show?" I ask, pulling the corner of my bottom lip into my mouth. I flex my abs a bit as she takes in my physique. It's mostly because I know she'll laugh, but she doesn't. It turns her on even more. Her pert, round tits rise up and down as her breathing speeds.

"Best in life," Harper finally responds. "When was the last time you were tested for rabies?" She meets my eyes with a small grin.

"Last week. Monthly. What about you?" I tilt my head and try to step forward, but she halts me with a head shake. "Come on, Harpee. You're killing me."

She reaches out and grabs my hand. "I'm clean," she replies. My cock jerks. No condoms. Skin. I crave it more than a man dying of thirst.

"You know how some people have a cheat celebrity they fantasize about having sex with?" I ask, committing her every naked curve to memory.

Harper grins. "Chris Hemsworth."

I let my eyes flare in mock outrage. "You're it for me, Harper. The one. The dream girl. The woman I'd break every rule to be with."

She clears her throat. "I was joking about Chris. You're mine too."

"Liar." I quirk up a brow.

"A little." She crosses her legs at her ankles. It's not supposed to be a sexy, fucking pose, but it's what I see. When my dick twitches in approval, Harper runs her hands over my pecs and abs.

"So, if I'm quick, you can't blame me," I growl. I hope I'm joking because I want to take it slow with her. This needs to last as long as humanly possible. The gratification I get from being with her like this, stripped of all preconceived notions, is the best feeling in the world, and my dick hasn't even slid home yet.

"Want to touch me now?" she asks, guiding my hand up the side of her body to end on her perfect tit. My other hand goes to the other without her guidance. "I want to feel you everywhere," she says, her voice breathy.

Sighing, I glide my rough palms over her nipples and up and over her sharp collarbones and down her arms. In the wake of my touch, her skin prickles, and her eyes close in pleasure. "You're so soft," I remark, watching my tanned, worked hands in contrast to her smooth, creamy skin. "Tell me how it feels," I command.

Her eyes open when one of my hands glides down her flat stomach and stops between her legs, on her smooth, wet pussy. She moans, her pink lips separate, and her straight, white teeth peek out. I slide one finger inside her, and the silky tightness grips me. I crook my finger against her G-spot, and I ask her again how my touch feels.

"Like I'm flying high in the sky," she gasps out, leaning her body against mine. The scent of her desire fills my senses, and my dick is pressed against my stomach in between our bodies. "So good, Benny. It feels so good. Nothing compares to this. Nothing has ever compared to this."

Somehow her using my childhood nickname and telling me I'm the best she's ever had makes my balls tingle. I need to hurry this up so I can have my turn.

With my thumb, I work her clit at the same tempo, and her petite body stiffens. "This feels good? If it feels so good, I want you to come." I brace her around her waist as the first grips of her orgasm hit. Her head thrown back, she swears in about four different languages.

In the mirror across the room, I catch a glimpse of our

naked bodies, and Harper presses so close I'm unable to tell where she starts and I begin, but for the differences in our skin color. Mine is tanned and weathered from a life spent in the elements, and hers is flawless and perfect. Taking a few steps back until my legs hit the bed, I pull her down on top of me as she catches her breath.

She lays her head on my chest for a second or two and then pops up. She doesn't say anything, and I don't have to either. I lick both my middle finger and my thumb as she grins and then leans in to kiss me. The kiss is cruel and torturous as she works her wet pussy over my steely cock, teasing, asking for more.

I grunt a few times when the head of my cock is on the cusp of slipping in. Cradling her head in my hands, I control the kiss. Her tongue is sweet, and her lips fit with mine perfectly, like a road map, and I know every subtle pit stop along the way. I lean away from the kiss and lick the corner of her ear. "Ben Wa balls in your ears?" I whisper.

"Hat tilt to the best twenty minutes in my history," she says, her slick lips brushing mine as she talks. The night we lost our virginity to each other.

I laugh. "It was less than twenty minutes." She's being generous. I was so stoked on her body and antici-pation I nearly creamed my pants the second she shut her bedroom door.

Straddling my knees, she orders me back on the bed. "I'm going to show you something that will take less than twenty minutes."

When she takes my dick into her hands, I raise my brows and fold my arms behind my head. "I won't tell you no. If you were asking."

She kisses my abs. It's more tongue than kiss, and my body hardens under the sensation. Another kiss by my belly button, lower again. Harper's hand is working my dick in slow, sumptuous strokes. When her mouth finally nears my cock, she leans up and spits on the tip—the saliva connecting me to her for a split second.

"It's almost criminal now that I know what I've been missing." Memories fade, but I know nothing in my history compares to this.

Instead of responding, she lowers her head to take me all the way into her throat in one fierce move, one hand on the base of my shaft and the other cupping my balls. "Ahhhh," I hiss. Controlling my hips is hard. I want to fuck her face, want to come right now, down her throat, but I want to be inside the slick warmth my fingers tasted more.

My view is something from a porno. Beautiful girl, wearing high heels, straddling me, with my dick sloppy wet, appearing and disappearing in her mouth. Harper's hair is swinging, and her eyes flick to mine every so often, and that's when reality hits me and the urge to come flickers more than it should at this point.

Not today, Satan.

"Harper, Harper. Stop. I need to be inside you." The sentence alone makes me desperate for my twisted, perfect request.

Wiping her mouth, she leans up, keeping her hands on my stomach. "Every muscle in your body is flexed," she remarks. "I like it way more than I thought I would."

"Happy to be of service. Back to the task at hand. Don't let my muscles distract you."

She snaps once in front of her face. "Hypnosis ended. Let's fuck, Ben." Her voice is a whisper, but her eyes are screaming for my cock. This is a version of Harper I've never had before. The person Marcus with bad breath has had all of these years. At the thought, my gaze darts to her neck and then the side of her face that he tainted by hate. A hate disguised as love and affection. A hate derived from her unwillingness to spend the rest of her life with him.

Shaking my head, I ask her to repeat herself. I need the dirty talk to get back to the root of our passion. She does, and then she slides on her knees up my body to hover over my dick. Using one hand, I bend my cock back to meet with her wet pussy.

Harper swallows hard, and I'm privy to her darkest fears by merely glimpsing in her eyes.

"It's me, Harper."

I let her sit down slowly, keeping my hands on her hips. Sweat beads on my forehead, and the willpower I have to use once I'm inside her is painful. The urge to fuck her like a bandito on a drug-fueled robbery is all-consuming. I want every part of her body to smell like me. I want every hole on her body filled with me. My cum. Every single thing on her body claimed as mine so strongly that every male in the country knows she belongs to me.

Harper tilts her chin to the ceiling and rides me, writhing her hips back and forth in a concoction of pure pleasure and ecstasy. Her arms are down by her sides, but she raises them to pull her hair out of her face on each side. Her pink nipples are hardened peaks on top of glorious, bouncing tits.

"You're mine. Do you hear me? This makes you mine forever," I say.

"Fuck me harder. I need it harder," she says, moaning. "Make sure I can feel you inside me forever."

Permission granted.

Tightening my grip on her, I fuck her like she wants. And also exactly how my dick prefers because the second the friction and pace quicken, I feel the sensations rise and know I'm going to come.

"Slow down," I ask, pulling her to the top of my dick

without disconnecting our bodies. My dick gleams with her wetness, and I can see the tip of my cock spreading her pussy open. "Dammit. My god, dammit." Slamming my eyes shut, I try to control my body, but she has complete control over my mind as well.

She slides off, and I feel her crawl next to me, her breaths ragged. "You on top. I'll come in like two seconds." She licks my ear. Then my neck, her lips traveling over to my mouth. I use my tongue to violate her mouth in a passionate kiss. My hands are holding her head in place, and the little moans and sighs of pleasure that escape her mouth drive me fucking wild.

I roll on top of her and cage her body under mine using my arms. Her hands run the expanse of my biceps, her eyes open and locked on mine. She blinks slowly, spreads her legs further, grabs my dick, and pulls it into her body. It's so warm and wet that it slips in. I don't move, but she works her hips under me to bring us together. "You feel so good. Stay inside me," she says.

The light from the bathroom lights the side of her face, and I lose my breath. "You're so fucking beautiful like this." I kiss her forehead and then her closed eyes one by one. "I never want to leave you."

She leans up and kisses me, and I thrust into her at a quiet, loving pace. This isn't fucking anymore. Harper meets my hips stroke for stroke. She didn't lie, it doesn't take her long. Wrapping her legs around my back, she digs her nails into my back as the muscles in her pussy clench my cock and draw me deeper inside her.

My neck muscles strain as I watch her face in orgasm. A slight sheen of sweat glistens on her face and neck. Her cheeks are red, her lips are violently pink from our kisses, and her eyes are hooded—nearly closed. "Where do you want me to come?" I ask, dipping my head into the crook of her sweet-smelling neck.

Her reply comes in a breathy moan. "Wherever you want." She digs her nails into my ass, pushing me in to the hilt.

Message received. I kiss her deep and hard. "I want to taste you when I come inside your pussy," I say, my teeth pulling her lips after I speak.

Pumping a few more times is all it takes because it's Harper. I'm finally taking her. She's panting and satisfied by my dick, asking me to blow my fucking load inside her hot snatch. It's all too much. I groan against our connected mouths and come inside her as deep as I possibly can—cock pressed to the back as far as it will go.

"I want to stay right here for a while," Harper says, wrapping her arms around my neck, keeping me deep inside her.

"No arguments there," I hiss out in between breaths, settling my head next to hers. "That was…everything."

Harper nods against my shoulder. Her heartbeat hammers against mine—matching it one love-filled beat for the next. My whole body feels weak after that mind-numbing orgasm. There's no comparison. Everything in my body is electrified, every sense heightened, my soul calling out to its one and only match in this twisted world. This is it for me.

She is it for me.

A sniffle fills the air, and I pull back to look at her face. A tear rolls down the side of her temple and disappears into her brown hair. Harper smiles and kisses me on the lips once. "I'm sorry," she whispers, her voice catching.

Narrowing my eyes, I ask, "What for?"

"For ignoring our truth for so long."

I roll off her small frame and tuck her into my body. She fits perfectly, her back against my chest and her legs bent around mine. Norah's lotion catches my eye, and I swallow down a bout of guilt.

How can I possibly feel guilt when I have, quite literally, everything I've ever loved in my arms? I kiss the top of her head, and she nestles in deeper, pulling my arm under her face.

I make a note to put away the lotion as soon as Harper goes to the restroom.

CHAPTER THIRTEEN

Harper

EVERY SINGLE MUSCLE in my body hurts. We had sex three times last night. There's not a spot on my body that doesn't have either Ben's saliva or his cum dried into my skin. Wincing when I sit up in bed, I throw a hand over my eyes when the sunlight blasts through the open curtain. "Oh my god. I think I'm dying," I groan.

Ben is already in the kitchen. Pots and pans are banging around, and I hear the fridge door open and close. Ben's white dress shirt is sitting on the floor next to the bed. "Perfect," I say, sliding my arms into the big sleeves and buttoning a few, leaving the top open. I catch sight of myself in the mirror over his dresser and find my lipstick smeared all over the collar.

Ben peeks into the room. "You're up!" His smile is bright, and butterflies flutter in my stomach. Part of me worried he'd think we made a mistake last night. I didn't.

"I was a right fine whore last night," I admit, turning to him so he can see his destroyed shirt.

He waves it off. "That's what Grace is for. She'll get those stains out."

"Grace?"

"My dry cleaning lady."

"Oh," I reply, feeling my cheeks heat. I wasn't drunk. Not by a long shot. Last night was all me.

He walks over and pulls me close. "Last night you showed me your best work to date. Don't be embarrassed. I had to physically restrain myself from pummeling your sweet pussy while you slept. It's why I made breakfast."

My core clenches at his words, but my stomach grumbles. "Can you pummel me after breakfast?"

"My god," Ben says, setting his thumbs on my lips. "I've entered heaven, haven't I? You're my gift for serving my country well." Ben leans in and barely touches his mouth against mine.

Everything in my body focuses on where he's touching me. "It was so good. I didn't know it could be that good."

He smiles against my mouth, and I have to open my eyes to view it. His dimples are out, and his hooded eyes tell me he thinks last night was more than good. "Just think. Today we bowl."

"Don't you have work?" I ask, pushing away from him to go into the bathroom. I pee with the door open as Ben tells me he's taken some time off work for a few days. It's because another team has taken over this week, so some of the guys were able to put in successful leave requests. I wash my hands as I survey myself in the mirror. Ben's back in the kitchen attending to our breakfast. Last night I told him this was the beginning of our new, truthful life, and I don't look the same.

I look happy. A truthful happy. The kind you find when you finally stop lying to yourself and give in to what you know you need. I need Ben more than anything else. He doesn't complete me. I don't need a man to do that. I need a man to love me more than he loves anything else. There's no question in my mind that he does. That regardless of his career choices or how busy he is, Ben will always love me most.

I smile at my wild-eyed reflection and head to the living room to search my suitcase for something to wear to bowling on our first real date. I mark the day in my head as the one where we started our forever over again. I'm sifting through my suitcase, folding and refolding as I organize.

"Move it into my closet, Harper," Ben says, appearing behind me, hands on his hips. "Solves the problem, right?"

"It does. You're okay sharing that space?" I ask, wiggling my eyebrows.

He shrugs. "You're doubting what I'd do to keep you here." He nudges me out of the way and grabs my suitcase and carries it to the bedroom.

The doorbell rings while he's gone. "Shit," I say under my breath. I pull on the hem of Ben's shirt. All of my clothes just left the coffee table and entered his room.

Ben runs out, his lounge pants slung low on his hips. "I'll get it," he says, eyes flicking from my bare legs to the door as he jogs.

Of course it's Norah, and blessed be, she didn't use her key to waltz right in. "Ben. Sorry I didn't call first," she says. If I'm correct, like I probably am, she's been crying. I have a reverse memory. The one where I barged into this house after Marcus ruined everything. Norah was so kind and gentle with me. The mere sight of me right now is going to be the opposite of that. My gaze darts around to find a hiding place.

I can't make it to the kitchen without being seen. I swear in Arabic under my breath and duck down next to the couch, getting on my knees to try to make myself smaller. "What happened? Are you okay?" Ben asks.

"I need to talk to you," she says, sobbing a little.

Ben clears his throat. "It's not a good time, Norah. Can we talk tonight?"

"Oh. I guess so," she replies. She's getting the brush-off, and she's still being perfectly polite. I know I couldn't do that. "What time works? It's important I speak to you about something, Ben." My stomach knots, and an uneasy feeling invades the place that just held nothing but love.

I peek out and Ben spies me in my hiding place, and his eyes widen. Norah steps inside and immediately catches sight of me. "I was just cleaning...something. Over here. Dirty. Ah, it needs to be cleaned." The only dirty thing is Ben's cum dried on the inside of my legs and on my stomach and neck, and I'm pretty sure it's in my left eyelash.

I stand quickly in one fluid movement. She's a woman. A smart one. It takes nothing more than a nanosecond for her eyes to dart to my bare legs, my appearance, and the smears of the lipstick on Ben's shirt. The same shade she helped me select the day before to know everything that matters right in this awkward moment.

"I'm so sorry, Norah," I say, swallowing hard. "I need to use the restroom." I excuse myself and flee the room with hot cheeks and a shame so deep I've never felt the likes of it before in my life. That's what happens when you follow the straight and narrow path without deviating. Last night felt like flying. This morning, as it makes perfect sense, I'm crashing.

The front door closes with a thud, and I think they're probably going to talk in the living room, but Ben strolls into his bedroom right behind me. "Harper. It's fine. Don't be embarrassed."

"How was that okay? She didn't do anything wrong. That was cruel."

He throws his arms out. "She knew! That's why we broke up! She knew. She didn't call. It's okay. Everything between us is fine." Ben takes me in his arms, and his scent comforts me even if it's the one thing that marks me as a traitor. "We weren't together. There wasn't cheating or lying. I was honest with her about my feelings for you, and that was when I wasn't sure if you felt the same way. This was always going to happen between us. Always."

"It doesn't mean I feel any better about it. I actually feel pretty shitty. Is she okay?"

He sighs long and hard—relieved I seem to be coming around to his logic. I'm not. But I can let him think so because I don't feel like arguing with him. "I'm sure she's just torn up about the breakup and wants to talk. I'll call her later on tonight. The scene in there, as awful as it was, was what she needed to see."

I widen my eyes. "No one deserves to see that. I would have sat her down wearing a nice sundress and strappy sandals in a little café, and I'd tell her over coffee. Like a real woman would. Not some dirty whore. You're all over my body. Literally. All over it."

"I'm sorry. It does make things easier, though, regardless of what it looks like. Plus, you just made my cock hard."

I scoff. "Don't be such a dude. We're having a conversation." I feel giddy I have that effect on him. "You're all over me," I say again, smiling this time.

He slides his right hand into his pants and pulls out his cock and starts stroking it in between us. He doesn't take his eyes off mine. "I want to be in you," he says, mouth slightly parted as his breaths come quicker.

I reach up and unbutton the few buttons I have done and let his shirt fall to the floor. "I'm already wet," I reply, bringing my hand down to slip my middle finger into my wet slit. Ben's lustful gaze watches, lighting like fire when I move my finger in and out to stroke my clit.

He drops to his knees and moves my hand with his chin. He scratches my inner thighs with his five o'clock shadow, but his lips and tongue? Oh, they lick and suck and fuck me into a wild orgasm that brings me to the floor.

Ben fucks me doggy style in front of the full-length mirror. He forces me to watch him in our reflection, holding my face in place with one hand. "I'm yours, Harper. Do you understand that?" he asks, eyes painfully serious as he pounds me furiously.

I nod, and he shakes his head.

"No. I want to hear you say it. You need to know I'll never belong to anyone else the way you have me."

"I understand," I moan. "I'm going to come hard. All over your cock," I say, keeping my eyes on his.

He reaches around with his free arm and strokes my clit until I explode around him, flexing and clenching furiously. Waves and waves of pleasure knock me over. Never in my life has sex been such blind bliss. His cock is a balm to my body, the only thing that brings it to life. He comes seconds later, driving his dick deep inside me, hot bursts spraying over and over. I feel the last jerk, and he falls on top of me, barely holding himself up.

We're both covered in sweat when he rolls off me to rub his knees.

"Guess we have it all sorted then," Ben says.

"For now," I pant, grabbing the soreness between my legs. "Ass later?" I ask, pulling one arm across my chest to stretch it, and then the other.

"Heaven, I tell you," Ben says, leaning over to kiss my lips. When he pulls away, he slides down to kiss my wet pussy. "Heal up, kitten. I'll see you soon."

Even through the sore pain, a tingle of pleasure still comes at his lapping tongue. How is that even possible?

"Let's shower," Ben says, hopping up. My heart is pounding out a staccato of everything I'm feeling in this moment.

He lets me have all the hot water and finishes me off for the millionth time with his fingers.

"We're never leaving this house," I murmur.

"Bowling," he says.

It sounds more like a threat than anything else.

The beer tastes gross, and the food has more calories than Grandma's pound cake, but I'm with Ben, so nothing else matters. I throw a spare and dance a little even though I feel like I've been ridden hard and hung up wet. We can't get enough of each other. That's saying something because we spent every single day together the summer when we turned eleven. We called it the summer challenge. I went on his family vacation, and he came on mine. Our parents took bets on how long it would be until we'd tire of each other. We never did, and they all lost.

Now that we're adults, it's a bit of the case of the summer challenge, except years of pent-up sexual frustration equals some seriously mind-blowing orgasms.

"That was lucky. You're cheating, though, so if you win today it's because you wore that skirt. I can't focus." Ben slides his fingers across the short hem of my skirt and takes them away quickly, teasing both him and me.

"Listen, I can remember multiple times in our past when I wore things far more provocative than this skirt, and you won. Weren't you paying attention back then?"

He nods, drying his hands on top of the hand dryer. "I'm always paying attention. I hadn't tasted your pussy minutes before throwing balls down the lane, though. That makes a difference. I think you're laced with illegal drugs."

I raise one brow. "Better hope they don't pop on your next drug screen." Laughing, I hug him around the waist. "Or maybe they should show up, and then you'll be dishonorably discharged for swallowing too much Harper Rosehall."

His chuckle reverberates through my body—buzzing, eliciting the new electric current that connects us. "In all seriousness, though. I love you, Harper Jean." He squeezes me. Just once. "Everything about this is right. Breathing is easier. Living makes sense. I love you more than anything else, and I can finally say it out loud." He taps some guy on the shoulder as he gets up to bowl on the lane next to us.

"Sir, excuse me. I need you to know that I love this woman. I love her," he says again, repeating himself just to make me squirm with embarrassment. Ben releases me, throws his fists up to the ceiling, and screams, "I'm in love with Harper Jean!"

The guy looks at him funny, flicks his gaze to me wearing a confused smirk, and points at his ball waiting for him on the rack.

I'm too smitten to be angry at Ben's insane outburst. Grabbing me again, he pulls me against his chest. "I love you," he whispers, confirming I understand the severity of his words.

While we've said I love you to each other so many times in our past, this time it means something more. It means the love we spent years cultivating through friendship finally gets the opportunity to break through and live on its own. Gazing at his face, so different, yet exactly the same, I finally reply, "I love you, too."

We're both smiling wide, stupid lovers' glee written all over our faces. "Enough to throw gutter balls for the rest of the game?" Ben whispers, tucking my hair behind my ear.

I shake my head. "Probably enough to throw gutter balls for the rest of my life," I respond.

"Damn," Ben says, sliding his hands down to cup my ass. "I like your enthusiasm." His dick hardens against me.

"The prospect of winning gives you a boner. There's something wrong with you," I hiss into his ear, looking to our side to see if anyone is watching us.

"You make my dick hard," he says, leaning close to whisper in my ear.

I fidget, trying to break free from our salty, completely inappropriate, public embrace. Ben doesn't let me. He kisses me on my neck, my chin, and then trails his soft lips to my mouth. His eyes fall closed as he kisses me, slowly, deliberately. Someone somewhere in the bowling alley celebrates a strike, and the sound of pins being pelted by heavy balls cascades around us. I melt a little, turning to a fine putty in the safety of his strong, familiar arms. I'll never worry if someone will be there to catch me or contemplate the way his mind works.

I lick the edge of his lip as I pull away from the kiss. "I can't feel anything except everything," Ben admits.

"Feeling everything is a gift."

He rubs his lips together, tasting me. "It's also a curse. I can never go back from here. It's an impossibility." His gaze skirts from the bottom of my face up to the top and back down again. "You're my blind spot, Harper. I can't see around you."

There has to be some negative connotation associated

with being a blind spot, but Ben says it in a way that forces me to realize the magnitude of his feelings. I decide on the truth as my retort. "If what you're trying to explain is that I'm your handicap, then I have the advantage. I can cause darkness whenever I want?"

He shakes his head, a small grin playing on his lips. "You blind with light."

He loves with his whole heart. A fact I can't fault because I do the same. It's also the first time he's wearing it on his sleeve. "It's your turn," I say. How do I respond to that? There's no follow-up appropriate enough, strong enough.

Ben grabs his ball and winks at me over his shoulder. He throws a damn strike and celebrates by moonwalking into our neighbor's lane. Everyone around us laughs at his antics.

"Stop breaking the rules!" I call out.

He does some other weird dance back into our lane.

Shaking my head, I take a sip of my piss beer. I wince at the awful flavor and grab my ball to go next. Ben's phone starts ringing on the table behind the computer. It's Norah, and I glance away, unwilling to ruin this moment. He kisses me quickly on the cheek.

"I'm going to grab this. Try not to lose too badly," Ben says, smiling.

It's a decent ball. I knock over seven. I'm waiting for a barb, but when I glance at Ben, he's ashen, the phone pressed against his ear.

Slowly, his eyes meet mine, and the sheer terror I see there is enough to incinerate the whole world.

Twice.

CHAPTER FOURTEEN

Ben

I'M MARRIED TO NORAH. If I say it to myself seven hundred times a day, it still doesn't sound right. Her birth control failed, and I'm going to be a daddy. Doing the right thing was the hardest decision I've ever made in my life. I made the decision to make her an honest woman after drinking a case of beer with Tahoe. Harder still was telling Harper that Norah was pregnant and I intended to marry her to make sure our child has both parents all the time. Sometimes you make things work for the greater good. I know this firsthand. I expected hostility, but what I got from Harper was even worse.

Pride.

Harper was proud of me for doing the right thing. Part of me hoped she'd tell me to love her, stay with her, that she'd be a great stepmother to my child, but Harper Rosehall will always do the right thing. The one time she deviated will go down as the best night of my life. Nothing is going to change that. Not a marriage of moral code and conduct, and surely not a child. Harper is too rational and calculating for that. Granted, tears started to pour down her face a minute later, which erased some of her proud words.

It's fitting that the one thing that could pull me away from Harper and our age-old love happened the moment I felt the most secure in all ways. It was a rug ripped out from underneath me when Norah called me at the bowling alley. She'd been trying to tell me earlier when she stopped by my house, but I was still in a fucking love cloud with Harper—too wrapped up in my perfect world to see how upset she was.

I'm a dickhead. No man has ever carried the amount of guilt on his shoulders that I do. I don't let it show because that would make the women feel even worse about this fucked-up situation. Norah wasn't easy to convince, either. She immediately went on to tell me she'd raise the baby by herself and that I could be involved as much or as little as I wanted to.

Once the shock of her insinuation wore off, I was furious she thought I was the type of man to not take care of his responsibilities. Especially one as great as being a proper father to a child. Everything else stemmed from there. My love and Harper's feelings had to take a backseat to the new life I helped create. Norah is still wary of my love for Harper, but with a baby girl coming, it's easy for her to get lost in the world of everything baby and pregnancy. She overlooks a lot. Or she pretends to.

The way I stare out the window waiting for Harper to pull up. The way I close my eyes when Norah kisses me good night. How I can't bear to look at the full-length mirror in our bedroom. How I haven't smiled in weeks. Don't get me wrong, I'm excited to be a father. More than I ever thought I'd be. I'm upset that it's not what I pictured in my mind, but then again, what ever is?

Norah gets out of bed to use the restroom. Again. I roll over to face the window and stare. The long window is naked as Norah is redecorating, so it's bright as fuck in the morning, but you can see everything at night. The stars. The clouds. The moon.

The toilet flushes, and I feel her crawl back into bed and hear her soft breaths. "Ben," Norah whispers.

I can tell by the tone of her voice this is going to be one of the conversations that make me want to jump out of that window and run fast and far. I clear my throat to let her know I hear her.

"You're not happy. You told me you needed some time to get used to the idea. It's a lot for me too. I don't want you to be unhappy. That's worse than co-parenting with two happily unmarried parents." She's more perceptive than I thought. Norah is my wife. I think that sentence three times. Norah is my pregnant wife. She's carrying my child.

"We're married. This is it for me," I say, my voice cracking from disuse. It's two a.m.

"Why does that sound like a death sentence when you say it?"

"It was the right thing to do." I roll to face her.

Her face is lit with moonlight. Her blond hair cascades over her shoulders in long waves. She looks ethereal—a figment of my imagination. A woman I should be worshipping. Not getting used to the idea of loving. A small smile appears on her full lips.

"I'll get there." I grin back and lay my hand on her stomach.

I asked her father for permission after I asked Norah for her hand in marriage. He knew right away she was pregnant. Norah is in career mode. Nothing would force her from that path except for one thing. "It's not an arranged marriage, Ben. You shouldn't have to try," she replies, laying her hand on top of mine. "When did you see Harper last? That's why you're so sad."

"Seeing Har—her isn't a good idea, and you know it, Norah. Don't say stupid shit like that. I'm doing what I think is right. What I want."

"At my expense. I don't want a marriage like this. You remember when I met your parents and they ended up talking about her? After, I told you I felt like I knew her even though I'd never met her?"

I nod. I can't think of Harper, let alone see her or talk about her.

"Because you are so entwined with her, you'll never disentangle yourselves. I don't want to be the interim wife you married to keep your intent pure just to have this crash and burn later on when you realize Harper is marrying someone else."

Jealousy, heavy and green, enters my chest and forces my heart to beat quicker. Norah is right. She's always right when it comes to Harper. "I love you. She can do what she likes. Can we get some sleep now?" I rub her stomach when the baby kicks.

"She's awake. I can't sleep when she's beating on my ribs."

I chuckle. "I guess I have you to thank for this deep, middle-of-the-night conversation, huh?" I say, lowering my voice for the baby. "Go to sleep, baby Robin. Let your mommy get some rest."

Norah laughs. "We haven't decided on her name yet." Pulling my face up to look at hers, she says, "One last thing." It scares me when she looks this deep. It makes me feel like she can see inside my soul, like she knows all of the promises I give her are dependent on something neither of us can control.

"Huh?" I ask, swallowing hard.

"Don't let me be the last to know. Not like last time. When you go back to Harper, give me some notice so I can prepare myself. Get my life together. For me and for her." She rubs her stomach.

I grimace. "That's sick. Don't talk like that. How can you live like that? One foot in and out of the door. Both of my feet are here. With you. Our life." I pat her belly for good measure.

Her eyes get glassy, and it's accentuated by the blue light pouring in the window. "Your heart is most definitely on the other side of the door. Feet don't matter."

She wiggles her cold toes against my legs, and I jolt. I pull her into my arms and hug her close. Pressing a kiss on top of her head, I close my eyes. "I made the first right decision of my life the day I married you." It's not a lie. All those times in my past I could have had Harper are my cross to bear, and it's painful to watch Norah deal with my mistakes. "I love you guys."

The fucking mirror catches my eye when I open my eyes. This isn't a bottle of lotion prickling my skin, this is a motherfucking ghost haunting my soul. "Try to get some sleep. I'll sing the lullaby Robin likes."

Norah nods against my shoulder and sets her head on the pillow. I scoot down so my feet are hanging off the bed and sing the song I created for the baby. My voice is low and raspy, but she stops kicking as soon as the first verse is out.

> Robin bird, Robin bird, I'll sing to you so sweet.
> You fly in the sky, and you're mine always to
> keep.
> Robin bird, Robin bird, you were born to soar.
> The clouds and the sun aren't enough, you want
> more.
> Robin bird, Robin bird, the stars and the moon
> are too far.

*Stay with me here for a while, but always be
    who you are.
Robin bird, Robin bird, I'll give you my all.
Robin bird, fly high. Soar free. Never fall.*

"We can name her Robin," Norah whispers into the dark.

Sliding back up to my pillow, I cradle her face in my hands. "Thank you."

"I'll be gone when you wake up," she says, smiling. "I have to check on a patient at five a.m."

"Sleep well," I reply, kissing her forehead. "I'll call you when I get up. I'm leaving for Arizona mid-morning."

Norah nods, rolls over, sighs contentedly, and falls asleep in a matter of minutes.

Tahoe is next to me, grumbling about his gun. Our Pelican Cases that contain all of our equipment are being loaded into our private plane. "Motherfucking thing isn't sighted in properly." He's eyeing the scope.

"Looks like you won't be killing anyone today," I joke. We have multiple guns, but we all have a favorite. I'm at ease this morning—existing in the area of mental Harper blocks. "What are you thinking? Twenty-four hours tops?" I'd really like to be home for the weekend.

"Who knows? They said there could be a few quads," he says, grinning.

I realize it's quite wrong of me to be disappointed, because that means it will take longer, and I don't even care. At this point, this is merely a job. One I enjoy for the moral benefits and the brotherhood. The excitement and thrill aren't too shabby either.

I'm screwing around with my kit, a pair of pliers in my hand, when my phone buzzes in my pocket. Pulling it out, I see it's my mom asking me to call her when I get a chance. She wants to have us over for dinner. The plus about this whole fucking mess is no one except Harper and I know exactly how atrocious the start was. My parents were shocked as hell when I said I was marrying Norah. They softened when they realized she was pregnant—that I was manning up. My father clapped me on the back and gave me a smile that looked more like a grimace.

Harper's parents were more upset. I think her mom even cried. She excused herself to the kitchen after I mumbled the words. It made my stomach hurt. She looks like Harper. She knows Harper. The pain transfer was evident. This is how Harper truly feels about my marriage. Not proud. Sad. Horrified that our bad fucking timing really did screw any chance we ever had for happiness. I text her back that hopefully Sunday we'll be over for dinner.

She texts back that Harper is going to be there, too. "Fuck!" I yell.

"You scared me, pussy. What's the deal?" Tahoe barks.

Macs and Smith, two other SEALs, walk by and shake their heads at my outburst. Macs mumbles something about getting my shit together. Shit ruins missions. Ask any SEAL. As elite a force as we are, we're also only human. With lives and loves, and pregnant wives we aren't in love with and will probably never be in love with. We have friends we're in love with that we'll have to be around for the rest of our lives even though it shreds our souls.

Groaning, I tell him. As quietly as possible. "It's complicated." I finish the story.

Tahoe grins, his toothy white smile seeming more like a kill face than a comforting gesture. "You have the least complicated issues of any of these fuckers. You realize that, right?" He nods around to our brothers. We all have our share of highs and lows, but at the moment I don't see how any of them can compete with the utter shitshow that has become my life.

I pocket my phone. "You're insane. I married her. I'm fucking married." Remember what I said about repeating the mantra? Obviously saying it out loud doesn't work either. It still tastes like chalk.

"I don't know why you went and did that," Tahoe says, cradling his gun in his lap, cleaning it before he packs it away. "A rash solution to a bad decision."

"What's the bad decision?" I ask, narrowing my eyes. He knows more about my situation than anyone else. I think it's because he keeps his relationship such a secret that his meddling in all of ours seems natural. He's a Yoda. A killing machine masquerading as a love whisperer.

"Letting her go," he says, meeting my gaze. "That's one you'll never live down. It's 2017, you don't have to marry your baby momma anymore. You be a father. I don't peg you for a deadbeat. You have some religious hang-ups I'm not aware of?" he asks. It's an honest question. He's trying to understand.

Shrugging, I say, "It seems crazy even to me. The thing is, doing the right thing regardless of cost is sort of my thing. It's why I'm not already married to Harper with a basketball team of kids right now. I joined the Navy instead of going to college with her. Do you know how many times a day I think about what could have been? How happy I'd be right now if I'd made a different decision? Then feel guilty for thinking it because I love my job. And I love my baby girl."

"How's that fair to Norah?"

I shake my head. "It's not. It hurts her more than me because she knows. Dude, every day I wake up and she's in my bed, I think how lucky I am she agreed to marry me."

"She's either stupid in love with you or just stupid," Tahoe replies. "If she knows you're in love with another woman, she won't be surprised when you tell her you don't want to be married. You'll be a good dad regardless. So many of these guys have kids from other marriages that they make work. Your morals and obligations don't change because your love is aimed at a woman who isn't her mother."

"I need to get over Harper."

"How are you going to do that?"

I've thought long and hard about this, and the only way to not love Harper Rosehall is to be indifferent. "Not think about her," I reply. "Or look at her. Blame her for this mess in the first place."

Tahoe chuckles, and it sounds like tits cutting glass. "Some moral high ground you're on. Blaming her for your indecision. I take it back, you're more fucked up than they are. Keep up the twisted game. Soon your daughter will be here to see it. That will be fun."

"Fuck you, Tahoe."

Closing his case, he stands to walk toward the plane. Over his shoulder, he says, "You only get one ride, bro. Make sure it's one with horsepower."

I board after him and fall into my own row. The window shades are up and shining morning light. I close them to darkness. Deep down I know how wrong I was to marry Norah, but Harper didn't stop it. She watched me commit the treasonous act without a word.

The engines start, and I take out my phone. I should text Norah. Or even my mom to respond to her last message. I text Harper instead.

> See you at dinner Sunday.

The gray bubbles pop up as she goes to reply, but they disappear as she deletes what she was going to say.

I write her a message in my notes but don't send it.

You loved me enough to let me break my own heart.

CHAPTER FIFTEEN
Harper

HEARTBREAK TASTES like bad curry and vomit laced with battery acid. Despite what everyone keeps telling me, I won't get over this. I work to merely forget the wedding even took place. Ben doesn't call or text, and I talk to his wife more than him. Every time I see her with her rounding belly containing Ben's child, it's like an electric current of envy. I want her stomach. Her baby. Her life.

I made my choices, and he made his, and even if they're bad choices, Norah made hers. The day she married Ben, she was well aware we were still in love with each other. It's sort of morbid. Like a Shakespeare play where everyone dies, including the animals. She wants to change Ben. Or change his feelings. She says he's excited about the baby, and I believe her. He's always wanted a bunch of kids. He was never the boy to shy away from playing house with me. He was a great dad to my baby dolls. Guess that's all I'll ever see him as a father in my life. Bad curry. Battery acid.

My stomach roils. I look out the window of my new house. It's a new construction build that cost more than I ever thought I'd be able to afford. I've saved for so long.

It was a beautiful moment that I could finally show something for my years of hard work. It's not anything grand, but it has a porch that wraps all the way around the house and hardwood floors. My voice echoes off the walls when I speak on the phone, and all of the bedrooms except mine are void of furniture.

Marcus came over when I moved in. I almost didn't open the door when I saw his face through the peephole, but Martina was over helping me decide what to do with the back patio, so I was confident enough to deal with him. He apologized, and he didn't make a move to step over the threshold. He looked sincere, and for a moment I thought maybe I could be with him again if he asked. Like, maybe I could erase the horrible night he accused me of loving Ben more than him. Maybe if I married Marcus, I could go back in time and rid myself of the torture I feel at the thought of Ben and Norah in bed together. In their marital bed.

I'm not an idiot, and in the end, I know nothing is going to take away the pain. Not even a DeLorean can fix my heart. I thanked him for stopping by and made small talk about his family. His brother is still living with him in our old place, and his parents still ask how I'm doing. He made a point of telling me he saw Ben and Norah's marriage announcement in the newspaper online. I wanted to ask if he was stalking it to see when I married Ben. I kept the catty thought to myself. I smiled, acted like I was happy for Ben, and excused myself back to Martina.

He hasn't come back since. I got a research job that pays well, and he stayed at the college as an assistant professor. Martina heard through the grapevine he may head back to the Northeast when his contract is over. I hope he does. That chapter is over and dead. Even as I closed the door on him, my cheek burned like fire, reminding me I made a good decision in stonewalling him. Martina is over again this morning before work. She's helping me make some final decorating decisions, and I think she's worried about me being here by myself.

"We're going to fix you up with our friend Matthew," Martina says, taking a sip of her coffee and tearing a page out of the *Z Galleria* magazine. She puts it in the stack with the other saved photos. "The chair in that one," she explains, pointing to a chaise. "That was a definite yes. Buy it for the sitting room."

"I love that one," I admit, taking the page for a closer look. "I'm not ready to date. God. The word is even scary. I don't know men. I've only known one," I tell her. "I didn't even know Marcus after all those years of dating." I'm starting to think I have something fundamentally wrong with me. I questioned myself in college, but now that I'm past that phase in life and should be on another level, I find myself floundering still. "Who's Matthew?" I ask anyway. The prospect of having male company is appealing. I haven't had sex since Ben, and I don't want to think about that for fear of weeping in loss or singeing from my toes up.

She gives me the basics on Matthew, and he seems harmless enough. "I have dinner on Sunday at Ben's parents' house. They'll both be there this week. I wonder how opposed he'd be to going out to dinner with me tonight or tomorrow and then accompanying me on Sunday." I'm getting ahead of myself, but that's a testament to my lack of dating.

"I gave him your lowdown. I bet he'd be more than happy to accommodate. He's a nice guy."

Nice. Those guys finish last. I don't know any nice guys, so it's probably time to try one out. I'm attracted to men who hit me and tear my heart into shreds by means of giving me everything one second and then stealing it away the next.

"You have to be completely open, Harper. You're ready?"

"I have to be, don't I?" I ask.

Martina looks sad as she glances at me and then back at the magazine. She nods.

I'm fine. "Give me his number, and I'll give it a go." She opens her cell, scribbles his number on the corner of the magazine, and rips it out. "I'll call after nine," I say, looking at the clock. "He'll know who I am?"

"He'll know," she says, smiling. "This will be good for you. I hate the idea of you being by yourself so much. Come over for dinner tonight?" She stands, grabbing her purse. "You can help me make that recipe you were telling me about last week. Your mom's."

"Yes," I say. "That sounds perfect."

Martina hugs me, kisses my cheek, and leaves. I set my house alarm and head into the garage to leave for work. Only true, blue adults have coffee dates with friends before work because they wake up so damn early.

My phone buzzes in my hand. Marcus. He's not a person who uses his phone to make phone calls. He's a text person. Answering quickly, I can tell by the pitch of his voice when he says "hi" that something is terribly wrong.

My heart sinks.

There's always a first day, and there's always a last. I remember the last day in vivid clarity because it was my fault.

After Marcus called me and asked me to come to the

hospital, I went. I'm not sure why. Maybe I was feeling nostalgic after talking to Martina all morning. Perhaps it was the destruction in his voice or pure stupidity for caring when I shouldn't any longer. Instead of driving to my office in the city, I turned to go in the opposite direction. He didn't give me any details on the phone, but no one can mistake terror when they hear it, and Marcus was terrified. Darren was in an accident. That's as much as I caught.

There's a hollow sort of feeling that accompanies tragedy. Even when it's not your own. If you wear the empty like armor, you have a thin layer between you and destruction. It's there for a reason even if you don't realize it at the time. The day the attacks happened I had this same empty feeling. When my father told me my aunt died, I remember nodding, like he was telling me what he cooked for dinner. It wasn't that I didn't care, I cared deeply, but all my shock was used up. I cried myself to sleep the next night, and for a month after that, too. It was an emotional delayed response.

The hospital is buzzing when I walk in—an unfamiliar destination that I try to avoid at all costs. After stopping by the front desk for a visitor sticker and a security screening, I head to the floor and area that Marcus directed me to. If the phone call was my first indication of how bad this situation is, the second is the heavily armed police officers standing outside of the room I'm supposed to be visiting.

In an effort to do something wise, I text my mom and Martina that I'm at the hospital and give them the basic information Marcus gave. Marcus exits the room and has to wedge himself in between the officers guarding the room. His eyes light, if you can even call it that, looking as horrible as he does when he sees me.

"Thank you for coming. I'm sorry. I didn't know who

else to call," he says, swallowing and stopping when he's a few feet from where I'm standing. At least he's wise enough to not overstep my imaginary boundaries. "It's bad, Harp. So bad," he says, eyes glassing over. "I didn't know who to call," he repeats.

I let my gaze flick to the officers and back to him. "Looks like an attorney, Marcus. What happened?" I ask.

He looks over his shoulder and then back at me. Shaking his head, he motions to the sitting area I passed on my way here. "Not here. Will you sit with me for a bit?"

Nodding, I turn and walk slowly to the seating area, my heart pounding out a warning. Why is he pulling me into this? Because he truly doesn't have anyone else to call on this coast. And it's my fault he's in this state to begin with. My inner guilt is having a field day.

Marcus sits in a chair in front of me, his back to the hospital door that's just out of sight.

"Is he okay?" It seems we're in some sort of intensive care unit. Doctors are buzzing around, and nurses with grim faces and tired eyes carry charts and push carts loaded with technical equipment. "He's okay, right?"

Marcus breaks down, his head in his hands. Shaking his head, he cries. "Even if he lives, it's not good. He messed up. He was drinking," he admits, raising his head to meet my confused gaze. In the past Marcus has been very forthcoming with information and storytelling. I nod for him to continue, or at least give me a little more to put the pieces together for myself. "He was drunk."

"This early in the morning?" I wrinkle my brow. All the years I've known Darren, a drinking problem wasn't something ever mentioned. Sure, I've seen him drink on one or two occasions, but not more than any other single man his age.

"He didn't come home last night. That's nothing new.

He's been drinking a lot since he got here. I've been taking care of him. His life went to shit when his girlfriend in Boston broke up with him. That's why he's been here for so long. His firm laid him off at the same time. He has nothing to go back to." Marcus clasps his hands together in fists and looks down at them. "He drank all night and was on his way home early this morning when he got into an accident. He's in a coma."

This is when my mind starts working. "What did he hit?"

Marcus squeezes his hands harder and then releases to grab his cell phone from his pocket. "I drove past the accident on my way here this morning and snapped a couple photos. It's so bad," he says. "He was going sixty in a thirty-five. The person in the other car died on impact."

He hands me the phone. The same phone, in the same navy-blue case he's had for the past two years. I take it from him, and the first photo is from far away, so it's hard to make out what I'm looking at. A bad accident, for sure. I recognize the horrible intersection, and I see shards of the silver truck that belonged to Darren. The other vehicle has been demolished, fully and completely. Tears spring to my eyes. "This is so awful. What was he thinking?" It's rhetorical, because I know that Marcus doesn't know—wouldn't know what he was thinking or why he chose to get behind the wheel of a car while inebriated.

I swipe right to look at the other photo. It's a closer view, and it is obvious Marcus took these from his car while approaching the accident from behind. Police cars and ambulances are swarming in this one, and I have to close my eyes for a second when I realize someone lost their life. I'm looking at someone's death moment, and it picks at my fragile emptiness. I turn the screen face down in my lap.

"Harper. I don't know what to do. They're going to arrest him and take him to jail as soon as he wakes up. I don't know what to tell my parents or if I should call his ex-girlfriend. It's all on me, and I don't know what to do with this."

Taking a deep breath, I tell him I need a few moments to process everything. I stand and walk to the little window that overlooks the bleak parking lot. Life moves on around us, as if it's a normal day. I shudder when I sense Marcus standing behind me.

"Please. Tell me what to do. He's a murderer. He's guilty. Nothing is going to change that."

"Even murderers get attorneys, I think. I don't know why you thought I'd be able to help you in any way. I think Martina's sister practices law, but I'm not sure what kind. What was that one friend we had at Harvard? He was pre-law, right?" I shake my hands to the sides. "This isn't my business," I say, shaking my head. "This isn't my mess. How could you bring me into something so... awful?"

"I didn't know who else to call. You were the only person in my life for years, Harper. You have to understand that fact. It was you and me and school, and then there was nothing. Darren didn't help me recover from losing you. He was basically using me for a place to stay while he got drunk and hooked up with bimbos impressed by his Ivy League degree and Ferragamo loafers. You were the person I wanted next to me, that's all. I lost all privileges to you, I know. I had to ask. Don't fault me for that."

I turn to face him. A doctor running down the hallway steals my focus for a second. "This isn't your mess. He's your brother, but it's not your mess. Go to work. Live your life, and he can deal with the consequences when and if he wakes up. Call your parents and tell them.

That's what I'd do. Don't complicate this any more than it already is. I really need to get going. I'm really sorry. I am. I feel for you, but I don't want to see you again."

I lift the phone when I realize it's his to hand it back, but the image pops back up on the screen. Once more, I look at it. Closer this time. Someone's death moment should be painful for me to view. It's hard to decipher where one vehicle starts and ends because of the destruction. I trace the edges of the windows and imagine what their last moment felt like.

As I envision what I'd think about during my last moment, I see the white sticker through the smoke. It makes it less visible, but now that I'm looking at it and know exactly what it is, I know what kind of SUV it is, what it looked like in perfect condition, and who drives it.

I cover my mouth with my free hand as the tears come in full force. "Do you know who was in the other vehicle, Marcus?" I ask, my tone low.

He clears his throat. "No. A woman. They won't give us a name until next of kin is notified." No one has to tell me. I slide down the wall until I'm seated on the floor.

"What's the matter?" Marcus asks.

Shaking my head, I hand him back his phone. I cry, burying my head between my knees. It's soft sobbing at first, but as the ramifications of this hit home, my cry turns into a soul-flaying wail.

In between bargaining with God and trying to convince myself I'm wrong, I hear Marcus asking repeatedly what's wrong.

I look him in the eye. "It's Norah."

CHAPTER SIXTEEN

Ben

WHEN WE LAND BACK in San Diego the next morning, my phone is blowing up. I make it a point to keep it off while I'm working so it doesn't distract me. I slept the entire flight, and I'm still exhausted. All I can think about is a dark room and my bed. My energy level after missions is completely depleted. I have to be on constantly. There's no breathing room. Perfection twenty-four seven. It's not as if I can make a mistake either. That could cost an innocent life or two. I like to call it the mental mush. Voicemails ping by the half dozen. Text messages from so many people I'm not sure where to start.

"Ah, I need sleep first," I whisper, trying to keep my eyes open. "Harper," I whisper, seeing a voicemail from her phone number flash across my screen as I walk toward my truck. It was from yesterday morning.

That's obviously the first one I click. "Benny. You need to call me as soon as you can. It's important. I'm not just saying that to get you to call me back. I'm saying that because nothing has ever been more important." She's sobbing hard, her words hard to make out. My brain that is finished for the week starts firing up again.

"Please call." The message finishes, and I'm left with a jagged hole in my stomach that's telling me something is incredibly wrong. I head to my truck, ready to be away from here and back on neutral ground—ready to be home.

I go to call her back, but I get a phone call from a number not programmed into my phone. I can tell it's a number from work, the place I'm trying to leave right now. Swallowing down my irritation, I answer. "Hello?"

"Ben?" a male voice rasps.

"Yes," I reply.

"It's Cage. I'm sorry I'm just now getting a hold of you. I couldn't track you down after you touched down. You already on your way home?"

"About to be," I say.

"We have some tragic news. Can you come back into the office for a second?" my boss says.

I sit up straight, realizing just how much elasticity my energy level has. No longer am I tired. I'm ready to fight —kill. I feel warm and cool at the same time as I open and close my truck door. I start the engine and turn on the air to full blast.

"Did you hear me?" Cage asks, waiting for my response. What if I don't want to hear anything right now?

"I heard you, yes. Go on."

"Can you come to the high bay?"

I glance to the right, to the high bay, where I just walked from.

"Just fucking tell me," I bark. Adrenaline hits me like a hot shot of whiskey.

Cage sighs. "Norah has been in an accident."

"Fuck! Is she at the hospital? Is the baby okay? Which hospital is she at? I'm in my truck now. I can be there in fifteen minutes. What happened?" I ask, my brain in a frenzy trying to process all of the information. He called it tragic news. "She's okay, right?"

He clears his throat on the other side of the line. "Norah was hit by a drunk driver yesterday morning. She was killed on impact. As was the baby. I'm so sorry, Ben."

"What?"

He repeats himself a few times. "Ben, do you have someone to drive you home? Please don't drive right now."

I don't respond. Norah is gone. Robin is gone.

"Ben?"

They say when you die, your whole life flashes before your eyes. Right now the whole life I was supposed to have blazes behind my closed eyelids. Every moment that was stolen from Norah. Holding Robin for the first time. Watching as she takes her first steps, kissing baby toes, watching a kindergarten play, first dates, learning to drive, and graduations. Robin. She never got to see the woman who loved her more than anything else in the entire world. It's so painful to think about that I might be sick.

"Who hit her? Who was driving the other car?" I ask, needing to know every last detail before I fall apart completely.

"The driver of the other vehicle is in a life-threatening coma at the hospital. His blood alcohol level was three times the legal limit. I assure you justice will be served. There's no way he's getting off, Ben. He will pay for this."

What if payment isn't enough? What happens then?

"I'm sorry," Cage whispers, his voice taking on the tone of a friend instead of a boss delivering the most horrible news of my lifetime. He rattles off several more details that I hear but don't quite process. Norah's father identified the body by sight. The intersection by her practice. The time it happened. The logistics of the accident. The speed of the other car. Cage tells me the things he knows I'll want to know, need to know, but he tries his best to detail them like a brief. Factual. Without emotion. Matter-of-fact. I appreciate his effort. Then he says Norah's name and mentions the baby.

Numbness takes over. I don't even feel the steering wheel in my palms. The edges of my vision go black. "Thank you," I say and hit the red button to end the call. I see Tahoe walking to his truck parked next to mine, so I get out and stop him. I'm on autopilot, my wise intuition forcing my feet and words.

He takes one look at me and asks what's wrong.

"Someone killed Norah and the baby," I say. Tears are falling off my cheeks, wet, warm, and heavy. Fucking traitorous salty drops that make what Cage said real even though it seems like a cruel lie told to destroy a human. A lie I'd eat and let wrap me for a lifetime if it meant it was false.

One eyebrow shoots up. "Who? What are you talking about?"

"I need you to drive me home," I get out. "I can't drive right now." I don't want to hit and kill someone in the name of grief. "I'll tell you what Cage told me on the way home."

Tilting his head to the side, he nods slowly. "Okay, bro. Let's go." No questions asked. A brotherhood. What would have been better is if he asked who we needed to kill. "Anything in your truck you want right now?" he asks, voice wary.

I don't respond. I climb into his truck and shut the door. When he gets in and starts the engine, I tell him in a flood of words tinged with fury, word for word, what was just said to me. Tahoe doesn't speak. He doesn't feed me bullshit lines about how everything's going to be okay. Because it's not going to be okay. Nothing can possibly be the same after this.

The attacks stole the nation's freedoms in almost every way. I made it my life's work to restore what small pieces could be salvaged. A drunk driver stole my entire life. The whole thing. There's no bright side or silver lining. There's a hole where my family should be, a regret and guilt for the time I spent trying to embrace them, a pounding in my chest that makes me feel like an infidel. Everything around me is foggy. I never pause when a life is taken in the name of terror. Evil people deserve death. How can I possibly rationalize Norah and Robin's deaths without feeling like a criminal?

Tahoe parks his truck in my drive and jumps up to hang on my roof with one hand while he searches for my hide-a-key with his free hand. He opens the door and looks back at me with a wary look. "We'll make a list. You have a lot to do." The funeral. "I'll help you, bro. We'll get it all handled. Why don't you get some sleep?" He nods to the sofa. A smart man.

"I'll clean up around here while you nap," he says, clapping me on the shoulder. I pull him into a full hug. "It sucks. Let it suck, man," Tahoe whispers. "Then when it sucks a little less, we move on. A little cracked, a little tormented, stronger than ever before."

I want to tell him that's what happens when brothers die. Somehow this feels differently. The same except the sting bites across my entire existence. My daughter. My future.

I fall back onto the sofa. Tahoe tosses me a blanket from the chair on the other side of the living room. A throw blanket Norah purchased last week because it had stars on it. Heaving a breath, I lean back and close my eyes, knowing there's no way I'll be able to fall asleep.

Except I didn't realize the pillow smelled like Harper.

It might as well be an Ambien laced with sedatives. The blackness pulls me under quickly. I'm covered in Norah and surrounded by Harper. My entire existence is in shambles.

It was a dreamless sleep. Void of anything. Black. My exhaustion won out, and I probably have that to thank for the short reprieve from my reality. When I wake fourteen hours later, Tahoe is sitting in the chair across the room, his head tilted back, mouth open, sleeping like the dead. Running my hands through my hair, I sit up as every muscle in my body protests. I'm still in my goddamn dirty uniform. Mud-caked camo pants and a white shirt stained yellow from sweat.

"You're awake," Harper says, strolling from the hallway. "How are you feeling?" Her eyes are wide, apprehensive, terrified by what she's going to find. "I let myself in. I hope you don't mind. I still had a key from… before."

Seeing Harper tears a wound open I didn't know existed. I close my eyes because the pain is back, but now it's multiplied by a thousand. "I need a shower," I reply. Tahoe snores, completely out for the count. I approach him slowly and shake his shoulder.

"What, what? I'm up," Tahoe says, eyes flickering open and meeting my gaze.

"Hit the couch," I say, hiking my thumb over my shoulder. He goes without saying another word, collapsing in a heap. He's back asleep before his head hits the pillow. Turning back to Harper, I swallow hard. "Shower," I repeat to her. "I'm fine. You don't have to hang around. Tahoe is here." My traitorous gaze flicks down to her bare legs and short ripped jean shorts with lace peeking out the bottom. A sliver of her stomach peeks out from her loose T-shirt. She crosses one leg over the other, self-conscious of my obvious appraisal.

"Benny," she says when my gaze finally finds hers. "Talk to me."

I shake my head and let out a small laugh. "I can't talk to you, Harper."

"Why not?" she asks quietly, peeking over my shoulder at Tahoe.

"He can't hear us. He's out for another half a day. We've been up for more than a day."

Harper wants to reach out for me. I see it in the way her hands flex by her sides. That's enough torture for now. I flick my gaze forward and pass by her without saying another word. I enter my bedroom and find it has been cleaned up, just as Tahoe promised. Norah's stuff isn't in sight. I see several boxes in the corner, and my chest aches.

Because my friend knows me better than I thought, and because it's all that's left of my future. I have nothing tangible except things. I don't want things. I don't need things. No one does, really. That's not what we as humans crave. The door clicks closed.

"I'm so sorry. Ben, I'm sorry. I feel so awful. I'm not even sure how to process something like this."

Sniffing my shirt, I wince and pull it over my head while focusing my gaze out of the window. It smells like Norah's lotion in here. I know how fragile life is. How it's here one second and gone the next, but this sensation is new to me. Harper calls me again.

"What?" I yell, spinning on her.

"Why are you sorry? Why do you feel awful, Harper? You don't have to process anything. This is mine to deal with. I can't make you feel better about this.

I can't save you this time. My wife and daughter are dead. So process how you want to, but do it on your own because I'm trying to figure out how to go on without them. I can't be on Harper duty this time." I shake my head and turn away when I see tears falling down her cheeks.

Harper walks forward, unperturbed by my harsh words. "I know you're upset," she says, reaching out for my hand with hers. "Your pain is more than I can comprehend." When I don't take her hand, she lets her arm fall back down to her side.

For a few moments I breathe and look at her. I feel better. Which makes me feel even worse. "You need to leave, Harper," I admit. "Just go."

Her whole body shifts, as if I stabbed her instead of speaking to her. Pain is etched into her facial features. She's not allowed to feel an ounce of what I'm bearing. "I'm serious," I whisper, gazing at the floor. "I can't be around you right now."

"Why?" she asks, striding forward and placing her hands on my arms. She grabs me firmly, grounding me to this moment. "Why?" Her eyes plead with me. She wants the truth.

I'm a glutton to give it. "The grief is killing me, dismembering my heart. The kicker?" I say, breathing several times to keep the tears at bay. "You're the cure I need. But you're out of my price range. Untouchable."

She shakes her head. Harper was expecting that, and it's comforting and infuriating at the same time. "I won't leave you here by yourself. I don't care what you see when you look at me. I'm not only the woman who loves you, I'm your best friend. The person who'd die to take an ounce of your pain away if I could. Don't complicate this. I'm your friend first, Benny."

I look at the ceiling because the tears came anyway.

"What if relieving my pain means you leaving and never coming back?"

Going up on her tiptoes, she grabs my face to force my gaze to hers. Her eyes are glassy, but she's holding it together. Because that's what I need from her, and she knows it. "Then that's your pain to bear because I'm not going anywhere this time. I should have stayed here all those years ago. By your side. I should have loved you through everything up until now, but I refuse to leave you during this. I'm going to love you through it. You will get through it."

My eyes widen as my mind, a clusterfuck of dark as the devil thoughts, processes her words. Her light. Her life. "What I wouldn't give to hear those words before. Love me from afar because that's what I need. That's what I want. Maybe forever. Definitely right now."

Voice loud and overbearing, Harper winces away from me.

"That's what you want?"

No.

"I have to tell you something." Her eyelashes flutter closed, and little lines form in between her eyes. It's anguish so great I've never seen her wear it before.

I stay silent and gesture with my hand for her to continue. She shifts around on her little black flip-flops, completely terrified by what she needs to say. "Did they tell you who was driving the other vehicle?" Harper asks, not meeting my eyes. In fact, she stares at the floor as she says it.

My stomach turns. Taking a step back, I sit on the bed. "No. You're about to tell me, though."

Harper meets my eyes, and her mouth forms a pout at the same time she finally frees her tears. It breaks the piece of my heart that wasn't damaged. "Marcus's brother," she whispers. "It was Darren."

Shaking my head, I try to remember what he looked like. I saw him only once, and he was piss drunk. I was so into Harper that night it's hard for me to recall his face, let alone details about the man who stole Norah's and Robin's lives. I keep my eyes on hers because I'm trying to remember, but I can tell looking at me and not touching me is distressing her.

"This is my fault. All of it, Ben."

"How?"

She steps toward me, but I halt her with a head shake. "If I had told you the moment I fell in love with you, none of this would have happened. The dominoes were set into motion because I followed my head instead of my heart. I should have stayed. I should have loved you. There would have been no Marcus or Darren. No moves from the East Coast. It would have been you and me. Just us. Nothing else. No one would have gotten hurt. It's my fault Norah and your baby were killed, Ben."

I've never seen Harper so upset. I recall the weeks after her aunt died, and she never showed this much emotion. If I weren't so detached, I'd be scared.

I open my arms to the side, and she rushes to me, wrapping me in a wet, salty hug. Her whole body shakes, her apologies flowing as copiously as her tears. She's barely breathing when she pulls away.

"Please forgive me. I'll never forgive myself, but I need you to forgive me."

I take a deep breath. It's not because I need one, it's because I want to inhale her into my system for the last time. She gave me exactly what I didn't realize I needed.

Someone to blame.

"Yes. I need you to go, though. I can't look at you. Stay away from me, Harper. I'm serious."

Backing away from me, she watches me, her face in utter anguish. From head to toe, I let my gaze roam her body. Every perfect curve, mark, and subtle nuance that's fully Harper Rosehall. I leave her neck for last. Pressing my lips into a smile that probably resembles a grimace, she turns, unable to stomach the rejection.

I watch her back disappear and listen for the front door to shut before I follow her. Everything in me wants to chase her. Tell her I want her, but my guilt would never allow me to have her. I watch her car leave through the front window.

"Burning it all to the ground?" Tahoe mumbles.

"And watching it incinerate," I reply.

He rolls over, and his loud snore is audible moments later.

Standing under the strong, hot water, I close my eyes and make mental lists of everything I need to do. I let practical Ben drive for a while because it saves real Ben from self-destructing. Watching Harper's pain helped me. I made the decision Norah would have wanted. I didn't honor her love enough during her life, but I can surely make it right after her death.

It gives me something to control.

Fuck knows I need it.

CHAPTER SEVENTEEN

Harper

I CALL his parents and Tahoe almost every single day to see how Ben is doing. He'll come around eventually. He'll let me back in. He has to. He's my best friend. Ben needs me, he just hasn't worked that out yet. I can make him feel better. I know what he needs. It's been six months since Norah died.

I went to the funeral, and it was just as tragic and sad as you'd expect. Ben wore his uniform, as did several of his friends. It was an enormous ceremony filled with so many people who loved Norah. Ben didn't get up to speak. The other vet in Norah's practice did. It's sort of fitting. Norah spent most of her life with her. More than with Ben, I'd fathom a guess.

Ben met my gaze once. He looked away almost as soon as he saw I was looking his way. It was the first time I thought maybe this was a permanent friendship break, and my own heartbreak intensified tenfold. Tahoe told me he's only doing well on the surface, that he doesn't trust him by himself, so he's been spending a lot of time with him on their off hours. Ben didn't take any time off work. He's been working even more, taking missions that aren't intended for his schedule. He's burning himself out. It's so he doesn't have to think. His brain doesn't ever turn off unless he's exhausted.

Darren died after suffering for several days after he woke from the coma. The masochist who wanted him to live out his days in jail was satisfied in the painful way he went. Marcus moved back to the East Coast. He emailed me last week to let me know he transferred to Harvard to teach linguistics. It sparked a glimmer of jealousy. The thing is, I'd never do anything about it. I'm where I'm supposed to be.

Since the accident, I get angry more easily. I wish I'd ruined Marcus's life. Filed a restraining order, made a black mark on his record so he'd have to suffer what he did to me for the rest of his life. He's seeing a girl, too. I wonder if she knows what he did to me, how he ruined a relationship with jealous rage.

That wasn't who I was back then, though. It's who I am now. Bitter. Hardened by a life that I feel has never been my own. I chose it, though I chose what I thought would serve me best instead of choosing what would make me happiest. I sacrificed my only opportunity to have my happily ever after by being selfish. It serves me right.

Martina and her husband just left. I had several people over to my house for dinner. Now that it's fully furnished and has all the charm of a Martha Stewart catalog, I've been hosting. It does make me feel better for a little while. My friends occupy my free time during daylight hours. At night, I'm so alone even my breath causes loneliness. Like Ben's surface happiness, I feel as if most of the people in my life are surface friends. Those that know me, but not deeply. Not every single detail and quirk. They know what I want them to see.

The one person who I savor a past with wants nothing to do with me, and I can't say I blame him.

It was Ben who tried time after time to tell me and show me what we could have had. It's wince-worthy when I think back. It's not equal parts pain and pleasure when I think of Ben. He saw what I ignored for years. You know how you can only cry wolf so many times? You can only turn a man down so many times before he believes you don't want him in the same way he wants you. Add in vehicular manslaughter, and you have a recipe to destroy any sort of relationship for the rest of time.

Once I've finished cleaning the kitchen to a spit shine, I shower and then call my mom. I'm seeing her this weekend. She told me Ben's parents were coming for dinner, and there was no way I could turn down the invitation. I want anything that has a connection to him. I flip the television on in my bedroom after I hang up with her and pull down my covers.

It's midnight when my doorbell rings. It's not a normal bell, it's a high-pitched screech that jars me anytime I hear it. This late at night, it might as well be a police siren. I let out a tiny scream as I trudge out of my bed, cell phone in hand. I slide over the peephole and look through.

It's Ben. And even from the skewed bubble version I see, he looks like absolute shit. Unlocking the door, I open it. There's still a glass door between us, so I slide down the storm window.

"Hey," he says, eyes brimming with red, dark circles. "What are you up to?" There's no other way to explain it. Ben looks haunted.

I decide against peppering him with questions and answer him. "Um. Bed. Watching some TV. What are you up to?" I glance at the driveway and see his truck and then eye him from his head down and back up again. Leveling him with my gaze, I say, "You finally popped on a drug screen? They kicked you out of the Teams?" It's a slight nod to his haggard appearance without commenting on it.

A small crooked grin appears on his face. "Nah. I just got home from work. I haven't seen your new house yet," he says, like it's a legitimate reason for stopping by in the middle of the night. He hasn't spoken to me in months. I know exactly why he's here. His hair is wet, and he's wearing a pair of sweats and a white T-shirt. The attire one wears lounging around the house.

"Ben. It's been months. You're not okay. It's obvious. You don't want to see my new house."

He swallows and looks up, pretending to examine the lighting fixture above my door. "I wanted to see you. I miss you, Harpee. Believe it or not." He adds the last sentence to acknowledge his absence.

Do you ever think about the space around you? The area that the wind blows around one individual? It doubles when you're next to a person, close enough to touch. There's more life, more oxygen, when I'm in his space. My body calls out to him. To be held by him. It wants more life. I want him.

I slide the lock on the glass door open, and with that click, I know there wasn't ever an option. Some may call it a weakness. I call it friendship. "Come in," I say. "You just got home. Are you hungry? I have some leftovers. I cooked my mom's chicken recipe. You know, that stuffed one she made for my birthday last year? I can heat some up for you."

Ben sighs, relief prickling every feature on his face, his body relaxing. "That would be amazing," he says. He doesn't look at my house the way any person who wants to check out a friend's house would. He stares at my bare legs, covered by only my oversized T-shirt. "I'm sorry it's been so long," he admits. "I, ah, I've been trying to get my shit together, and work has been busy."

Because you've made work busy, I think.

"You never wanted to see me again. I didn't expect you to knock on my door…ever," I say, my tone mocking.

He sits down at the table in my kitchen. It's where I eat breakfast and have coffee. Drumming his fingers on the table, he says, "I'm sorry. I figured you knew I didn't mean it."

"How could I not think you meant it? It made perfect sense. I understand, Ben. I hope you didn't come here trying to make me feel better about everything. I don't need your apology. I have to live with the part I played."

"Harper. I came here because I need you to make me feel better," he says, grabbing my waist as I pass by him on the way to the microwave. "I need you. Do you understand?" If I didn't, he's made it perfectly clear with his touch.

I swallow and eye him from the side. I can't deny what his hand on my body does to me. A riot of sensations bleeds to the surface—all those things I try not to think about because I knew I'd never have them again, knew no other man could play my body so precisely. "I'm not sure that's a good idea," I say, turning in his grasp to meet his lust-filled gaze. "You look like shit, Ben. Being with me isn't going to help you how you need it to."

His eyes glass over. "Don't make me beg," he whispers, lips barely parted. "For once, don't overthink it. Do you want me?" What a cruel, unfair question to ask.

A stronger woman would deny him. Tell him to grow up and deal with his emotions like a big boy. A stronger woman would have grabbed this passionate, beautiful man when she could have. A stronger woman wouldn't have been afraid of the power of the love we shared. "What do you need? Tell me."

"What I've always needed," he replies.

I set the cold plate of chicken down on the table, all but forgotten.

"We need to talk first," I reply, my heart hammering in my ears. I want to ease his pain, steal the hurt away from his body as soon as humanly possible despite any hardships in our past. I think I'll always feel that way. "Can we talk?"

Ben's weary face hardens. "Everyone wants to talk. Talking doesn't fix anything, Harp. Please," he pleads, standing, taking the sides of my body in his hands. "Please," he whispers again, voice cracking at the end. "You can fix me. Only you."

I let him guide me to my bedroom and settle into my bed. When we're lying down face-to-face, I admit, "I can't fix you. You know that. You need help. I can talk to you as a friend." It's an offer my body rejects. It wants what he's after. The friendship needs to come first. It's obvious he's in pain.

"What if I don't need a friend right now? What if I never needed you to be my friend? What if right now I need the woman who loves me? A woman who wants to steal away my pain? The woman who promised to love me through this? Fix me."

His chest is heaving, and the first tear has fallen. Leaning over, I kiss it away, and Ben shudders at the slight contact from my lips. "Yes," he says. "More. Touch me more."

I trace my lips across his stubbly face and end with my mouth hovering over his. "This isn't a good idea," I whisper.

He closes his eyes. He wants this so bad I can feel it in the air. How desperate he is for our connection. In turn, it makes me delirious with desire.

He pulls me so close, our noses are smashed together.

197

His breathing becomes jagged as he pulls breaths through his mouth. His eyes are closed tightly, the pain of holding himself back twisting his features. He's taking my oxygen and making it his own. I realize maybe I can fix him by giving myself to him, laying down my life, and my air, for him to bend at his will. I'd do that, and more, to make Ben happy.

Unable to hold out any longer, I kiss him. His whole body comes alive when I slip my tongue into his mouth and wrap my hands around his neck. He groans in complete relief at the contact, and I'm so happy I cry, a small tear leaking down my temple. The hollow, empty place is filling, and I don't know if it's just for tonight, but I have to take it regardless of the price.

Ben pins me to the bed with more force than I'm expecting, his hands holding down my forearms. He traces circles with his tongue on my exposed neck and chest as my T-shirt rides up to expose my panties. My whole body prickles with goose bumps, and my stomach flips. I'm so anxious and excited there's no controlling my reactions. Moans escape as he releases me to slide my underwear down my legs. Sitting up, I take off my shirt, and he makes haste pulling off his clothing. No boxer briefs tonight.

He stares at me from the foot of my bed, chest heaving, eyes heavy, and cock pulsing in preparation.

"Come here, Ben. Let me love you." I hold out my hands to him.

His eyes turn down in the corner. Sadly, he shakes his head, his brows pulling together. "That's not what I need," he whispers, licking his lips.

I nod, understanding. Swallowing hard, I reply, "Fuck me. Right now. Fuck me."

Crawling up the bed, he rests his head in between my legs. It's not a soft, light, feather touch. His tongue and mouth are rough. At this point in my sabbatical, it doesn't matter. Ben's face is pressed against me, and it's more than enough to have my pussy throbbing out a love song of wetness and lust. He doesn't want love, and maybe I don't either.

I'm about to come, and I scream it to the heavens to let them know, too. Ben doesn't let me. He wipes his mouth on my inner thigh and then drags his lips and mouth up the side of my body. He kisses the side of my breast, moves his tongue over my nipple, and trails the kiss up the front of my neck.

"This neck," he moans out, moving his kiss back down again.

I arch my chin to the ceiling and relish the sensations.

I can feel the head of his dick brushing softly against my core, and I move my hips to let him know I'm ready and want him to take me. Ben is kissing and licking every inch of surface on my neck. He's taking it slower than I thought he would. His eyes are closed as if he's relishing every second. It hurts my heart to see him like this. I want to give him what he needs. My body at his disposal —for him to lose himself in something familiar, something steadfast, a body filled with life.

Leaning up, he lays a palm, fingers spread wide across my chest, and says, "Your heart is beating so fast." He swallows hard, feeling my heartbeat.

I laugh a little. "You make me excitable," I reply. "You should finish what you started."

Ben replaces his hand with his ear, leaning his head down to listen instead, a complete change of pace. "I'm talking to you, heart," he says, smiling. "I'm gonna give you something to really beat about."

"Do it," I say, smirking when he meets my eyes.

He's back for a second. My Ben. Then he enters me in one hard thrust, and he's lost in an entirely different way.

He kisses me every so often, but its rough juts and feral shouts, anger fluidly swallowed by terror and rage.

I can't even hang on to his shoulders, it's so rough. It's not pleasurable for me, and I think he's forgotten I'm even in the room with him. Leaning back on his knees, he pulls my hips to him instead of thrusting. He fills me over and over, and I think he's trying to fill me with everything he's trying to get rid of. He looks up at the ceiling as he pulls me onto his cock at a furious pace. I clutch at the sheets and try to keep myself in place. I keep my eyes closed. There's no need to see Ben right now, because this isn't my Ben anymore. He pulls me all the way onto him and comes. Ben screams out. It's a cry of anguish.

My whole body is tense when he pulls out. I don't dare open my eyes. I listen to his harried breaths mixing with my soft whimpers. More tears come as I try to squelch the tightness in my chest, the hurt he's caused.

"Harper," he says.

I hear the apology in my name.

He's looking away from me when I open my eyes and sit up. Swallowing the lump in my throat, I wipe another tear away lest he see what he's caused. He sobs and retreats to my bathroom.

I scoot off the bed, sore and terrified of what just happened, and walk in behind him. Ben is bent over the counter, forearms pressing on the granite, the ultimate picture of male prowess. Naked, stunning, muscles coiled, and chest heaving. He's also a man completely destroyed. A stray delicate petal on a steel flower.

"Fuck," Ben hisses. "I'm fucked up, Harper. So fucked up."

I stay silent but stand next to him, the mirror reflecting our images in an unfamiliar way. Ben meets my eyes in the mirror. "How many times have I transfixed your face on Norah? At least a million. Only the times when it matters? When I was fucking her? Definitely when I was marrying her. When it counts? This is my punishment from Norah after death. Seeing her sad, second-best face anytime you're in front of me." The man I love transforms into a ghost.

"Oh my god," I sob. "I can't do this. You shouldn't have come here, Ben. I love you. I do," I whisper, grabbing his arm. His gaze darts to where our skin meets in the reflection. "I'm not sure we can get over this. Or you need more time. This is breaking my heart. Fucking me isn't going to bring back your dead wife. I won't do that for you, and I'll do a lot."

One side of his mouth quirks up. "The heartbreak club. At least we'll be in it together. Fucking you helps me. It does. It's the only thing I can think of."

My stomach roils as my heart splinters.

I point to my bed. "I'll never do that with you again. That's a promise. I'm not some toy." Swallowing hard, I cross my arms over my chest, suddenly feeling too exposed.

"I need to go," Ben says, brushing past me to get his clothes. "I'm sorry. I am. This was a mistake. I'm a weak bastard." Shaking his head, he does look remorseful. He doesn't apologize for using my body as a Norah vessel, and the thought makes me shiver. "I'm out of my mind." He mutters under his breath, something about how he can't believe what he's done and how he needs to shackle himself to his house.

I grab my T-shirt from the floor and notice the bloody, mangled sheets.

"Can we forget tonight even happened?" he asks, finally speaking loud enough for me to hear each word. I can tell he's not going to try to convince me of his point of view, like my Ben would. He's going to ask this of me.

"You'd ask that of me?" I ask, biting my lip to stifle tears.

He sighs. "My best friend would forget."

When he gets to the front of my house, I open the door for him. "Maybe I can't be your best friend and your fuck buddy at the same time. You said you didn't need a friend. You didn't need that version of me." I stifle a hiccupped sob and pinch my lips together. "I'll forget more than tonight. That's a promise," I reply, shutting the door in his sad, haggard face.

I drown out the night with a stiff drink and pass out in the sheets that prove I won't forget that quickly.

Or ever.

CHAPTER EIGHTEEN

Ben

EVERYONE HAS those few mistakes they'll never live down. Mine are the unforgivable sort that stick around even when I'm not thinking about them directly. They influence everyday decisions and the way I approach the world. Two months have passed since I crashed Harper's house...and heart. She texted me once to make sure I wasn't going to be around for one of our parents' dinners. I tried to get her to talk to me then, but she refused, telling me some bullshit excuse about being busy. There's no way I can ask for forgiveness for that night. I was out of my mind.

I could only think of her and how much I missed her. Blind love. Furious lust. Pent-up feelings for denying my mind and cock what it desperately desired. I missed her friendship, sure, but most of all I missed her understanding. I knew damn well if I went there she'd understand and give in to anything I wanted. The lonely greed won out.

I'm driving to my parents' house, trying not to think of this shit, but when my mind isn't occupied at work, these thoughts are on repeat. You don't know what you have until it's gone. That saying is the motherfucking soundtrack to my life. I took everything for granted in every area of my life except for my career. That will always be there, unfortunate as it may be. Everything else is a loss.

No wife or family. No best friend to call. I have my brothers. A promise to make the world a safer place. My only life goal at the moment. After I pull into their drive, I vow not to let my morose demeanor show. I put the front on like a mask—an actor perfecting the skill of convincing the people he loves that he's fine. I walk slowly up to the door, not looking left for fear of seeing Harper's parents, and knock once before opening the front door.

My mother rushes me. "Benjamin. Oh, it's so good to see you, honey. Why haven't you come sooner? I know you weren't working last weekend. We aren't getting any younger, honey." Her arms are around me in a vise grip. "You've gotten bigger!" she exclaims.

"I've had more free time at the gym," I tell her, grinning over her shoulder at my dad. He's watching the exchange with an amused smile. There's no telling Mom anything. "I've missed you, too. What do you have cooking today?"

"Oh, I have so much cooking. You're never going to want to leave. Mr. and Mrs. Rosehall should be here any second." That's when I start to sweat. Like a sixteen-year-old boy caught having sex on a living room sofa. "Go help your dad out back. I need you two to wipe down all the furniture on the patio."

Swallowing, I glance out the side window. "Oh, just the Rosehalls tonight?" I ask, keeping my tone level. "Harper isn't home this weekend, is she?" It will be a fucking disaster if she is. I wanted to talk to her on our turf. If anything unfolds here, it's going to get messy. I panic, an unfamiliar feeling of dread and excitement.

The doorbell rings, and next Harper walks through, a bottle of wine tucked under one arm and a pie in the other. Her parents trail behind, their faces void of smiles. "Ben," Harper says, raising one brow. "I saw your truck out front." Not even giving me a passing glance, she greets my mother with a kiss on the cheek and approaches my dad with a joke and a hug.

The Rosehalls greet me cheerily and ask how I've been. Everyone's expressions always change when that question comes up. It used to be a standard answer, now I'm the widower with a dangerous job. I'm like the liability no one wants to talk about. My mother frowns as she overhears me talking about the most recent mission we did. I'm comfortable talking about it, as it was all over the news. Several top leaders were nabbed and brought in for questioning. It will lead to a slew of more arrests.

From my view, I can see Harper helping my dad clean the furniture outside, and I'm envious. What are they talking about? Is she telling him about something I don't know about? "Harper told me you've been busy with work. I guess we didn't realize just how busy," Mr. Rosehall says.

"Ah, you know. It makes everything at home… easier."

Mrs. Rosehall lays a hand on my shoulder. "Is it getting easier then?"

My mom walks away, my father following her. I nod as a response. Norah is a subject that will make her cry no matter what. My cell phone chimes, and I read the text nonchalantly. It's Tahoe checking in to see what I'm up to. I tap back quickly, Welfare check confirmed. Mrs. Brahams has your back tonight.

He sends back a smiley face, and I think how out of place that is. "I, ah, hurt Harper," I say, wincing a little. "I didn't mean to. I just want you to know."

"Which time, Ben? You must be talking about now, because I haven't seen her this upset since you told her you weren't going to college with her." Such a trivial thing now.

I grin a bit. "True. I'm not sure I can make it right this time," I tell her.

Her face wilts. "You're the only person who can make it right. It's high time you guys realize what you have."

"What's that?"

"A love a lifetime in the making."

It takes a moment or two for her words to settle where they need to. She continues, "I've watched you two grow up. I've watched your love grow and change over the years. It's time. It's time." She repeats herself one more time, sadly, though.

"I've ruined everything." I sigh.

"Talk to her. Don't think you know what she's going to say, because she might surprise you. For as well as you two know each other, I think you're completely blind to what's right in front of your faces."

I stumble back a bit. Harper comes back into view through the glass door. She's beautiful, like she always is, but her mom is right. She's not the same person she was in the past. This is the Harper of my future. If I can right the varying degrees of wrong I've committed. I shrug, shaking my head. "I can try."

Mrs. Rosehall pats my shoulder and walks away smiling. I catch Harper's hand when she tries to head for the hallway behind me. I can't ask her to talk. "Want to go shoot some hoops?"

Harper rolls her eyes. "I have to use the restroom."

"I'll be outside dribbling the ball," I say, making the motion with my hand and juking back and forth with my body.

"You're such a geek, Ben," Harper says, pulling her

arm out of my grasp and closing the bathroom door behind her.

The trap has been set. I walk out through the garage and grab the basketball from the basket in the corner. Palming it, I find it has enough air. It's faded from the sun and missing most of the black ribs. It's just an orange ball all these years later.

Arms crossed and eyes narrowed, Harper opens the garage door and crosses to me. "Don't think this means anything. My mom made me come out here." We both chuckle after she realizes how childish it sounds.

I pass her the ball. Awkwardly, she catches it and then brings it up to her nose to give it a sniff. "If I'm a geek, what does sniffing a ball make you?" I ask. "Freak," I mutter.

Harper shoots a basket and makes it. "It reminds me of something," she says.

Walking over to her, I take the ball back.

"Something good. I like to remember the good things. Before all of the bad swallowed most everything else up. Shoot it."

I do and miss by a foot. "After dinner, want to head up to the water tower? Someone said you can graffiti on it without repercussions."

She wrinkles her brow. "Where did you hear that? The bar?"

I shrug and shoot the ball. Nothing but net. "I have my ways."

"You want me to be your friend now then, huh? I'm getting whiplash."

"I'm sorry. For so many things. If we talk through it, maybe we can get back on track."

Harper sighs and closes her eyes. "Which track?"

"Whatever one you let me on."

Harper makes another shot and wipes her brow with

the back of her hand. "I need to go wash my hands and see if they need any help in the kitchen. If we can pick up snacks, I'll go to the tower with you."

I go down on my knees and press my hands together. Harper turns around and smiles when she sees me.

"Friendship track, Benny." The smile leaves her face slowly. "Dinner truce?" she says.

"Thank you," I reply.

Then she leaves.

I have all of Harper's secrets. Even the ugly ones she doesn't want another soul to hear. She has more of mine. Although our parents don't know the extent to which our lives are entangled, we both know they sense the shift in the atmosphere. They didn't bring up anything untoward. That's the first time they've been polite.

We filled up an entire shopping basket at the 7-Eleven, and she's made me hold the enormous bag as we climb the ladder up the old water tower. It's walking distance from our house, and we spent countless hours here as children. It was safe here. We could talk about anything we wanted, away from prying ears and parental eyes. A no judgment zone. We haven't been back since I brought her here to tell her I wanted to enlist in the Navy instead of going to Harvard.

Harper climbs slower than she did back then, her feet more tentative on the rungs than they were all those years ago. I try to keep my eyes away from her short shorts, but when she brings her foot up to the next step, I slip and see a glimpse of her hot pink panties.

"Pink," I shout.

"Oh my gosh. Stop looking! I should have known

better! I have Jenny Megly to thank for your obsession with female underwear."

"I'm only obsessed with yours," I toss back, laughing to punctuate my old-school game. "I love when you wear short shorts."

Harper speeds up after groaning a frustrated sigh. We go all the way to the top and sit down on the metal ledge, our legs dangling out of the lowest barrier. The pink and orange horizon in front of us is beautiful. "I forgot how pretty the sunset was from here," Harper says, catching her breath. Leaning forward, she folds her arms on the metal bar and puts her chin on her wrists. "We probably had no clue how pretty it was back then," she amends.

"It's always been this beautiful," I say, speaking to the side of her face.

Looking at her, looking at the sunset, brings back all of the memories. Mrs. Rosehall is right. I've never truly looked at Harper in this honest light.

"Tell me something, Benny. Anything worth saying."

Her gaze doesn't waver. It's unflinching in the direction of the sunset. "Okay," I say, trying and failing to form the words I want. "I'll tell you what I think you need to hear."

She nods. "Probably a good place to start."

"This is my punishment for my evil, lying crimes of the heart. You know how I hid from the truth, you did it too. I have to live with this for the rest of my life, and Norah and Robin paid the price for my bad decisions." She looks at me but then thinks better of it and looks away again. I go on, "They were innocent in all of this."

"I've thought about this a lot because of Marcus and Darren and everything," Harper says, voice a whisper. "You can't blame yourself. It was an accident."

I shake my head, a lump forming in the back of my throat.

Harper's gaze locks onto mine. "You can't control everything. It was an accident. It didn't happen for any reason other than she was in the wrong place at the wrong time," she remarks.

I've thought about this, too. "No. It's never just an accident. Things happen for a reason. Everything does. Nothing is happenstance. The world is too cruel for that. The things I've seen? I know for a fact there are no true accidents." I look up at the sky, a broken man bargaining with someone who took away the only things more important than my own life.

"What if everything is one big accident? If you're saying nothing is an accident, I'm telling you maybe everything is. Me sitting next to you, holding your hand, is because of an accident. Maybe your mom forgot her birth control pill. Poof!" Harper says, twinkling her fingers like magic. "You're here. An accident. My dad accidentally got a job, and we accidentally moved next door to you. We became friends by accident, and you fell in love with Norah by accident. We never told each other just how we felt about each other because, you guessed it, an accident. We both know Robin was an accident, so there's no arguing there. Darren accidentally drank too many drinks that night, Ben. Everything is an accident. If there's one thing you can trust, it's that I'm here for you. I'll always be here for you. Not by accident, either. Because I want to be here for you. Because I love you."

Harper's words strike a chord, stirring the cold place inside my chest. I've considered every possibility, and she could be right. I'm not ready to admit that, though. Scooting closer to her, our legs touch. I hold her hand on top of my leg, and we watch the sun vanish together. There are silent breaths and tiny sniffles, but no words. "I love you too," I whisper. "Thought that's important, you know."

"This isn't how it's supposed to be. Our chance is gone, regardless of how much we love each other. You know that, right?" Harper says as she squeezes my hand.

"How can you say that? Look at what happened to make circumstances for us!"

She nods. "That's exactly what I'm talking about."

I tell her to explain, and I know she will, but the silence between us spans on for longer than is comfortable. "You've always lived life unapologetically," Harper says.

I scoff. "Because I spent the first half doing nothing but apologizing."

Harper blows out a long, jagged breath and finally turns to face me. The pain in her eyes is crystal clear, but she wears a peaceful smile on her pink lips. "Sometimes when something bad happens and everything falls apart, it's not so something better can come together. It's unrecoverable. There's no silver lining, and dreams turn into unimaginable nightmares. You're left scarred—irretrievable, in a zone untraceable by lifeboat, by hope, by love. You disappear completely."

"I'm here. With you. That statement is a tad dramatic," I deadpan.

Her smile widens. "But it's the truth." She shakes her head. "I'll be your friend. I'll always be your friend. To be anything more than that would be dishonorable to our past. We're so much more than lovers," she says, leaning her head on her shoulder. "We're lifers, Benny. Forever."

It hits me hard and fast. A swift break, a sharp pain. "You're serious. You've made up your mind for good. Not like the times in the past when you've lied and tried to forget what we could be. This is real this time, isn't it?"

"It's sad, I know." She kicks her legs, and both of her flip-flops fly into the air. They turn into tiny black dots as they hit the ground. "Time is a luxury we can't waste.

Not anymore." Shaking her head, she steels her resolve. "If Norah taught me anything, it was that. Time. So much of it was wasted and squandered in the name of fear and indecision. I can't let you hurt me again."

My heart hammers. "Why would I purposely hurt you? It's like cutting my own heart! I have the scars to prove I've done it in the past, that's for damn sure. I'll never hurt you again. You have to trust me. Trust me! What if I don't accept your decision?" I ask.

She laughs, shaking her head softly. "You don't have to. I'm strong enough for both of us."

The clouds are turning a shady purple color as the cool of night layers the air. She points at the cloud cluster. "Vada Sultenfuss, *My Girl*. Sitting on the end of the dock."

"Shit. I actually see it," I reply, letting out a loud laugh, trying to accept her decision as coolly as possible. "Keeping the sad trend alive, I guess."

"You cried like a baby every single time we watched that movie," Harper says, wiping her nose. Sitting back, she opens the plastic bag, pulls out a pack of Sour Patch Kids, and opens the bag. "Every single time." She offers the open bag my way.

I take a handful and pop them in my mouth. Around the sugary sweetness, I admit, "You liked to torture me. I don't even know why you're my friend. All you do is torture me." I shake my head. "I should banish you."

"That's what best friends are for. Don't be lame. You can't banish me. You love me."

I groan. "The root of all of my problems."

Harper pulls out a thick black marker and pulls off the cap. She crams about seven red kids in her mouth and leans up on her knees. "What do you say we leave our mark, huh?" She motions behind us to the water tower. It used to be a sky blue, but now it's covered in spray paint and marker. You can barely even tell what color it used to be.

She scribbles in capital letters: Vada + Thomas J. BFF

I take the marker from her hand and shield my work with my free hand: Ben + Harper = Life

I take my hand away so Harper can see. She stares at it for a few seconds. "I want to kiss you right now," Harper says, looking at me.

I raise one brow. "You should. Don't be strong enough for the both of us," I tease.

She sighs, hands me the bag with all of the Sour Patch flavors she doesn't like, and digs in to find a different candy. She pulls out the Bubble Yum and puts a piece in her mouth.

"You planned this. You planned to take advantage of me. That's the only reason you'd bring my chewable kryptonite," I exclaim, pointing at her mouth.

"A first kiss and a last one. It's the only way," Harper says.

My smile falls, and my stomach flips. Not from the sugar, but from the prospect of never having her lips as my own after tonight. I don't ponder long because Harper's leaning toward me. I halt her, taking her head in my hands. I place my thumbs on her lips. They're warm and sticky, and I inhale greedily. She smacks her gum and then closes the distance between us, sealing the finality of this moment with a kiss.

I taste her forgiveness and feel her soul. I hold her face, and she clutches me tightly. Tears and love war with the inevitable future. The sun is long gone now, and from the ground we look like two tiny specks entangled in an embrace, neither ready to let the other go.

Eventually, reluctantly, we do part ways. I chew her gum that ended up in my mouth for hours, trying to figure out what exactly transpired tonight. I think about love and life. I think about heartbreak and pain. I try to figure out what to do next—where to go from here. What Harper wrote on the tower was a right-now sentiment. What I wrote was meant for forever. It's always been that way with us. The turtle and the hare. I'll never give up hope. I can't. Not after everything we've been through.

As I fall asleep, I'm left with only one thought: Love sews souls together. Life picks at the stitches.

CHAPTER NINETEEN

Harper

"A. S. L," I say out loud, reading the newest message in my dating website inbox. This one is a real gem, although the photos of dicks are probably more offensive. This proves that not only isn't he a match, but he didn't even take the time to read my damn basic info. The test to pair me with matches took exactly a week. It's supposed to be foolproof. It will find me the man of my dreams, or I get my three hundred dollars back.

Not that I doubt their diehard promise, but I already have a pair of shoes picked out that cost two hundred ninety-nine dollars. I'm hoping they're on sale when the refund comes.

I'm feeling frisky, so I type back, Older than your mom/yes please/Earth, and hit send. Giggling, I make my way into the closet to choose something to wear to a dinner out with friends. It's my welcome back party. A couple weeks ago I returned from a year traveling abroad. My parents pointed out my linguistics degree could serve me well wherever the wind may blow. Blow it did. All over the map.

My workplace in America set up so many meetings and lectures that I was constantly on the move, and being on my own in unfamiliar territory gave me a sense of freedom and security I never would have dreamed of in my bubble of a safety net in Southern California. I made friends that will last a lifetime. I tried foods I never would have given a second glance. I said yes. I went out dancing. I dated a man in Spain for two whole weeks. He took me to dinner, served me sangria, dipped me back like men do in movies, and kissed me in the rain. He was beautiful and temporary, and I was alive—my heart beating for the first time since it was destroyed completely.

I felt everything. Travel changed me. I spent hours lost on subway cars reading books and took bumpy rides in bicycle taxis. There were days of tears when living abroad made me crazy and highs from learning something new. Oh, did I learn. Not just about languages and communication. I learned about myself. Harper Rosehall. I wouldn't go as far as to say I found myself while traveling, but I will say I defined myself.

Ben and I speak on a semi-regular basis. It's usually via a quick text to check up on one another, nothing too telling. We never speak about our love lives, and our parents know not to bring it up. It's back the way it was before, except completely different.

My laptop pings a new message, and I groan. "I should turn it off. Cancel this thing before I get one more cock shot," I mumble, touching the track pad to wake my screen up.

The little pink star lets me know it's from a match—a person the website says is compatible with me on every level. It's the second match since I finished the test. The first one followed up a funny joke with, you guessed it, a dick pic. This new message is from mancandy2011@matchmemail.com and the title says, Are you a robot?

There aren't photos on the website, and they say it's purposeful so you get to know the person before you see their face, but they do take into consideration turn-ons and turn-offs and preferences in body type and size. If he's a match, I'm trusting he has abs like Adonis, dimples, and a cock that doesn't resemble a carrot. I figure this might be the one that gets me my pair of shoes. I'm in my panties and bra, a black dress draped over my lap. "What do you have to say, Mancandy?" I click his message.

"Hi RJamour7068,

I love the Internet. Porn is fun. So is social media. But those are visual things. Images. This website tells me that photos aren't good to start off with, that we should exchange photos via email when we're ready. They say you're the one for me. A match so perfect, my mom will finally have grandchildren. What remains to be seen is if you're a robot or not. I'm not a robot. I'm a pretty awesome dude. Check out my profile. If you like what the words say about me, send me a photo. I like what your words say about you. For the record. But…are you ugly? I told the computer I was only interested in dime pieces with brains. I'm not sure if we're reading from the same dictionary, though."

I laugh out loud, and I probably shouldn't be as entertained as I am, but it's a good message. I'm drawn to the quirkiness in his tone. He doesn't know any facts other than what the test results give him. He knows I'm local, but that's it. He doesn't know my background, or my profession, or anything telling. Guess that's the website's way of keeping creepy stalkers at bay. After taking about ten minutes to read his characteristics and personality type, I type back:

I like the Internet too, to an extent. I don't think I'm ugly, but I wouldn't consider myself a dime piece, nor would any woman who also has an above-average IQ (which you requested), but my dad says I'm the prettiest girl in the whole world. I'm trying to trust the process and keep photos and appearances hidden until the bitter end. I'd rather get to know you as a person first. Are you okay with that? It does look like we matched on every single tier of this stupid program. If a computer can choose a person for me better than I can choose a person for me, I might jump off a cliff. Just a warning. Not really, though. So, the first question (if you want) it's prompting me with is, "Tell me your ideal first date?"

P.S.) This may sound odd and a bit forward, but I'm not looking for a friendship. I need passion to punch me in the stomach and keep me lying on the ground. Can you dig?

P.S.S.) I'm a size 4. Brown hair. Brown eyes. Girl next door meets Minka Kelly circa Friday Night Lights. What about you, Mancandy?

I send the message and watch as the window tells me it's been read. "I'm going to be late," I whisper, checking the time. I throw the dress on and fire off a quick text to Martina, letting her know I'm on my way. Not really, but I'm never, ever late, so I'm sure they'll forgive me for being fashionably late to my own party. It's so euro. I queue up an Uber and find they're only ten minutes away.

Cracking my knuckles, I stare at the screen, waiting for his response. Maybe he won't respond right away, I tell myself. He does, and my heart nearly leaps out of my chest. I blame my lack of a sex life on my giddy, overzealous character these days.

> You sound more like my type than I would have guessed. I won't tell you what envisioning Minka circa Friday Night Lights did to, um. Never mind. You're my type physically. I'm excited.

> I'm tall, 6'3", sort of goofy, muscles, straight teeth. Funny you mention friendship. I'm sort of allergic to it. Throw me in the passion pit any day of the week. I'm not saying that because I'm a man. I'm saying that because I want the all-encompassing hunger that can't be staved off by a…friendship. I hope you don't think I'm being too graphic. I'm really a pretty strait-laced guy in real life. It's so odd you brought it up, though.

> The ideal first date for me would be something low-key, away from the public, and quiet so there's plenty of atmosphere for talking and getting to know one another. I'm not into wasting time, you see? I've done that in the past, and I'm ready to find the one and make the rest of my days count. The beach would be a great first date. A blanket, a basket of snacks, and a day with nothing else in it.

> Sound interesting? How about it?

I waste no time replying.

> Are you asking me on a date to the beach or the passion pit? You didn't even ask me my ideal first date yet.

I hit send. His reply is quick.

> When you know, you know. Your choice on the passion pit, but beach first. Tomorrow afternoon? 4 p.m. Blacks Beach. Salk Canyon Road entrance. I'll be wearing a baby blue T-shirt and a white smile.

Drumming my fingers on my desk, I stare at his short message. I could sit here and try to decipher it all night, or I could go with my gut instinct and trust the three hundred dollars I put into the computer's hands. My cell phone chimes with a text from Martina asking where I'm at. I have to deal with this message now. The type of people who come back to stuff like this later confounds me. It's an impossibility to put this off. Plus, I'll probably be drunk when I come home tonight.

> It's awfully presumptuous of you to assume I don't have plans tomorrow afternoon. I don't, though. I don't have time to meet with an axe murderer either, so I really hope you aren't some creeper. I'll wear a long, tan dress. Also, I'm not a fan of baby blue. Wear red.

Before I lose my nerve, and also before I make myself later than I already am, I send the message and fold my hand over my mouth. I've shocked myself with this bold move. Maybe it is desperation, or perhaps I was able to bring some of my new, brave qualities home from overseas. Whatever it is, I have a good feeling about it. Mancandy sends another message.

It's a date. Candy Apple Red.

I haven't smiled this wide in a long time, not since I've been home. I close my laptop and fly out the door when the Uber driver honks to announce his arrival.

"Tell us the story again," Martina gushes, her chin in her hands on the other side of the table. They love my stories from Spain. Well, they love my stories about Ricardo from Spain, mostly. I've had several drinks, and the night is winding down. Mancandy stayed safely tucked away —a secret until the very last moment when I had to tell someone lest I end up on the side of a milk carton or the front page of the newspaper.

I rattle on about the time he scooped me up on the handlebars of his bicycle and rode me through the farmers' market on a Sunday afternoon. It was romantic in the best kind of way. I'll never mind repeating that story. He was suave and spoke with a slight accent because his dialect was from a smaller town toward the south, and I broke up with him before I moved to Japan. "I don't know why you didn't stay with him. He was so obviously into you."

Raising my brows, I say, "Yeah. If you're into that sort of thing." My sort of thing is a little more stable, but it was fun while it lasted. The red straw between my fingers, I swirl my drink that's mostly ice water at this point. "Thanks for welcoming me back. You know how to make a woman feel special. Somehow my mom baking a pie just wasn't as fun as this." Everyone at the table giggles, and we toast, some glasses a little more sloshy than others.

A song, one of my favorites, starts thumping through the speakers. We all stand to dance, or as the alcohol dictates, sway along to the beat. I'm hot when the song finishes, a sheen of sweat glistening on every part of my body that isn't covered by the black dress. The cute bartender stops by our table to clear our empties. All it takes is one look at each other to know we're all on the same page.

"Until Janine's birthday next month, then?" I ask.

We make plans for the weekend after next. Janine is turning thirty-five and wants to make a big deal of it, figuring it's really the best birthday to go all out for. It's the age where you're definitely not a child anymore, but you're still fresh-faced. It's a good birthday. We make our way to the front door of the club, holding on to each other as we go. When the cool SoCal air hits us, I see my Uber, the same one who dropped me off.

"It's no Ricardo. But he'll do for the night," I joke and tip my imaginary hat in Martina's direction.

A sad smile plays on her lips as she holds me by my shoulders. "It's going to happen for you soon, Harper. I can feel it in my bones. You glow in a world of darkness."

She hugs me, and I wave her off. "I'm not a lightning bug." I think better of it. "Maybe I'm a different breed of lightning bug. I shock potential mates. To death."

"You're sick, Harp."

I get into the back seat of the white car and roll the window down. The neon lights of the bar shine behind Martina's head. "I'm joking. I bet you're right. Thanks for tonight. Lo pasé muy bien. Ricardo would have approved."

Shaking her black curls around her head, she smirks. I

wave, and we set off for home. There are at least twenty emails that need my attention. Even still, after years, after our lives have passed us by, I find my thumb hovering over Ben's number in the wee hours of the morning.

I don't call him. I like to think I'm stronger than that. Tapping his name, I send him a text: They played your song at my party tonight.

It's two a.m., so I don't expect him to reply.

His response: I am everywhere. And then another right away. I hope you danced.

We've held fast to the decision we made two years ago. Friendship only. The year before I left to travel was difficult—my body and heart wanted nothing more than to stay wrapped up in his arms. Right around the time when I felt like there was no way I could keep my promise and honor the only decent decision I've made regarding Ben, my mother told me to get the hell out of here. In the nicest, *I'm your mom, and I want what's best for you*, type of way.

Then the year away changed everything, and I knew I'd finally gotten over my hang-up on the man, the myth, the Benny. I don't need him to complete me like I once thought. I never needed any man for that. The best thing you can do when you're lost in a sea of doubt? Get lost in another country by yourself. If you can't travel to another country, drive a few cities over, park your car, and wander. Listen. Open your heart to the possibility of being enough on your own.

See you at Ma's on Sunday?

Ben texts again.

I glance at my lap and smile. Ma is my mom, not his.

> I'm making dinner Sunday! Come early and help me.

I send back.

> Done. I need to get some sleep. Gotta be up in a couple hours. Text me when you get home. Is the Uber driver a creepy fuck?

We round the corner to my neighborhood as I reply.

> Ha. Ha. No. Seems a nice lad. Tall. Dark. Handsome. Wait! How did you know my boyfriend wasn't driving me home?

The gray bubble pops up as he types his response and then disappears when he deletes whatever he was going to send. I wait. We pull into my drive, and Ben still doesn't text back, so I pocket my phone. Thanking the driver, I wait for him to pull away to unlock my front door and go inside. I shower because my hair smells like stale cigarettes and I have raccoon eyes. It's almost three thirty a.m. when I finally down some Tylenol and crash into bed. My sheets are cool against my bare legs, and the temptation to check my laptop for a message from Mancandy is strong.

Luckily the vodka is stronger, and I fall asleep a few seconds later.

Fate Ballet

HARPER

I TOOK TOO long to get ready, so I'm arriving at Black's Beach ten minutes late. Now that I'm sober and the prospect of meeting a stranger looms large, I'm fucking terrified. "What was I thinking?" Multiple times throughout the day I thought about messaging Mancandy to tell him something came up. I'm not sure why I didn't. Some niggling sense of curiosity, I suppose. I don't even know his name.

When I pull into a parking spot, I text Martina, my mom, and Janine just to be safe. I'm officially accounted for. I tell them the bare minimum, hoping I don't alarm anyone so much that they follow me down here. Martina texts back,

> Text/Call if you need a quick exit. I'm getting a bikini wax right now. That can turn into a bad case of herpes at the free clinic if the situation requires it,

I text back a joke about her bikini line being more of a priority than my rescue. I pop my trunk and find my beach bag. It has one of those blankets that doesn't let sand sit on top and a novel I've been trying to finish for

225

the last few weeks. I toss the book back in my trunk and stuff a towel inside instead. I lock my car door, and a message from my mom pings:

Have fun.

God, Mom, I think, *shouldn't you be at least a little concerned?* That's the point where we are in our lives. She wants grandbabies. Well, she wants me to be happy with someone, and grandbabies would be a nice side dish. She's telling me to have fun with a potential serial killer with little regard for my well-being.

Thanks, Mom.

I text back while making my way down the trail that leads to the beach. Thinking about what my mother must think of me at this point in my life keeps my nerves at bay for a second. As soon as I put my phone away, my heart moves into the cardio zone. "Candy Apple Red," I whisper to myself, shielding my eyes from the sun to scan the part of the beach visible from my location. Sliding off my flip-flops, I slip them into my bag and step into the packed sand.

Nothing. No red shirts, so I keep walking. I see a family with a golden retriever running around the beach, turning his fur a dusty black color, a stick in his smiling mouth. There's a woman and her little boy, an older man walking, a fanny pack strapped to his waist, and a woman running. Narrowing my eyes, I let my gaze wander farther down.

"If I get stood up by a man with Candy in his name, I'm buying a pair of cats," I mutter under my breath. There's a white gazebo set up, which is completely out of place for this beach, so I head in that direction. It's far from the place he told me to park, so I'm not holding my breath. I make up a song in my head, one that's in the tune of a Katy Perry song. The chorus is, Harper is a hare-brained harlot.

It passes the time as I walk. "I should have brought my book," I say when I begin to shame spiral. I pull out my cell phone and check my social media accounts to pass my walk. A friendly speed walker wishes me a good day. I respond with a smile and like a photo of my friend's new baby. It looks like a little alien wearing pink sitting in a spaceship. I scroll down a little further and see a photo posted by Marcus's wife. She's tagged him, so I'm able to view it. The caption reads, #tbt #bestday-ofmylife. "Puke," I groan, thumbing down immediately. Next is a picture of my father in the garden, holding up a tomato. They planted a few things, and it looks like he got over a case of the black thumb. I type in a comment, Way to go, Dad!

I shunned social media all through college and a bit after, but then it got to a point where I was missing too much by not being on it. Marcus's Instagram photo scandal is what spurred me to be a little more conscious about the social interweb world. It was one more way for me to try to fit in better and connect in a disconnected world.

I look up to see how far I have to go and to scour for a red, muscle-filled shirt, if I'm being completely honest. The white cabana is empty but for a large lounge chair and a table in one corner. The white curtains billow against a slight breeze, and my phone pings an alert.

I look down and click the red number one. It's a tagged photo from Benjamin Brahams. It's a photo of a beach. Black's Beach. He's added two stick figures using the draw feature. The caption reads, Fate Ballet.

"You weren't supposed to see that yet," Ben says, his voice coming from beside me.

Jumping, I let out a little scream and then recover by covering my mouth and dropping my cell phone into the sand. "What are you doing here?" I ask.

Ben picks up my phone and hands it to me. His fingers brush mine as he sets it in my palm. "Conducting a ballet. It's so hard to get my dancers to do what I want, though."

I wrinkle my brow and smile. "You're insane," I remark, looking behind me. "Seriously. How did you know I was going to be here?"

"You're serious, Harper? Really? You don't know? I mean, I knew there was a possibility you weren't one hundred percent sure, but I figured you'd be a little more intuitive." Ben extends his hand. "Mancandy. Nice to meet you."

"What? No way." I step away from him. Like he's some criminal who's meddled in my files or stolen my email password or something. "There's no way. No fucking way. We were a perfect match. The program said so."

He extends one bulky arm to the cabana. "Welcome to the Fate Ballet, Harper Rosehall. Where every part of the dance has been leading up to a grand finale. I know we're perfect for each other. You know we're perfect for each other. The fail-proof computer program knows it too. Your mom told me you were doing some stupid online dating site."

Swallowing down this insane truth, I walk to the lounge chair and sit down. Ben sits next to me, his red shorts glaring against the white fabric.

"I knew which one you'd use, and I joined too. Figured if someone else told you we were meant to be, you'd believe it. There was never any doubt in my mind." He clears his throat.

"This can't be real. You hacked the system. You had to have. There was nothing in there about me. How did you know it was me?"

He laughs, his angled, perfect jaw tilting back a touch. "I'll always know it's you," he says. "You're back now." Ben strokes the side of my face, his fingers a featherlight touch on my skin but a heavy bowling ball to my soul. "I've missed seeing you."

"Fate is a pretty superfluous word for you to use," I say, straightening my thoughts. "Not a word my Ben would use."

He shrugs. "Maybe I'm not your Ben anymore. I'm Mancandy," he says, extending his hand. "It's nice to meet you. What was your name again? Amour?"

"You want to start over?" I ask. "I don't see how that's possible."

"Anything is possible. We aren't getting any younger," Ben says, looking at the ocean and then back at me. White hairs have started peppering his temples and sadness fills my heart for all of the years that have passed since we fell in love and did nothing about it. "Before you tell me nothing has changed in two years, I beg to differ. A computer matched you to me, and the statistics of that happening are a million to one. Don't say no to the computer, Harper."

"How do you know my name?" I smirk.

Ben slides closer to me. "You look like a Harper, that's all."

"I think a fresh start is the only way to make something as complicated as this work out, and I don't have the first clue as to how to make that happen," I admit, looking at him. Shaking my head, I go on, "I still can't believe you wrote those messages. Well, I can and I can't. I'm still looking for a dude in a red shirt."

Ben smiles, but it's sad. "I'm tired. I'm so, so tired. It doesn't have to be complicated. You'll agree to a fresh start? Something new and different? You and me?"

Biting my lip, I try not to get upset. I've pushed these emotions away for years and years. It was my armor. My security. My heart's way of protecting what has never been a wise choice. I shake my head. "Our past, though. How? How do you overcome that? We'll never forget that. Don't fool yourself. It will always be there. How do you propose we make a fresh start?"

It's now that a traitorous tear sneaks out of the corner of my eye. Norah and Robin. Marcus. The space between us and our friendship. Big pink balloons at airports. Almost kisses. First ones. Last ones. Then before that, stalwart friendship. Fights and games. Basketball. Push and pull. Give and take. Loss and grief.

Ben brings a thumb up and swipes at the tear. So many tears over this. Over us. "Funny you mention it," Ben says, shifting in the chair next to me. His shoulder bumps into mine. "I have a proposition for you."

Ben kneels next to the chair, and that's when I lose it completely. These aren't tears of sadness and regret that have washed my face so many times in the past. They're happy tears falling over a smile so bright it's making my face hurt.

Ben shakes his head. "I'm going to keep this real short, Harp, okay?"

He opens the box to expose my great-great-grand-mother's engagement ring. It's exactly the same as I remember. A piece of jewelry I've always admired inside my mother's chest. Benny and I played wedding one day long ago, and I stole it from her room to use. Ben almost dropped it down the air conditioner vent when he went to put it on my finger.

"Don't want to drop it," I whisper.

Ben nods, taking in a huge breath—a man unsure of the outcome. "One question, about our fresh start then."

Wiping my eyes, I clear the pooling tears from my line of vision. I want clarity in this moment. I stay silent, waiting. Wondering if this is all one sick twisted joke. In my dreams this happened ten years ago.

"Now or never," Ben says, removing the ring from the black velvet. "That's the question." Holding my left hand, he hovers next to my ring finger.

I nod. "Now," I say. "Always now. Never never."

Ben slips the ring on my finger, a perfect fit. I can't take my eyes off his gaze to admire the ring because he's looking at me with such a fullness that my heart aches. Not a happy ache either.

A *finally* ache. A lifetime of love culminating in one good decision.

A decision a computer made.

"Fate Ballet," Ben says, eyes glassing over, arms pulling me into a strong embrace.

"Now," I say once again.

CHAPTER TWENTY

Ben

SO MUCH TIME has been wasted. I can't even call the decisions that kept us apart bad. Life kept us apart regardless of how much we wanted to be together. We aren't wasting another goddamn second.

"What if you get called away last minute? What if you can't make your own wedding, Ben Brahams?" Harper squeaks out underneath my body.

I raise one brow. "Someone can fill in for me," I reply, dipping my head to kiss the hollow of her neck. "Like they have for the past few weeks." I had to take time off work for the first time in a decade merely to get my fill of Harper. I wouldn't be able to focus properly had I not taken the time to relax and just be with her in all ways. My mind has never been in a better place. With the truth came this calm clarity.

Harper grabs my arms and pushes me back to a kneeling position. I moved into her house the same night I proposed. She was a little stymied that I already had my stuff packed, but when I told her I put all my money on black, she had to appreciate my Herculean effort to claim what I wanted and rode me on my living room floor, front door wide open.

She scrambles up to kiss my mouth, her tongue dipping in and out, teasing me, and then runs her mouth down my pecs, abs, and down to my dick. She takes it into her mouth. I groan out a long string of curse words mixed with her name. I lay my hand gently on her head as she bobs up and down, but I don't push down. She hates that. Harper sucks and licks at her own pace that just so happens to be frightfully maddening.

"I need to be inside you, Harp," I say. "We don't have enough time for this."

I have to go to my parents' house for the night, so we don't spend the night before our wedding together. As it stands, three of Harper's friends and her mom are in the kitchen behind our closed door. We're supposed to be in here working on our vows, but we've done nothing but each other in the two hours the door has been locked.

"There's always time for this," Harper mumbles around my cock. She sits up. "But I'd rather like it if you were inside me."

My dick jerks. "You're speaking my love language," I exclaim.

Harper presses a finger over my lips. "Quiet, they'll hear you."

I roll my eyes. "They heard your second orgasm when my tongue was fucking your pussy then, too."

"My god. Say that again. I'll come a third time," Harper says, smirking. "I mean it," she adds when I don't speak.

I say it again, whispered in her ear, while dipping a finger inside her slit. Sliding closer to her, on my knees, I push my cock down so I can rub her clit with the head of my dick. "This is what you want?"

"Yes," Harper moans. "I want it now."

Her face is flushed, and she has a red beard stubble rash everywhere. I'm so fully all over her body that looking at her is the ultimate turn-on. Harper is mine. Tomorrow she will be mine in the only other way she's not. Officially. For the rest of time, I'll get the girl I've wanted my entire life.

Harper reaches between her legs and guides me into her, leaning her body to position my cock deeper. She opens her eyes to meet mine. "Now," she says, a ghost of a smirk dancing on her lips.

Grabbing her hips to take some of her weight, I fuck her, watching my dick disappear as I fill her. She clenches around me as I rub her G-spot from this position. I go slow, taking it in, appreciating everything happening in front of me. I'll never get tired of this, will never take Harper and our connection for granted again.

"How does that feel?" I ask, trying to control my breaths. The urge to come is always there if she's naked and in front of me, but when I'm watching my dick spike into her cunt, it's another world of desire. Filling her with my cum is the only thing I can think of after she orgasms around my dick.

I want her to have my babies. I want to see her round with my children. See how she changes over the years, time granting me the ability to love her in all of the phases of life we have left. She went off birth control the day we planned the wedding two weeks ago.

"It feels good. Rub me like that. I'm going to come so hard," Harper says, trying to keep her voice down. She realizes she didn't speak quietly and throws a hand over her mouth.

I keep up the slow assault on her until I can tell she's about to go out of her mind. She circles her hips, and that provides a completely different sensation, and I groan. "Keep doing that, and I'm going to come before you," I whisper, but it comes out more like a growl through clenched teeth. "Stop. No, don't stop, keep doing it."

Harper smiles, eyes narrowed, happy her little game is driving me insane. "I want you to fill me with your cum, though. All of it. Fuck me," Harper says, using her tongue to trace the bottom of her lip. My mouth goes fucking dry as I alternate my gaze between her hot snatch eating my dick and her face, which might be just as much of a turn-on.

"Your filthy mouth makes me want to come down your throat," I say, using my thumb to rub her clit in tight small circles. Harper's leg muscles tighten, and her eyes fall closed. Then she comes, her pussy grabbing on to my cock like a death grip. Once the waves of her orgasm subside, I thrust into her deeply and change position so she's fully on her back and I'm on top of her. "But I want to come in your pussy more."

My pace doesn't match my words. I'm slowly gliding in and out while my lips play with hers. Opening and shutting in a passionate kiss, our tongues dancing in a way that lets us know we were made for each other. "Come in me," she says, words a breathless plea. "I want you to be a part of me."

Her request is hotter than a million filthy things spoken from another woman's mouth. Leaning down to rest my face in her neck, I whisper, "You already are."

Harper clings to my neck as I jut between her legs a few more times and spill inside her deep and hard. I don't want to move, and Harper doesn't want me to go anywhere either, her heels digging into my ass, holding me inside.

"I love you, Benny," she says, her words lighting my ears like my favorite song.

"Tomorrow I'm going to make you my wife, Harper Jean, and it's going to be the best day of my entire life."

She sighs, content and warm under my body. "It took so long to get here," she says.

"And it will be that much better because of it," I reply, leaning up on my hands to gaze at her face. She has a huge red mark on her shoulder and neck from my five o'clock shadow. I kiss one of the marks. "I need to get away from you before my dick gets hard again."

Wincing, I draw my cock out of her body slowly, deliciously, every inch feeling her tight walls. "Dear God in heaven, thank you for Harper's body," I murmur, closing my eyes. "You have no idea how much you affect me," I admit, palming my cold dick. I want her wetness on my hand.

She sits up, hair a tangled mess, body flushed, and face mirroring the satisfaction I feel. "And you have no idea how much that makes me want you back inside me."

I groan, throwing myself away from her, backing into the dresser. "Wicked woman, with your magic pussy powers. Stay back." I hold out a palm in her direction.

Harper giggles and climbs off the bed seductively, hips swaying, hands tracing every curve I want on me.

"No magic here, just Harper." She winks. Like a sex panther in heat. I want to devour her in the wild. Fuck myself to death. Die in a Harper orgasm fog. Her essence on my lips and my cum pooling inside her body. She makes her way to the restroom, and I watch my cum leak down the inside of her legs.

"When you look in the mirror, you're going to wish you had some magic. There's no way they're going to believe we've been writing vows in here with how well fucked you look right now."

She shrugs. "It was worth the scrutiny," Harper says, sitting on the toilet to wipe away what I just worked so hard for. "I have to go make the bouquets for tomorrow. You need to get out of here. What are you doing tonight?

Strippers? Killing bad guys? I'm not sure what it is a man like you does the night before he gets married."

She flushes the toilet and tries to fix her hair with a comb. She curses when it doesn't work. "What does a man like me do the night before he gets married?" I ask, walking up to wrap my hands around her naked body. "I thank God I get to marry the woman of my dreams and count down the hours until it happens, while simultaneously praying the world doesn't come down around us before it happens."

Harper grins, pressing her lips to one side. "You're trying to woo me right now. I'm swooning, Ben Brahams. I didn't know you had it in you."

"You want it in you one more time?" I ask, joking.

Harper's smile widens at the same time as her feet. Then she bends over, pressing her perfect tits against the cold granite. "I need a shower anyway," she purrs, reaching back to spread her butt cheeks. "If you're game, that is?"

"How the fuck am I supposed to say no to that?" I ask, stroking my dick while I stare at one of my favorite sights in the entire world. "Hold that fucking thought," I say, holding up one finger.

I pop my head out of our bedroom door to find Martina sitting cross-legged on the area rug with what looks like a million white flowers spread out around her. "Twenty more minutes," I say, teeth gritted.

She rolls her eyes. "Take thirty. Her mom left during round two. Keep it down."

I don't think about what that means and lock the door, grab the bottle of cherry lube from a nightstand, and find Harper in the same spot as when I left her.

The profile of her body, ass popped out, back arched, causes the Neanderthal that lives inside me to come barreling out, pounding his fists on his chest. "Where were we?" I ask, sauntering slowly, appreciating the absolute vision Harper is. "We have twenty minutes."

"You were going to put it in me one more time," Harper says, pressing her lips together in a mischievous smirk. "Wherever you want," she says, spreading a bit wider than she was before.

I drop to my knees and lick her pussy and ass. It's a dick-throbbing mixture of Harper and my cum. She pushes back into my face as I wrap my hands around her thighs and pull her onto my face further. "You have to keep it down," I say, pulling away, licking my lips. "Or else no more fun."

I see her nod in her reflection, eyes closed. If you told me last year I had the ability to come back-to-back the way I do with Harper, I would have called you a fucking liar. Not only is every single brain cell attracted to her, but my balls work overtime to mass produce loads meant specifically for her.

Sliding two fingers into her pussy slowly, she fucks them by rocking back. I rub her G-spot while I dribble some lube on her ass. It puckers from the coolness, and my cock flexes at the visual. "Relax," I coax, laying a hand on her lower back. "Arch and relax."

Harper obeys.

I pull my fingers out of her pussy and line up my dick and slide into her ass in tiny juts that eventually seat my dick all the way in. I close my eyes when Harper moans.

"Fuck me hard," she says, meeting my gaze in the mirror. It reminds me of a time I fucked her so long ago. Even then, I didn't feel like she was mine.

This time when I fuck her ass and watch her come, I know without a shadow of a doubt she's mine. When my balls feel like they might explode, I grimace, fuck her to the hilt, and come in her. Again.

And it's never enough. Will never be enough to make up for all the time I didn't have this connection. This power.

This love.

CHAPTER TWENTY-ONE

Harper

I'VE NEVER BEEN HAPPIER in my entire life. That's a bold statement. One I'd repeat a million times if it means I get to feel like this every day for the rest of my life. My dad is walking me down the aisle, just sand marked by white flowers on either side, to the man of my dreams.

Ben is standing barefoot by the water wearing a white shirt, untucked, and a pair of khaki pants. We're getting married in the exact spot he proposed. There are about ten chairs on either side of the aisle, all filled with our closest friends and family who could make it on such short notice. We didn't send out invites or make a registry or do anything stereotypical brides and grooms do. That's for everyone else. They can keep the customs and pomp. We just want each other. My dress, a white, lacy, curve-hugging number, flares at the bottom in a mermaid cut. Ben came with me when I tried on dresses and said if we're doing it on the beach, I should get my Ariel fantasy.

"I love you both so much, baby. You don't know how happy this is making your mother and me," Dad says, squeezing my arm. "After all this time. You're finally doing it." It's a statement as much as it is a question.

I squeeze his hand resting on my arm. "Thanks, Dad. Took a little longer than it should have," I whisper, laying my head against his shoulder. The pride that oozes from his body is enough for a million daughters instead of just one. He's always been proud of my scholarly and work accomplishments, but somehow validating my lifelong love for Ben is enough to wash all of those away. It's because I'm finally being honest with myself, finally taking the chance I never took. "I love you," I tell him.

He sniffles next to me, and I have to focus on Ben to keep from tearing up and ruining my makeup prematurely.

My hair is down because I know that's how Ben likes it. I took a photo of Lyla Garrity, a.k.a. Minka Kelly, with me to the makeup artist. She did an amazing job replicating the look, and it's a small tilt to a weird way this was all brought to a close. The sun is setting just enough so that the heat isn't severe and the clouds are that beautiful color they become just before night hides them away.

Ben's smile is this huge, beautiful work of art. It reminds me of when we were kids and we had the inability to stop laughing at some stupid joke. We'd look at each other and start cracking up all over again. This is a smile he won't be able to wipe away. My dad hands my hand to Ben, and they share a quick man hug before he takes his seat next to my weeping mother. She has a tissue in each hand and a smile that matches Ben's.

Ben hugs me straight away, ignoring all normal wedding rules. "Harper, you are stunning. The most beautiful girl in all the world."

"Thank you," I reply. "You look pretty handsome yourself." I squeeze his biceps, and he laughs.

His eyes are so happy, so jubilant, that I'm truly trans-ported back to when we were innocent, happy children. Smiles for miles and not a care in the world. And isn't that how you want a marriage to start? I lean up on my tiptoes, and Ben's on the same wavelength. He kisses me on the lips once, very chastely, and then on the bridge of my nose.

"Get a room," Tahoe calls out, causing everyone to giggle.

Ben glares at Tahoe and turns the megawatt smile out to everyone else. "I've waited too long for this! I'll kiss her when I want!"

More laughter is followed by clapping, and my mom sniffles some more.

The pastor starts in on the simple ceremony. We listen, but we don't take our eyes off each other, like maybe the words he's saying will telepathically melt into our systems. Ben touches my face, my neck, and my shoul-ders instead of merely holding my hand. He's checking to make sure it's real. I'm real.

"Harper and Ben have written their own vows to each other, and they would like to share them with you today. Ben," the pastor says, clipping a small microphone on the edge of my capped sleeve and one to the open collar of Ben's shirt. "Whenever you're ready."

Ben bites his lip in a grin. "I love you, Harper Jean, sneeze queen. Every moment and mistake in our lives has led to this right here. It could have happened earlier," he says, looking at the audience when they laugh. "But it wouldn't have meant as much as it does right now. Standing here after trials and tribulations that would make Gandhi question our sanity means that despite everything else in our past, we choose each other. You are the part of my life that has been constant because of how much I love you. I've never been scared of the depth of my feelings for you because I fell for you gradually. A little bit at a time during each phase of our lives. Now I'm at a level so deep I'll never make it back to the surface in this lifetime. It's only deeper from here to eternity. I vow forever to you. You hold all of my yesterdays, and I vow to give you all of my tomorrows." Ben works down a hard swallow and cradles the side of my face. "You're my girl now. I knew you'd be my last dance."

It's my turn to sniffle, sob, and halfway choke on emotion. "I love you," I say to Ben, laying my hand on top of his. "How am I supposed to follow that?" There's tittering from our audience as I try to compose myself enough to get my vows out.

Ben smiles wide and pulls me into another hug. "Finally!" he announces. "I made her cry out of happiness!"

Everyone roars with laughter at that comment, and while highly inappropriate, it's also pretty endearing at the same time. We're allowed to poke fun at our torrid past.

I pull away from the hug. "All right. I'm ready," I reply, sucking in a deep, cleansing breath.

The sun is almost gone, and the sky sets the perfect backdrop for this moment, and I'm overwhelmed with gratitude. How could I possibly appreciate a life with Ben without realizing how challenging it's been without him?

"I could say a million things to you about how our marriage will be one that stands the test of time, but you already know that. I could tell you how everything about you is what I love, but you know that too. The fact that we're standing here right now is a testament to our love. A weaker variety would have run in the opposite direction, would have sneered at computer pairing logistics." I smile when I see tears form in Ben's eyes. "My vows to you are simple, because after all these years I think this is the vow that means the most." I have to clear my throat. "You are the person who knows me most in this world. Every single piece of me, down to the cellular level is imprinted with your kindness, your understanding, your love of country, your persistence, your knowledge, your love."

I pause, pressing my lips together. "I vow to be your best friend because those are just as important as wives. I promise to never take another breath for granted. I promise to take all of you and love it the best way I know how." If you don't believe in magic, I'd tell you to look skyward. The answers are out there. You just need to know how and when to look. I've never seen it so clearly than I do in this moment.

I cross my hands in front of me, and with tears filling his eyes, Ben does the same, grabbing onto mine. I take in a deep, jagged breath and say, "Harbenny, Harbenny, getcha, bitchen some, we rule the world, you're my life plus one."

Our parents stand, cheering like maniacs, the only people in on the joke, and the pastor pronounces us husband and wife. I leap into Ben's arms, and we kiss like our lives depend on it.

At this point, they kind of do.

A Look At:

ALL THE WAY UNDER

She chased freedom, but danger and desire caught her first.

Saylor Wyndham has everything money can buy—except the freedom to chase her dream of sailing solo around the globe. When her family and boyfriend call her ambitions reckless, she leaves them behind and sets sail alone, only to be captured by ruthless pirates off the coast of South Africa.

Navy SEAL Brody McCoy's mission is clear: infiltrate the pirate camp, rescue the hostage, and bring down the terrorists without blowing his cover. To succeed, he has to pose as a captive himself, getting close to Saylor in ways that test his patience and his self-control.

Saylor thinks Brody is just another man trying to cage her spirit, while Brody sees her as a spoiled heiress with no clue what real danger is. But as their risky escape plan unfolds, tension turns to heat, and one wrong move could cost them everything.

AVAILABLE NOW

Author's Note

There are those stories that speak to an author on a soul level. The Destined SEAL is one of those stories for me. I honestly can't think about Ben and Harper's love without getting a little misty eyed. There are different kinds of love everyone experiences throughout their lifetime, but the kind that is the most devastating is the kind you don't embrace fully. In the first draft of this novel, the story ended at the water tower. Ben and Harper looking into the distance—a sky half-dark and half-light, the atmosphere tinged with equal parts sadness and happiness. I envisioned their future, and it always, always ended in a forever after, but showing it was hard, painful almost, because of all of their missed chances and because of how much time was wasted not embracing this epic, life-altering love.

To my readers: thank you for coming on the journey with me. You make my dream possible! Thank you to all of the people that made this story possible: my early readers, my Racy Readers, my editor, proofreader, and formatter. They take my blood, sweat, and tears, and polish it, validate it, and hold my hand through the process. Your support means more than words ever will.

Thanks, as always, to my ultimate, lifelong muse, my husband. You're all the best parts of my characters and I wouldn't have them if I didn't have you. You choose to run in the direction of chaos and destruction. Like Ben,

9/11 was a deciding factor in serving your country, and that is the greatest, most respectable decision one can ever make. You're my destined SEAL. Always.

Rachel grew up in a small, quiet town full of loud talkers. Her words were always only loud on paper. She has been writing stories and creating characters for as long as she can remember. CRAZY GOOD and SET IN STONE, and TIME AND SPACE, three of her Navy SEAL novels are INTERNATIONAL BESTSELLERS. After living in San Diego, Virginia Beach, and then Fairfax, VA, she now resides in colorful Colorado with her badass husband, two children, her Sphynx cat, & her dog, Polly.

www.racheljrobinson.com
Rachel Robinson's Racy Readers

Rachel grew up in [...] small town [...] dreamt of living in a big city. [...] two dishevelled son[...] and [...] cat [...]. She has been [...] childhood [...] and compu[...] consultant for as long [...]
[...] bachelor's degree in [...] CISSP, and SCRUM [...]
TIME AND SPACE, [...] of THE [...] SPACE [...]
CENTRAL STATION [...] and [...] STALL[...]. AND [...] are HE[...]
Please Comma, [...] Beach [...] and [...] are [...] the now
[...] a cellular Colorad[...] with her [...]

[...] www.[...].com/authorr[...]
[...] or in book [...]